Dottie graduated from Arizona State University with both Bachelors and master's degrees in English Education. For 24 years, she taught a variety of high school English classes. Her favorites were Creative Writing, Science Fiction and Western Literature. She loves to write Historical Fiction and has completed 4 novels.

Dot Jay Gomez

ALUMINUM HIGHWAY

AUSTIN MACAULEY PUBLISHERS™

LONDON * CAMBRIDGE * NEW YORK * SHARJAH

Ordering Information
Quantity sales: Special discounts are available on quantity purchases by corporations, associations, and others. For details, contact the publisher at the address below.

Publisher's Cataloging-in-Publication data
Gomez, Dot Jay
Aluminum Highway

ISBN 9798886936995 (Paperback)
ISBN 9798886937008 (ePub e-book)

Library of Congress Control Number: 2024910715

www.austinmacauley.com/us

First Published 2024
Austin Macauley Publishers LLC
40 Wall Street, 33rd Floor, Suite 3302
New York, NY 10005
USA

mail-usa@austinmacauley.com
+1 (646) 5125767

Special Thanks to:

Grant the Great, Janie, James, Andy, Denny and Monica, for all your patience.

Special thanks to Dad for his years with the Army Air Corps and all of his stories as a Hump Pilot. 1945-1946

Special thanks to Becky, Dee, Rosemary, and John for whining at me to "get it done!"

Favorite Mottos:
It's not what you know, it's what you do with it.
He who is bored, is boring.

Dot Jay Gomez
IMPORTANT: NEED TO KNOW!

1944

HUMP pilots of WW II were the 20-21 year old Flight Officers (AKA F/O) who flew over the Himalayas, the "Rock Pile," the "Roof of the Earth," under treacherous weather conditions risking their lives and that of the crew to fly the new C-46 Commando and the new C-47 Sky Train loaded with cargo. These first of its kind missions, air lifted supplies from INDIA bases across BURMA to the ALLIES in KUNMING, CHINA to support the war effort against the *JAPANESE.*

AIR TRAFFIC CONTROL--ATC, originated the CHINA-BURMA-INDIA--CBI Theater in 1942 after *JAPAN* had invaded BURMA at Rangoon cutting off all livelihood to CHINA. Together, 28,000 ALLIES and 35,000 CHINESE, labored to secure BURMA and CHINA *in the 1940's.*

BAIL-OUTS were frequent when the huge planes encountered severe ice and wind while flying over the HUMP, surviving the worst weather in the world. Over 600 planes crashed at a loss of 2000+ crew men, 550 of which were pilots.

AIR TRANSPORT COMMAND (ATC) originated for dual purposes:

#1—Fly supplies 500 miles over the HUMP from INDIA to CHINA on a northerly route to avoid enemy fighters.

#2—Construct a new leg of THE BURMA ROAD between Ledo, India and Kunming, China.

The massive air-lift faced three major problems:
1) Monsoon Rains in summer; 2) Heavy icing on planes in winter; 3) *Japanese Zeroes.*

Mount Everest at 29,000+ feet and Mount Kanchenjunga at 28,168 feet, were always within sight. On a rare sunny day and a rare moonlit night, the routes from INDIA to CHINA sparkled with the remains of downed aircraft---a trail negatively referenced as:

<u>THE ALUMINUM HIGHWAY</u>

Foreword

Dear Reader:

Ninety percent of the stories in Aluminum Highway actually happened as taken from the stories of those who flew the HUMP so long ago, and these events are re-told through the lives of many characters.

Of the millions who participated in WWII, there must have been a leader like HOLT, a multi-talented LUCKY LARRY, a tough PALOOKA, and an always handsome BOBBY JOHNSON.

CHAPTER ONE—June 1944 LEDO, INDIA

Tensions mangled in the ASSAM VALLEY of NE India, all teams waiting for the landing of the crew in an empty C-46 Commando returning from a 500 mile trip to Kunming, southwest CHINA. The pilot had dumped the payload of supplies—guns, ammunition, food boxes, airplane parts, etc, and was heading home to the Ledo base.

Although this is June and the beginning of heavy monsoon rains turning all make-shift landing fields to muddy quagmires, the plane's problems most likely started over the HUMP, flying at 14,000 feet where icing occurs most of the time at 10,000. De-icers break off easily due to the rough landing strips, most of which are rough edges of mountains hurriedly transformed into craggy landing strips. Planes easily freeze, first one engine than the other. Distress signals radioed in for the last thirty minutes put the entire field crews on edge as the pilot circled 360's above in the giant sputtering plane. Blurred calls from miles away of engine failure hurried ground necessities to get ready to evacuate the crew from the C-46, nicknamed the "Gooney Bird" ship.

Anything can happen. Crashes are common, unfortunately. This is Ledo, Assam India, a popular landing strip, the main hub of common stops with supplies for General Stillwell's new leg of the BURMA ROAD, one to meet in Wanding, Burma and attach to the existing one leading out of Kunming, China. When added, the 1000 plus mile road, a task in unbelievable conditions, will help deliver supplies to China's allies, a hurry-hurry task as the Japs have control of Rangoon, Burma, the main supply route to China, and they are heading north to control Myitkyina (Mit-Chee-NAH) and all of Burma.

High pitch voices on the ground shouting and questioning, put everyone on edge—again so soon.

"Who's the F/O?"

"Flight Officer Cooper."

"Where is the home base?"

"Chittagong, India."

"Are they fully loaded?"

"No! Thank God! Ground control reported they already unloaded 30 litters of patients with the help of MAETS." (Medical Air Evacuation Transport Squadron).

Two Search and Rescue teams with emergency aid kits are waiting in the perimeters far out of the way, their parked Willys Jeeps running and ready.

Chinese laborers shout at each other to move away from the end of the field where they have been working with mules and water buffalo clearing the end of the runway of debris, vegetation, vines and bamboo, a usual repetitive task. "THE LONGER THE RUNWAY THE BETTER," is an order from base commanders of the ATC-(Air Traffic Command) that takes top priority.

WEN WU shut his eyes while shaking his head. "Too many! Too many!" He whined. Again he would have to report the sighting to Base Commander HOLT as he had been trained to do…now, too many times over shots of whiskey at the tent's make-shift bar.

"Another tent mate down," voiced PALOOKA pacing.

"Not yet," said a nurse clinging to him.

PALOOKA chewed vigorously on his cigar stub. "I've lost half my tent buddies! Hell-of-a-note!" His shout of anger matched the roaring, sputtering plane approaching the strip. Nervously he stomped around, red hair sticking out of his cap while puffing and chewing anxiously. He spit the dirt out of anger.

"Land the ship!" Someone shouted.

"Land the ship!" PALOOKA joined in.

"Land the ship!" Yelled another as they all gawked, stomach cramped, some pacing, others frozen clinging to one another.

WU in the distance watching and fearing the worse, turned the water buffalo around facing the jungle a few yards away, turning away from the terrible scene.

PALOOKA remembered all the unnecessary crashes that occurred last year due to a mechanical malfunction—a check valve honestly installed for safety was the culprit of crashes, starving engines of fuel. Many planes and crew were lost in 1943 until Pratt and Whitney made changes. Now, this year is different. Causes are not from mechanical malfunctions but usually the extreme Himalaya weather brings ships down by the dozen per week. It is a magnificent machine, the C-46, maxing speed of 270 miles-per-hour at 10,000 feet. First of its kind and first flown in 1940. Now, demands of high altitude terrains, difficult weather conditions and rough landing strips hewed out of mountain sides, are the causes of current crashes. Some days, too many to count.

LUCKY LARRY, the AMO (Aircraft Maintenance Officer) is the top dog no-nonsense main mechanic in charge of the crews that keep the C-46 Commando and others in the air. His truck loaded with salvage from downed planes is his toy. "Parts salvaged keep planes in the air."

Now he sits in his truck in the far perimeters and prays for the crew in the plane. Luckily it is not loaded. To capacity, its cavernous fuselage harbor capabilities of transporting the most troops—50 fully loaded, and greatest tonnage of supplies, over 10,000 pounds more than its sister the C-47 Skytrain.

LUCKY LARRY removed his cap numerous times to scratch his early balding head, a nervous tick which helped him think. He earned his name as "Lucky Larry" last year as an F/O, (Flight Officer) after flying the HUMP fifty times. To his credit are two bail-outs and one crash landing. All before he convinced ATC that he is a better mechanic than pilot and earnestly wants to live passed his twenty-five years. Since mechanics are rare and there are more planes down than there are proper parts, ATC handed him the hot job as Aircraft Maintenance Officer, referenced as the AMO.

Now he felt sick with past memories as he watched the injured Commando gear down for a crash landing. Recognizing the nose art of "*LUCKY LULU*", his favorite paint job that took a month to finish—the voluptuous brunette babe with only a flimsy skirt as cover and a no-where top—his best piece of art, now descending too fast—too low—wavering wings—smoking engine and <u>NO WHEELS!</u>

"No Wheels!" Everyone yelled. Men rolled up their khaki sleeves as women grabbed them at their elbows for needed support. Chinese laborers bunched together in a flock holding their animals tightly, turning them away from facing the extremely loud noise that is to come from the descending machine. WU whined orders.

Unfortunately, crashes are not too uncommon to the animals and workers. Continuously flown from one base to another, animals and workers labor to keep landing strips clear of debris in NORTH EASTERN parts of INDIA, NORTHERN BURMA and SOUTH WESTERN CHINA, all along the HUMP route. And, they knew the treacherous monsoon weather. ASSAM, INDIA, was the rain capital of the world. Over 600 inches per year employed many men to reroute the constant streams that flowed near and over runways.

ALL stared in sad anticipation, too aware of the crashes of these premier cargo ships, the C-46 and the C-47 that were in for the big haul of supplies keeping the countries safe from the ruthless Japanese. Tonnages of 50 gallon drums of gas for fighter planes, along with food, medicine, clothing, jeeps, mules, horses and whatever the ALLIES in KUNMING and other locations in China demanded—are delivered. And they, the workers, loaded and unloaded everything—over and over—daily.

DING HAO!

CHAPTER TWO—June, 1944

Brits, Aussies and Canadians are the bulk of allies fighting the Japanese in this part of the South Pacific War. Goal is to push the Japs out of Southern Burma where they are currently in control of routes to China. America's assistance with the war effort meant supplies—supplies—supplies!

And here come Cooper and his crew, victims of this massive air lift, praying for their lives, circling above in the empty plane….young men barely out of high school, all American made.

Now, crews in tents away from the field and those in office barracks, rush out to see the landing, hoping for a successful belly attempt which has become more and more common. It is a storm of khaki among the misty green of the Indian Jungle, a beauty among tragedy and devastation. Elephants far enough away bellow, their trunks ready to load the stack of 50 gallon drums. Standing out of danger, pacing, waiting, knowing what is to come, they lift their trunks.

The pilot circled again.

The second time low enough to afford a view of the half demolished plane the ground crews shout… "Left engine's on fire!"

"That's near the fuel tanks!"

"The fuselage is ripped and torn!"

The smoking C-46 skidded to a stop at the end of the strip and exploded, only seconds after the young crew of four…pilot, co-pilot, navigator, radio operator…jettisoned out the cargo door. Running helter-skelter towards the jeeps, they barely hit the ground racing when the ship exploded. Ducking small shrapnel and larger pieces of plane, they scooted on all fours as low as possible.

First to scoop up crew members are two Willys Jeeps, one driven by PALOOKA as he flies down the muddy mess of a runway, tires sometimes in the air. "Hell-of-a-note" he shouted helping two climb in his Willys, now fittingly a transformed make-shift air ambulance. They ducked low in the Search-and Rescue vehicle as it sped away on two wheels, than four.

LUCKY LARRY in the other Jeep almost collided with PALOOKA while scooping up the other two disheveled-wild-eyed young men. Yelling "Holy-Mackerel," while looking back at the flames, he continued "How'd you guys escape?" Medics, nurses and aides waiting for the shaking crew, grabbed each arm and took the men to Army green canvas chairs and cots in a larger than normal tent labeled "Emergency Medic and R & R."

Everyone was shouting and talking except the four young crew men who sat shaking in shock, ready for aid to be administered to cuts and abrasions. After sipping from metal canteens held by nurses, water was gently poured on their heads and faces by gentle hands for cool down. Hands peeled off khaki shirts that seemed to be smoldering from the smoke, dust and humidity.

And, since this is Ledo, India, where hundreds of men and trucks labor daily on the BURMA ROAD, medical attention is always necessary. Supplies of medical bandages, Sulphur, morphine, iodine and other staples are available to be hastily administered. The BURMA ROAD so far has taken a toll of "a man a mile".

Now, Flight Officer (F/O) Cooper shaking from trauma, begins to speak in staccato while nurse Polly sops blood from a deep scrape on his cheek. One long sleeve was gently ripped off by another medic checking for burns.

"A-a-after a routine landing at Myitkyina (Mitchee-NAH) and the unloading of ammo for the B-29 Bombers, I was headin' back to India when we got attacked by Jap Bettys swooping in thru the river valley, straffin' my plane and other transports that were still unloading." He attempted an arm wave illustrating the diving swoop. His arm flopped carelessly at his side. "A.a…a shell exploded in the cockpit shattering the instrument panel and fragments tore at my cheek. We had taken off and my plan was to land as quickly as possible before we exploded in the air. Crew members were yelling that the left engine and fuel tanks were on fire."

"And as one of the fighters made another dive at us, he was unable to pull up and crashed in a hill," the Co-Pilot added while listening.

"I nursed the ship here," said Cooper. "I don't believe it!"

Navigator Luke added with a deep sigh, "I didn't think we could make it."

"And we lost contact," interrupted the Radio Engineer shaking so badly that he spilled whiskey on his chin while sipping from a small metal cup. He continued, "Is everyone aware of the Japanese dummy-homing-stations that are there to throw us off?"

"How's that work soldier?" Petite young Nurse Judy administering iodine on scratches to his hand, couldn't help getting involved in the dramatic conversations. After all, this War was everyone's War to live and work to the end.

Navigator Luke continued while staring at Nurse Judy holding his shaking hand. "They pretend to be us by using our call letters to send us crashing into one of the many mountain tops."

"How do you know the difference?" she continued softly…too softly.

Luke gulped while now looking into two pools of brown eyes…long lashes…brightly colored lips… curls cascading around her face.

"Style" he said. "It's different."

Judy shook her head in understanding, yet afraid to ask for more. She continued helping the surgeon add special cream to burns on Luke's hands and a place on his upper arm where the khaki cloth had torn off exposing flesh from the exploding plane. She smoothed hair out of his face, back along his forehead, much to his pleasure.

Flight surgeon PALOOKA helped Nurse Polly start sutures on Cooper's cheek than stood back and let her take over. After setting his cigar on a small table, he opened a new pack of Lucky Strikes and casually offered a cigarette to each of the stunned crew. Mercifully grateful to be sitting there alive, they shook in their blankets even though the temperature was warm…very warm for a June day in Ledo.

"Coop was the hero of the day," James the Co-Pilot said. "Enemy gunfire was raking the aircraft from the rear." Two nurses hovered over him, attending to a cut on the top of his head and the numerous scratches on his arms. They smiled warmly and kept patting him on the back for comfort. James shook less and less, although the Lucky Strike wobbled while hanging loosely from his dry lips. "I'm happy to be alive," he continued. He let the cigarette fall to the ground at his feet and stomped on it. "They came up through the Irrawaddy River Canyon and got to us flying low out of Myitkyina (Mit-cheeNAH)." He spoke slowly, still in a bit of shock.

Radio Operator Martin mumbled. "I can't believe this. It's my first crash and I've lived to talk about it. July 24th I'll be 22 and I'm having a humdinger of a party. All are invited." He was hurt the worst and lay on the cot not smoking, but breathing hard. Blood was spurting from an ear lobe and also from the top of his head. He tried to touch his hair line with his index finger to stop the flow from dripping in his eyes. Quickly, Nurse Linda dabbed blood away with a heavy pad of gauze and pushed his hand slowly to his side. "I'll take good care of you soldier." She spoke soothingly. Only a miracle enabled the men to escape the flaming plane, and she knew it. She has seen too many planes go down with lives lost while landing. How was this one different? In her one year of service, she was no longer a new nurse. New in age, but old in experience she knew how to care for the desperately injured. Nurses are usually transferred back to the states after one year, but she had asked for an extension.

"We will all be at your birthday party," she whispered close so he could hear. Noticing his daze and shallow breathing, she waved for help from Flight Surgeon PALOOKA.

CHAPTER THREE—June 1944

PALOOKA PENNY ready to do what he could to save the life of the expiring young Radio Operator Martin, worried about his desperate shallow breathing, and the blood that spurted non-stop.

"Talk to me soldier." Nurse Linda did not want to lose him like she had seen so many others breathe a last puff of air. She smoothly stroked his hand hoping for a show of life.

Working quickly, PALOOKA strapped an oxygen mask loosely over Martin's face securing it with straps over the ears.

"Birthday party—twenty-two," he mumbled. His hand went limp in Linda's hold and his face fell to one side.

PALOOKA PENNY quickly checked for a pulse. Soon, he walked away shaking his head and rubbing his eyes with a few fingers.

"Hell-of-a-note" he repeated as others close by ducked heads in silence. Martin's flight crew wept openly.

Now he and head nurse Polly held each other for a long, long, time. A silent heaviness endured by all was soon broken as the other three were now more soothingly attended to. Cooper, Luke and James would be sent to the closest Field Medical Center, then on to a station hospital in Kunming, China. Recuperating in Darjeeling for Rest and Recreation was last on the list. Rehab was an important step for the flight crews because of the constant dangers they faced.

"I'll notify HOLT," he said sadly.

Everyone knew HOLT, the Base Operations Officer who traveled around the bases and posed as a liaison between the crews and Brass. He had connections everywhere. "Keep everyone happy and the War running smoothly," was his motto. "I need your chutes, or what's left of them," said PALOOKA.

The four men had kept them on as a necessary precaution when they knew they were in trouble and before they jettisoned out the cargo door during the crash. Now the three remaining men were glad to be free of them. Martin's would be tenderly cleaned, folded, and sent home to the grieving family. And too, Radio Operator Martin's body would be prepped for the long ride home.

PALOOKA PENNY was not only a flight surgeon but became a regular with the Jungle Wallas, a group "jump qualified". Jungle Wallas became the nickname given to tough guys, out-doors-men, loggers, rough necks and dare devils who attended the British Training School in Rawalpindi, India. Main issue teams for personnel recovery and return, was their priority. Each man was required to master the skill of re-packing chutes appropriately. So, PALOOKA soon became a man of many skills. Most importantly, his Search and Rescue team kept him busy and away from base problems.

Open to Americans who can "rough-it", PALOOKA immediately signed up a year ago after med training. He soon learned the difficulty of joining and the troubles inherited with such a group when tempers flared in bars over competitive toughness. Until the Brits felt the red-head's left fist and broad shoulder punches, they soon left him alone. Admirers offered him drinks and his adversaries learned to stay clear. He was notorious for no nonsense.

Nightly brawls relieved tensions of War, but were also the backaches for Military Police wielding clubs to break-up fights.

While everyone chatted and paper work was completed, the day dimmed and only the clinking of a nurse's Royal typewriter sounded in the distance. PALOOKA took the stub of cigar out of his mouth that he had been working on, cleaned it, wrapped it in a piece of wax paper and put it in his shirt pocket. Next, he smoothed his long moustache outward with his fingers. Thinking it defined his toughness, he would never shave it off.

"Hey, I have to meet a buddy of mine in Sookerating for a birthday party. You wanna come?" Palooka looked at Polly who was now washing medicine off her hands from contact with the injured crew. He sounded cheerless as was expected for the circumstance. But, this was War and the cadence of life marched on…and on…and on.

"When you going?" She asked, while wiping down counters and instruments with a bottle of alcohol. Her tone was neither one of excitement nor indifference. This would be an event like all others, and she needed to get away from death for a while.

"Tomorrow. A group of us are meeting in Sook at the Swing Canteen for an evening birthday party for F/O Bobby Johnson. He's flying today but has tomorrow off."

"Can't miss it!" She said.

PALOOKA watched her folding small, clean service towels stacking them neatly in a closed basket. Soiled ones were over-flowing in another. He lingered and watched for a few minutes. One side of her brown curly hair clipped back securely behind an ear with Bobby pins while the other side loosely framed her face in hiding. He wanted to touch the curl that plopped around her face and tiny nose pulling it out of the way. But, this was not the place, nor the time.

"Talk to me soldier," she said sadly and continued working. Periodically, she tried to blow the sprig of hair out of her face.

"BOBBY JOHNSON turns twenty-one tomorrow. We joined the Army Air Corps together back in Arizona. He and a group of us."

"Group still together?" This was important to her considering all the deaths and misplaced servicemen. "Yeah." He began to name them. "We all started out together as F/O's but have changed jobs. Still we get together often when possible. There's HOLT, LUCKY LARRY, JOHNSON and me."

"Who's me." She smirked.

"PALOOKA's the name," extending his hand.

"You say Sookerating?" She had too repeat it. Keeping the conversation going was important. Drying her hands on the service smock of apron wrapped around her tiny waist she asked, "At the Swing Canteen there?" They shook hands.

"You know where it is?"

"Sure do soldier. It's this side of the Brahmaputra River."

He held her hand a little too long, not wanting to let go.

"Polly's the name." She gently pulled away. LUCKY LARRY approached all excited. "I've been over there with the watering crew fighting the smoldering plane and it looks like I can take the rivets out of the metal flap, remove it with my paint job nose art intact, and salvage it for re-use." "And <u>LUCKY LULU</u> can ride on another plane." Polly's remark put a smile on everyone who heard. "You going to the Swing Canteen tomorrow night too?"

"Wouldn't miss it, but I need a date." He looked around as PALOOKA moved closer to Polly.

"Who needs a date?" Nurse Louise was standing by with a group of five nurses all arranging medicines, emptying and filling bottles with precision.

LUCKY LARRY raised his hand and grinned.

"You're all invited. I'm playing sax with the band." "Hell yes! It's Saturday night party time," PALOOKA shouted.

"No bar fights?" Polly asked, raising a brow while staring at Palooka. "I've heard about you."

"What?"

"Your left fist. I want to dance and not play nurse."

LUCKY LARRY folded his arms at his thin middle and turned around in a tight circle rubbing his bare chin. "Seriously, how do we keep the Brits away?" "It's a secret," said PALOOKA.

"And we're not sharing our women with them," LUCKY LARRY stated as the nurses grinned. "I'll drink too that." PALOOKA re-opened the locked grey cabinet of whiskey bottles and brought out a new one.

LUCKY LARRY grabbed the small shot glasses and helped pour. "Hubba hubba!"

The few soon became a group as everyone needed an out from today's crash. WU was waved in to join the group. As the top interpreter for all of them, he never left the group. Orphaned as a child and raised by an elderly British couple in Kunming, he was bi-lingual.

Chinese workers were busy with mules and carts helping clear debris from the run–way. WEN WU whined orders as backhoes shoveled smoldering pieces into a pit on the sides to cool and be added to the huge stock pile of parts. He knew how it was to be done. HOLT had taught him well. He rubbed his eyes, shook his head and sighed deeply. HOLT would ask for a precise description of what happened today…with the crash, and WU would have to relive the scene as he has done many, many times.

Noise dimmed with the day as workers bedded animals in stalls, corrals, and barns for tomorrow's work.

Another day done.

Planes flew overhead continuously.

June rain came pouring down.

DING HAO!

CHAPTER FOUR—June 1944 Jorhat, India

HARRY HOLT walked out of Base Operations with a large pad of paper in one hand and tacks in the other. Under the porch awning and attached to the wooden wall a huge ten foot bulletin board covered with cork matting clung tightly. Size was important considering all the notes of multiple orders, flight plans, news from home and other pertinent announcements. Loose papers flapped in the warm breeze, some yellowed and some fresh. He had new written instructions from headquarters in his hand for all pilots and co-pilots to read, and as Base Operations Officer, one of his many titles, actually a liaison of sorts, his job was to ensure messages from upper brass were always delivered in a hierarchy pattern, a timely chain of command. That meant from top to bottom. But, who was on bottom in this wet-moist-humid, swamp of a land?

Easy answer.

No one!

After attaching the new instructions on the bulletin board, he needed to talk to the young crew men who were busy with their off duty chores and remind them to READ THE DAMN orders. In his pocket was a personal note from home, a Western Union message he had received last night. After reading it for the tenth time, he tenderly folded it before putting it back in his shirt pocket.

Unhappily, he gritted his teeth too firmly and kicked at a green moss covered rock in his path reminding him that he needed to keep ridding his feet of toe fungus from this fetid jungle. At one point, everyone suffers from jungle rot in one way or another under the guise of amoebic dysentery or toe fungus.

He glanced over at the medic tent and at the nurses bustling about. Again, he took the Western Union bulletin out of his pocket, the one he had received last night at bedtime. Tenderly, he put it away in his shirt.

He walked back to the make-shift building and decided to talk to the crew in a few more minutes. For now, he sat on a wooden bench and watched the action. Noise was everywhere and the new young crew men seemed to bounce with too much enthusiasm, he thought.

Planes roared overhead, jeeps and trucks were noisily hauling supplies to planes out on the fields for loading the C46's and C47's in formation for continuous twenty-four hour delivery to Kunming, China. Holt had confidence in his friend WEN WU who made sure that the Chinese laborers completed their dangerous jobs of loading and un-loading with precision. Because it was a constant unrelenting effort, there were many near fatal accidents. One in particular stays with him always. At the end of a hazardous late night flight, and as he, PALOOKA, LUCKY LARRY, and BOBBY JOHNSON, brought the ship in for a so called perfect landing on a narrow strip, laborers started walking across leading water buffaloes hauling carts of supplies for an early dawn loading. A wing tip cleared the group by inches.

DING HAO.

Now, he continued to watch the crew men out front. Since Burmese girls were helping them with their laundry, they had time to throw a baseball back and forth. One missed ball flew towards him. "Hey!" HOLT caught it with one hand and threw it back.

They laughed. He frowned even though he knew this was all good.

Daily he witnessed youthful spirits dampened by treacherous icy flights over THE HUMP. He thought about buddies who bailed out over melting jungles and the rock pile to never making it back. Never heard from again.

Bailing out over the Himalayas meant freezing to death before hitting the ground in weather 20 to 50 degrees below zero. On the other hand, Jungle bailouts meant facing primitive tribes or landing in deep rivers only to drown from the pull of parachute and gear bag. PALOOKA, his best friend now in Search and Rescue, has told him many stories.

Shaking his head to eliminate negative thoughts, he took his pipe from the upper pocket, filled it and put it in his mouth unlit. Next, he took off his cap, finger combed his wavy brown hair back off his face and decided he needed a haircut next trip to Sookerating.

Demands of today meant authorizing clean up and re-use of the landing strip where Cooper and crew crashed. Since WU was in charge of workers, he knew with confidence the job would get completed. This was one of HOLT'S aircraft and crew.

Of his many jobs, he acts as Senior Officer with six aircraft and crews, commanding flights from and to the three North-Eastern bases in Ledo, Chabua, and Sookerating. Since these flights originate in India, Burma and China—the so called CBI routes of the Pacific Theater, the hazards are many and the Jap Bettys play upon these hazards, every one of them targeting shoddy handmade landing strips they can attack with their Zeros.

He lit his pipe, sat back and watched the baseball game commencing out front and thought, *this is good.* At thirty, he is the old man, been to many dangerous places and seen too much.

In the last six months of 1943, losses due to weather, mechanical problems and pilot error, included 135 aircraft crashes with a loss of 168 air crew members. Some were his closest friends. There were many unanswered letters circulating around camp. Families back home wanted to know more. He tended to the ones from family of crews he knew. Writing accounts of heroism— treasured words they wanted to hear back home about their loved one, he simply combined an unopened family letter written to the deceased with his letter of the airman's accomplishments and sent all back in one envelope. *This is good!*

He set his pipe down after a quick smoke, dumped its contents, and thought about his friends.

Tent buddies he gambled and partied with for years—gone.

Crews he flew with—gone.

But, nothing matched the open letter he carried in his shirt pocket.

Taking it all in on this steaming hot day, he planned to cling to the last few that he has known the longest—PALOOKA, LUCKY LARRY, and BOBBY JOHNSON.

A short distance away, soldiers were constructing a privacy screen in front of an open air latrine, a row of ten seats. Like HOLT, they rolled sleeves above elbows and cuffed their pants to the knees in the stifling heat.

"Typhoon blew the roof off our latrines." One airman looked his way and assumed he needed validation for what was going on.

"Cooler that way," HOLT said. "When finished, all of you need to read the bulletin board with the new instructions. Initial next to your name that you read everything." His voice was now loud and commanding. "Brass is complaining that you fail to read and initial."

"Will do."

"Yeah."

"Next job to do when finished here." HOLT didn't like the new order about—*No additional fuel will be available when flying back from CHINA. Use normal climbing and cruising power.* He knew the dangers of "minimal fuel". Orders assumed ships could stop at Chabua and Sookerating for more fuel if the gauge is low. HOLT knew the high winds which threw the planes off course were responsible for low fuel crashes. He himself had to switch power from manual to autopilot—back and forth many times in order to have enough fuel to land. Twice he landed without enough fuel to taxi the length of the short—always too short--runways. As a result and as a mature precaution, he ALWAYS uses a measuring stick to determine that he is not short changed of the appropriate fuel allotted. And after all, since fuel is hand pumped from 50 gallon drums, mistakes can easily be made and fuel sabotaged. Who would do this? Probably some careless new person not paying attention. Another item on his list to solve.

He just sat on the bench, watching and listening to the youthful group out front, building a new cover to the latrines, doing their laundry and singing.

"Roll me over in the clover, roll me over lay me down and do it again. Oh this is number one and the fun has just begun…"

Burmese girls, half of them bare-chested, laughed and giggled as they helped with the drudgery of laundry, shuffling quickly to the clothes line and back again.

All was good, Holt thought.

Today was his day off and he had downed two shots of whiskey from the locked cabinet in the office. He knew that he needed to deal with the shock of the letter in his shirt pocket. He'd put it off until later.

LUCKY LARRY parked his Willys Jeep close by and jaunted over with the almost empty whiskey bottle in hand, the one used for the horror of Cooper's crash in Ledo. His usual gate, a walk with springs in his knees, and that of a thin man, always put a smile on HOLT'S face.

"Eat something before the wind blows you over," said HOLT while playing with his now unlit pipe, smacking the butt of it against his cheek, his usual habit. "Read," he said to his best friend and pointed to the bulletin. His arm waved out of control and he almost lost his balance. With the movement, the envelope with the air-mail coloring on its edges containing the letter inside, flipped out on the ground. HOLT quickly retrieved it before the wind took hold. Dramatically, he kissed the envelope before shoving it back in his shirt.

"Holy mackerel, what's your problem?"

CHAPTER FIVE—June 1944

Since HOLT was in his non-speaking mood, LUCKY LARRY decided to read aloud from the new instructions.

"It has been noted that there is a marked laxity of pilots reading the bulletin boards…" LUCKY LARRY noted a new roster of names needing the initials of each pilot as indication of having read the bulletin. He read on.

To date there are less than five percent of the pilots who have initialed the roster. All pilots and co-pilots WILL read and initial the bulletin board at once!

LUCKY LARRY looked over at HOLT for a reaction, but he hadn't moved from the step where he was sitting, still thumping the butt of his pipe on his cheek in a dismal state.

He read on. *It is the responsibility of the pilot to instruct the co-pilot before flights just what he is to do. In case of engine failure or other emergency on take offs, they can function as a crew.*

"Hey HOLT! How many engine failures and near take off misses have we had?"

HOLT muttered almost silently, "Not enough toes and fingers to count."

Not accepting this as an answer, he pushed on. The current condition of his close friend bothered him so he decided to taunt him with a discussion and out of his stupor. He sat next to him elbow to elbow and watched the laundry scene out front. He took the shot glass from his upper pocket, poured it half full with whiskey and handed it to HOLT. Next, he drank briefly from the bottle, emptying it and throwing it down at their feet.

"We were fully loaded with fifty Chinese Nationals"—HOLT began hardly audible—"and the nose wouldn't lift going down the runway. Crew and I shouted for all of them to move back to the tail-end as far as possible to lighten the front of the plane. We barely made it clipping the tops of the banana trees at the end of the runway stripping the trees and filling our wheels with leaves."

"I remember it well," his friend answered. "We barely made it. Thankfully, the leaves had blown out of the wheels during the long three hour flight to Kunming, China."

Next, he briefed HOLT descriptively about Cooper's crash and the demise of Martin, the young radio operator. All happened hours ago in Ledo, and HOLT had already heard the details. Now, they sort of leaned on each other sadly. Too many thoughts about crashes to relive.

"Need to leave for a bit," LUCKY LARRY said. "I'll be back to discuss the birthday party tomorrow in Sookerating for BOBBY JOHNSON."

An un-responsive HOLT sat staring out front at the action. He patted his shirt pocket that contained the opened envelope with the letter positioned over his heart.

His friend did his usual hop into his door-less Willys and headed toward a C-47 that was being loaded with pieces of disassembled machinery heading out to China to be assembled and welded back together after landing. As the main AMO Aircraft Maintenance Officer, he made sure he kept busy so that a drifting brass from headquarters will always see how important he is and won't ask him to pilot a plane over the HUMP as an F/O. He has all the necessary credentials of a Flight Officer and has put in his time, but never wants to go back to the dangerous job.

He was one of the early graduates of the Army Air Corp and HOLT had been his instrument flight instructor a couple of years ago, then test pilot and on to station chief pilot in charge of training. Somehow the two had been paired together with PALOOKA and BOBBY JOHNSON.

"Comradeship is a good but dangerous thing," HOLT had said over and over having lost best pals numerous times.

HOLT sat on the low bench a long time watching the men construct the new privacy screens to the row of latrines when a Brit in knee length shorts and short sleeve khaki shirt approached. Stepping out of a jeep, looking too fresh from a cooler somewhere, and with both hands on his hips he spoke. "Who are these raunchy men?" While accenting the word raunchy he left out the 'r' letter and raised his eyebrows in contempt.

It was Saturday and break time for the flight crew of about thirty men who were working on the latrine screens. Some were lolling around in boxers under green open-air tents, sitting on canvas folding chairs, all soaking feet in a fungus fighting solution. Half were smoking and playing craps, yelling, laughing, and drinking whiskey somewhat wildly in the bone melting-sweltering-heat. The skimpy clothing was sweat soaked.

CHAPTER SIX—June 1944

"Spitz, you new here?" A raging HOLT jumped to his feet a little too fast blowing smoke in the newcomer's face from his freshly lit pipe.

He savored the name Spitz and tagged it to anyone he didn't like or care to know. Noting the Brit's shirt of badges and stars, he assumed this guy of rank had the audacity to intimidate others. Swaying from the heat and the extra shot of whiskey, he grabbed the nearest post and leaned on it.

"Spitz, you're looking at boys fresh out of the Army Air Corps training school having the guts to fly through the soup over the Rock Pile facing winds of over 100 MPH to get supplies to China." He swayed.

He had not seen Spitz before, not even at the popular SWING CANTEEN frequented by Brits, Aussies and Yanks in Sookerating.

Raging battles between Brits and Americans were a Saturday night fist festival keeping the military police busy. In the old days, two years ago, the two lefties—husky HOLT and powerful PALOOKA--earned money from on-lookers placing bets. Of course, look-outs were stationed at the doors in case military police were coming with their batons.

They were young hot heads flexing muscle. And as always, after fights and brawls among testy groups, drinks were offered all around the canteen and blood blotted before brass and military police arrived.

Nevertheless, now Holt became furious and much later in retrospect blamed it on what—the letter he tenderly pocketed? The fetid stinky environment? The whiskey? Or simply the ostentation displayed by the freshly dressed newcomer? He blamed it on the latter.

Red faced with temper rising he continued in a low shout causing others to stop what they were doing and watch. He swayed again.

"These youthful spirits are dampened by amoebic dysentery, icy flights, landings on primitive strips cut into sides of mountains and bailouts over jungles inhabited by dangerous primitive tribes!" He shouted.

The louder he talked, the madder he got. With shoulders squared and chest flexed he puffed on his pipe one last time before dumping the lit contents on the ground near Spitz. Too hot to put back in his pocket, he simply tossed the sacred tool back on the porch where he had been sitting and clenched his fist ready for any confrontation.

Spitz lit his limey cigarette, blew smoke in the red face of Holt who had advanced too close, and laughed! He threw back his slim upper back in a sway and laughed again, this time more loudly, open mouthed, showing bottom layer of crooked teeth.

HOLT, not realizing his condition from the heat, the whiskey, and tiredness, fell in the arms of the Brit as he swung his fist in full force capturing air, and while doing so stumbled on a rock.

Spitz walked him back to the porch in the shade and sat him down.

Immediately, HOLT felt for the letter making sure it was still there in his upper pocket near his heart. Dazed, he leaned on a porch pole, grabbed his pipe and straightened his cap which had been askew all along and the cause of Spitz's laughter.

"Snake!!" LUCKY LARRY coming around the building, yelled as the venomous varmint came winding from the edge of the jungle anchoring itself to a latrine where an airman was sitting behind a make shift piece of screen, boxers at his ankles. The snake snuggled too close.

All froze.

"Sonofabitch," said HOLT.

Spitz began a low whistle—a tune of some sort and backed toward the jungle. No one moved as the giant Cobra began to follow him in undetermined spurts, than moved away on its own into the deep green undergrowth of the sweltering jungle.

Laughter and thanks followed as the airman leaving the screened latrine white-faced and shaking, hurried away.

"Spitz, I owe you," said HOLT taking his pipe in his left hand…his toy, his security blanket.

"We're throwing a birthday party for BOBBY JOHNSON'S 21st at the SWING CANTEEN in Sook tomorrow night. Join us." LUCKY LARRY intervened, smoothing out the volatile situation that could have taken place.

"I'll be there with some friends." Spitz left without another word in his dark grey Jeep weaving down the muddy trail of a road.

After he left, LUCKY LARRY mumbled, "What did he mean by 'friends'? And what's wrong with you?" He looked at HOLT who had walked away to their tent near headquarters and sat on his cot. For the tenth time, he took the letter out of his top pocket and with a grim face read it.

"Hey," whispered a soldier standing next to LARRY. "That better not be a 'Jade' letter…you know for the Jade wall."

True. There was a wall in all the barracks containing a pin-up area from the girls who wrote 'Dear John' letters to a specific young man stating, *"I found another and simply can't wait for you…"* The goodbye letters were usually cold and precise. Soldiers felt jaded. There was always comradery with loss, and this was usually played out in some way at the SWING CANTEEN. Here, nurses became beautiful with sympathy.

LUCKY LARRY saying nothing, had followed his good buddy into the large tent of cots and cabinets. Lighting a Camel, he sat on his cot and watched him nearby, wondering why the short fuse today.

HOLT opened a locked cabinet, took out a bottle of whiskey, and drank from it long and hard before capping it and tossing it on the ground. He flopped spread eagle on his cot with the letter in his hand and passed out.

The opened letter lay on his chest, of course inviting LUCKY LARRY'S curiosity.

"Sorry to write you about a terrible loss. Your family begged me to inform you that Babs met with a terrible car accident and is now deceased. Everyone here feels your sorrow…."

LARRY neatly folded the letter, placed it in the envelope and shuffled it back into HOLT'S pocket. Next he put the almost empty bottle of whiskey back in the cabinet, locked it and hid the key among his things in another cabinet.

In a tent nearby, a group was singing his favorite marching cadence.

I've got six pence. Jolly, jolly six pence. I've got six pence to last me all my life.

A radio signal of an injured plane coming in for a landing interrupted. "Mayday! Mayday!"

I've got two pence to lend and two pence to spend and two pence to send home to my wife, poor wife…

"Mayday! Mayday!"

CHAPTER SEVEN—June 1944

"BAIL OUT! BAIL OUT!"

F/O BOBBY JOHNSON, yelled to his crew and re-checked his chute for the third time to ensure he was buckled in properly. His dis-attached oxygen mask and heated electric suit lay at his feet as he prepared to jump.

A lightning bolt memory of the catastrophic death last month of his tent buddy Tucker flashed through his mind in seconds.

Tucker was the F/O of his crew and after yelling "BAIL OUT" everyone made it out, safely floating to the ground except Tucker. His chute was loosely buckled and he fell out of it when the billowing silk opened, plummeting him to his death. The three members of his crew found each other through shouts and made the half-mile trek to the scattered pieces of C-46 per directions from brass—"Stay with the plane so Search and Rescue can find you." This is the number one directive from Air Traffic Command, the ATC.

Chuck, the Radio Engineer, had contacted Bed Post, the nearest high frequency tower about their dilemma. They were flying the upper ABLE route from Tezpur to Myitkyina (Mit-chee-NAH) fully loaded with gas for the B-29s when they hit a black cloud and had no choice but to plow through it on instruments. This route hugged the Himalayas and its dangerous peaks. BOBBY JOHNSON and crew feared for their lives high above the Patkai Range. Quickly using call letters 860 and direction finder "King Charlie", Chuck was able to give the radio tower their bearing. Assigned altitude was 15,000 and all four were on oxygen.

Previously, after about one hour of extreme icing from the weather, they were dropping altitude. Ice formed on the inside of the cockpit window. Although this had never happened to BOBBY'S plane before, he had heard stories from others as a warning. Also in the last hour of panic they rolled about ten, fifty gallon drums of fuel out of the hatch in vain.

Props and throttle froze. Both engines failed.

They bailed out through the cargo hatch and cleared the ship just before it hit a mountain top and exploded. Two hours ago they had left north Assam, India, high above the Naga Hills and were east of the Patkai Range over northern Burma. A silver streak on the ground was the Chindwin River and Bobby knew the area from previous flights with his buddies HOLT, LUCKY LARRY and PALOOKA.

F/O's regularly identified areas by ridges and rivers. First ridge flying west to east was the Patkai Mountains and before the second ridge of Himalayas was the Irrawaddy River which flowed from the high mountains of Tibet to Burma forming a lake near Mandalay. Crew members feared drowning with full gear weighing them down and pulling them under swift currents.

Bobby had mentally marked the route via the rivers they crossed from Tezpur and other areas of the Assam, India Valley, to their main destinations of Kunming, China, where they were to empty their load and pick up Chinese National soldiers and the injured. Always the injured.

Now, floating, floating down and than up by the thrusting wing, he worried about freezing to death. Luckily he was bundled in three layers which was his usual attire when flying the upper Able route. Horror stories of crew members freezing to death after jumping, played on his mind. *Breathe deeply— don't fall asleep!*

Problems of all kinds flashed through his mind as he slowly descended. Thoughts of the crew members' oxygen tanks and his, all thrown aside for the jump and the dangerous sleepiness that quickly accommodates the altitude they had just left, plagued him now. At fifteen thousand feet, swallowing hard every few seconds was necessary as lungs gasped for air and hearts pounded.

Down, down, he descended. *He had done his best. The tricky air pockets had tossed the ship up and down violently. But the accumulated ice on wings did the negative as the C-46 thrashed around headstrong before he lost control. Ole Dumbo had lost out to the Himalayas.*

Far, far away he saw the three other chutes open as expected and the men floating down from the air hopefully within calling distance, down into NAGA INDIAN territory between the Dikoo River and Kohim. Here the NAGA is a manly, cheerful fellow preserving his tribal customs and dances. But, northeast from the Dikoo in the Margherita direction, the customs and morale of the NAGA groups degenerate dangerously. So he had been told. And this was Head-hunters' territory.

Bobby had memorized tribal information that was important to note in case of a bail out—like NOW! And currently on his mind was the display of heads he had seen in a Burma Village—heads neatly tied on a board—about twenty of them. Was it his imagination or did the two short Indians nearby stare extra-long-and-hard at his thick blond shock of hair? "Holy Shit!" Was the simultaneous reaction among him and his group. They were told that the heads were captive souls becoming future servants to the hunter.

Floating, he shook with the ghastly memory.

Immediate thoughts were to locate the crew. Copilot Harry, Radio man Chuck and Walt the Engineer bailed out first and would be close by. He was sure of it. Since he had radioed in to the closest station in Mohanbari their plight, he believed one of his best buddies, PALOOKA of Search and Rescue would be coming for them. "Hang tight" was his mentor.

With the wind at his back pushing him down, down out of the freezing cold, he considered luck was with him so far. Since it was the middle of June and not the first months of the year, warmer currents greeted him as he landed in a green, bushy forest of wild tea plants and banana trees. So soon? How long had he floated?

THINK! THINK!

Rolling as he landed, he cushioned the final contact crouching with the chute billowing over him. *I'm alive.* Breathing deeply he sat for a while gathering his thoughts.

It was a weird feeling to be on the ground after flying above. Shaking as he stood, his knees were wobbly while rolling his chute per training. When finished, it became a tight back pack and a life saver with its many uses.

Next, he patted his flak jacket and his canvas bag making sure the Jungle Kit was intact. He would check all necessary tools for survival when his mind adjusts. Since his hands were bleeding from numerous cuts and abrasions sustained from the landing, he scolded himself for not wearing his gloves in the plane. He swiped at a cut on his cheek as blood ran down his neck. Gingerly feeling his cheek for wound assessment, he determined it was deep and short.

From his kit, he took the Sulphur powder and applied it on all his open wounds. Occasionally yelling out the names of the crew, only echoed in the empty air. He listened. Keenly aware of sounds now, his heart pounded too loudly in his chest as he held his breath to concentrate on surrounding sounds.

Leaves thrashed from intermittent winds. Rain was coming. This was June, the month of weather change from cold to torrents of rain.

The quiet sound of water running far, far below caught his attention.

A river flowed somewhere in the far distance and he feared for his crew. Where were they? Had they drowned in a swift river after tangled gear pulled them under?

Two shots from his 45 were all he could afford.

What if he needed it for an emergency?

There was no response.

All the hill tribesmen are friendly and your gun will not be necessary as they are not a threat. Sure, he thought cynically. Brass had not seen the board of mounted heads.

Shivering, he noted the coldness and searched for his gloves in his canvas kit, a large bag worn over one shoulder that contained his survival kit. Carefully, he pulled them on over the small injuries. At the beginning of June, the weather changes from cold to wet as the start of the monsoon is under way. He hoped for warmth and feared icy nights. His decision was to continue walking down towards the river he heard and out of the higher altitude. Staying with the damaged plane was unthinkable. He would have to climb back up the mountains that he had drifted from, and by now, he was many miles away. Luckily, the winds had floated him down to warmer currents and away from the lofty mountains of ice. If he could make it to a sandy river bank, PALOOKA with Search and Rescue would find him. Again he repeated this thought as a goal. His friend had successfully rescued many, landing on a sandy river bank with his small L'5. In the extreme last minute confusion for survival, he lost sight of the river markings. Surely, the river he heard was the Chindwin which flowed below the Naga Hills, home of the Naga Indians, both good and bad. Searching for trails in the thick brush was mandatory. Trails made by animals and people would help him get out of here. With thoughts that the many hill tribes had never seen foreigners before, he worried. They were a simple people.

Mitch's words during his last poker game with the guys pounded his thoughts. He would have to survive and meet his tent buddies of F/O's, Radio men and Navigators, all the boys planning a 21st birthday shin-dig. He was proud to be one of the Hump Pilot boys of the CBI and was eager to celebrate. Stories—stories—stories were shared by all, bringing laughs and fear of near disasters. Comradery kept them motivated. PALOOKA would find him. HOLT would demand it and LUCKY LARRY would be part of the Search and Rescue. Surely, laughs and tall tales were in the immediate future.

Again he listened.

Where were the other three?

So this was loneliness. Move out and get out before dark. Thoughts of his twenty-first birthday party motivated him with positive encouragement.

And there was the nurse named Bonnie. They shared fresh hot coffee before his flight early this morning because she was heading out on a rescue assignment. Although she was in the familiar khaki outfit—baggy in places and tight in others—she looked like a movie star.

"See you at the Swing Canteen," she had said while her thick blond hair held back behind her ears by two shiny silver barettes, swirled around narrow shoulders. Large green eyes sparkled above ruby red lips. Her fleshy smile opening to perfect ivories mouthed, "See you later."

Remembering how he simply nodded instead of grabbing her for a kiss, left him feeling whipped and empty at this moment. But, how did she know about the party for him, when and where?

Pleased with determination that he would meet her again, he sighed, readjusted his pack over his left shoulder and tucked the cumbersome roll of chute in the pit of his right arm.

Consoling his fear of the unknown as he searched for a trail, the last flight piloted by PALOOKA and his crew came to mind. They had tricked Brits out of crates of whiskey when they were on the same flight heading to Kunming.

Now from his kit, he sipped a swig of whiskey from a flask and recounted the story that was told. *Flying supplies to the British in Burma was always a good time for the American G.I.'s. Because there were no land entrances for them in Burma, due to the Japanese occupations at Rangoon, all supplies had to be delivered by plane—including their month's ration of whiskey for officers and men. A British soldier always accompanied the boxes of whiskey, standing guard with a loaded machine gun as a watch dog. He usually sat by the back door with gun propped against the cases and snoozed from the plane's vibration. On this particular run, the crew chief came back and asked the Brit if he would like to come up to the cockpit and fly the plane. "Yeah, I sure would," he said with excitement. Joining the staff, he stood between the pilot and co-pilot for a short while watching the scenery of picturesque mountains floating by.*

Soon the pilot asked, "You want to fly it for a minute?"

"Yeah, I sure would!" "Here sit in my seat."

The Brit sat in the left F/O seat, all smiles.

Then, "Here, push down a little and it'll go down. Up, and it will go up."

Meanwhile, the conniving crew member got busy loading the Brit's boxes of whiskey in the 'john' of the plane, clear to the top. When finished, he walked up front. The F/O seeing the crew member said, "I better take her now."

The Brit went back and sat down again next to his gun and the last few boxes, unaware of previous mischievous circumstances. The C-47 droned on. ALL were happy. The Brits would have to pay for their own whiskey at the SWING CANTEEN.

His smile was weak as he thought of the successful deed.

Looking around, he tried to determine how far down he had floated. On paper, the map was clear and distinct and the rivers were well outlined in black. Yet, reality meant confusion. Where are the earthy landmarks? His compass would help once he finds a known recognizable place—like the sandy banks of a river.

The lower the altitude, the more plush the jungle. Above 3,000 feet, the terrain thins. He had learned that tribal habitat was high on the hills, above the running rivers and streams. Yet, along the river he heard below, there could be some villages. Should he climb upward toward the hill tribes or keep heading downward toward the river?

CHAPTER EIGHT—June 1944

He stayed with his decision to travel down to the river below, where ever it is, and now needed to hurry due to cloudy weather and darkness. He figured that he was in the upper hill country and not too far from the Brahmaputra River that runs from the Himalayas on down to meet the Ganges, finally joining other tributaries emptying into the Bay of Bengal between Burma and India.

But, what does all this mean now that he is on the ground, lost, disoriented and in somewhat of a daze.

"Get your head together!" Words from one of his five sisters rang clear and loud. He could sure use their comforting words now.

It seems they had flown over the wide river hours ago. From a previous lecture about jungle conditions, he learned that North Assam and North Burma were extremely dense during the rainy season, like now the start of June. Most hill tribes stay at home and only travel to adjacent villages. It is during the winter when the jungle thins that travel is easier and the area becomes busy.

Is this good news or bad? He needed people for survival, but still worried about the tribes.

He never felt so alone with his decisions.

Knowing all the dangers he could face did not help his dilemma.

Where were the others who bailed out with him? The high winds must have separated them from each other. Or maybe they were together and he was the only loner?

From his pack he took out a coach's whistle and blew it staccato like an S.O.S as part of his plan. PALOOKA, the Jungle Walla pro, medical surgeon, F/O partner, had told him to do this in order to be found. PALOOKA, the red head with the wild red mustache, always originated plans for survival and had given him this special whistle. *"Could save your life someday"*, he had said. For now, BOBBY JOHNSON decided to keep it handy and ready. From his survival pack, he took out extra shoe laces. Tying them together and then to the whistle like a necklace, gave him a feeling of confidence. Periodically he would use it to signal for the bailed out crew.

The Jungle Walla. Five years his senior and his idol. So resourceful! What would he be doing right now in this circumstance? And now while listening for sounds, he recounted the stories told by many pilots having trouble taking off with such heavy loads that they had to tell their passengers to *"Move on back so the nose will lift!"*

For another full minute Bobby listened for sounds without moving. The return of another whistle would help him find the crew.

Nothing. Only echoes.

Taking a deep breath, he decided he needed some chocolate. He took out a small piece and thought about how crews before him had lived on small amounts of chocolate while lost for days. Remembering their stories, he knew the importance of rations.

He counted the squares. Since there were ten big ones, he decided to have one a day and would search for small fish to eat as trained, in the many streams and larger tributaries. He needed a supplement in addition to the chocolate. The area was filled with rocky streams this time of year and small fish three or four inches in length darted under flat stones in shallow water. When necessary, he knew how to catch a small fish and smoke it on a thin bamboo grid over a campfire. He and his buddies had accomplished this during survival training. Good old survival training. Thankfully, he didn't sleep through the lectures like some others did. *"Make friends with the good natives and they will help you survive,"* was an important motto. Sewn on the inside of his flight jacket was a 12 X 12 leather square identifying him as an American pilot with instructions in Mandarin stating that he is here to support the people and that they are to help him. For those who could not read, graphic pictures accompanied the letters. This square had saved many lost crew members.

He patted his jacket with confidence.

Looking around he saw no trail of any kind. But, nearby was an area of high flat land, a plateau. Perhaps from there he could better survey his surroundings.

Heading there, he made sure all gear was intact. The bag with survival kit was flung over one shoulder and his rolled up parachute was under an arm. Moving cautiously, always looking around and listening for any unfamiliar sound, he became more aware of small cuts and abrasions that now began to sting. Feeling the cut on his cheek with the back of his gloved hand reminded him that he needed more Sulphur medicine to spur the healing process and keep out infection. And, what's with this limp? Suddenly, he realized that his left ankle hurt and maybe it had become twisted after landing. Why hadn't he noticed it before?

From the plateau, he looked down on an extremely thick jungle, so dense that he could not see the river he heard flowing out there somewhere. And it began to rain. The downpour was instant and powerful. He expected much more to come since this was the middle of June and he was in Northeast India somewhere, the rain capital of the world.

Ducking under a small tree, he escaped the torrent a bit while constructing a small tarp overhead from the silk of his parachute. The shelter held as he stood next to the tree afraid to sit down on the muddy ground. He was on a high piece as fierce rolling streams raced down and around him heading towards a tributary. Later he plans to follow the streams to a source. For now, he needs to thoroughly check his survival kit for all its contents.

The jungle kit was originated for airmen who risk danger of a forced landing in N.E. Assam or Burma. "Ok", he said aloud, "this is for me." His mind was a little muddled, but he thought he remembered the kit's contents and now needed to reassess for livelihood.

Most useful for the moment was a light-weight, oiled –silk ground sheet which he could use as a cape from the rain. Or, better yet, ground cover for sitting. Laying it on leaves that were under foot, made a pad of some sort from the mud. He sat huddled, waiting for the rain to slow and continued his kit search.

A small canvas bag contained a compass, small flash light and a sharp cutting knife. In another package he found a service type mess tin, and a spare pair of thick woolen socks. Although there was plenty of fishing tackle in another tin, he is no fisherman. However, the twenty yards of fishing line will come in handy for smoking fish above a fire per example during survival training. "How to" examples were usually led by the Abors, one of the Hill Tribes in the area.

He pictured the extremely well-built, stocky group of natives who wore only a short sleeveless vest and a flap of cloth over their privates. Both men and women wore their hair the same—fringed in a short bang and cut short around the head. They laughed a bit as they served the bunch of us the tasty pieces of smoked fish.

He wouldn't mind meeting this group of people. Before reviewing the pamphlet about the main groups of Hill Tribes in N.E. Assam and the Northern Frontier of Burma, he needed to take care of the pain on his cheek.

Of the medicines, he took out the iodine for his face and a three inch crepe bandage to cover the cut. The sting was harsh and he gasped. Could he get blood poisoning from his scrapes? He noted that in the medicine kit, there were one dozen M&B 760 Tablets available for this sort of thing.

He wishes he could ring HOLT on what to do, or send him a telegraph. *"Tough it out!"* He would only say.

"And use your tin to boil water. There are not enough Quinine Bi-hydrochlor tablets to help you if you get diarrhea."

BOBBY remembered these survival notes and double checked his waxed container of matches--which he would do often.

Ration packs included dates and raisins.

He ate one date and six raisins. Like stories he had heard of previous crews, he would ration everything until making it out.

Next, there were maps of this area plus how to construct a shelter from the Wild Banana and the Jeng leaf. He was told that these plants grow profusely in the Patkai Range and North Burma. But looking around, nothing seemed familiar. He had spent a good year with Air Transport Command flying B-29's, C-46's and the C-47 to Africa, Australia and on to Ledo and other bases. Now, here he was on the ground looking at foliage he flew over. It was all too foreign.

Most importantly, he was looking for the necessary items needed to high-tell it out of this dangerous place, and those are the screw-in studs for his shoes. He read, *Highly recommended by others from previous bail-outs in this wet and dangerous territory, these studs, when attached to the bottoms of shoes, enabled crews to move quickly through the mud and thick brush.* Makes sense, he thought. Normal shoes and boots slip with every step.

While sitting on a nearby boulder, Bobby worked quickly and efficiently with the small auger and screw-in key, strategically placing three studs in the holes of each sole while listening to sounds. The gripping shoes were a miracle as he stomped around trying them out.

"Ouch!" He forgot about his foot.

Rain splattered noisily to a sudden stop. He got out from under the small tree that had been his refuge, folded the oil cloth he had used as a cape and added it to his bag again. Numerous veins of mud and water rolled downward where he must go if he is to find a river bank. Now, this is his goal. PALOOKA would be looking for him and the others early tomorrow. He was sure of it. Meanwhile, the descending darkness meant to find another place to hide-out and stay put.

He had a compass, map, warm clothes, and a survival kit. What could possibly go wrong?

An extremely loud noise of someone or something running through a path of bushes came closer and closer.

He turned sharply and yelled the crew's names.

No response.

The noise stopped.

"Who's following?"

When he walked he heard movement as if an animal or person was following. Each time he looked around.

Nothing. When he stopped, the movement stopped.

Now he felt the rawness of the wilderness where no soldier had walked— no white man. Hundreds of miles of raw adventure lay in each direction and he knew that the only people were the local natives who lived in small villages along the hillsides and flat areas of the river valleys.

The flight from Ledo, India to Kunming, China was around five hundred miles by air and over one thousand miles by foot. And here he was on foot with mandatory thoughts about survival.

That rustling bush sound again.

He had been still. It wasn't him. "Hey! Anyone there? Hello!" Nothing. No response.

Cupping his hands he yelled—"Chuck, Walt, Harry!"

Holding his breathe, he listened. Nothing.

Making circular turns, watching, he saw where the sound was coming from as a bush behind, on an upper mound, moved with a rustling effect so pronounced that he figured a native or animal was making serious efforts to frighten him. Animals don't frighten. They pounce.

High above, the drones of planes in the clouds seemed a vacant mystery. Quickly looking at his watch, it was now five in the afternoon. With a break in the cloud cover, the crew above could see the smoking plane and call PALOOKA at Search and Rescue. This was his hope.

A footpath he now followed went in various directions meandering this way and that, but always down. He decided to stay on it keeping his gun handy knowing something was following him.

Aware of the increasing throb from his sore ankle he now kept his sight on the pathway for a stick or pole length piece of sturdy plant.

After finding a piece thick enough to lean on, he hobbled faster, away from the rustling sound behind him.

Or so he thought.

He felt warmer now while moving around, plus he was not in the fifty below zero weather over the hump. Especially where he is headed, the weather warmed every few degrees sloping down to a river or one of the many large streams.

He knew that PALOOKA'S rescue crew flew the small K-9 down through the river canyons successfully and even landed on sandy banks when necessary. Half the time, bail-out crews made it to one of the many small huts and villages seeking help. Word was plentiful all over India, Burma and China to help the "fly-boys" and servicemen when in need.

Rescue leaflets were dropped in great numbers near remote mountainous villages. There were pictures of pilots parachuting down and natives helping. This gave BOBBY JOHNSON some comfort as he tried not to worry about the mystery of being followed.

Suddenly, there were sounds of a large knife cutting through the brush closely behind him.

Too close!

CHAPTER NINE—June 1944

BOBBY panicked for the first time since bailing out. Where could he hide?

Was this an enemy tribesman?

Earlier lectures mentioned that dangerous animals and snakes are almost non-existent in upper Assam and upper Burma. And that the jungles contain a small amount of elephants, tigers, leopards and snakes. India Bison border near the lower river banks.

Yet, he distinctly heard a knife.

BUT, he remembered stories contrary to the lectures. And now, he had reason to worry and be frightened.

He thought about the *small amount of tigers and leopards and snakes.* Ridiculous! All it takes is one to put him down. He took his 45 pistol out of the holster slung over his left shoulder concealed under his flight jacket and got ready for the surprise.

Since all the Army Air Corps members and all crews are living in tents and Bashas near landing strips, they are vulnerable to threats and disasters from the wild life. He had heard a repertoire of gory stories that bothered him now.

The two headed snake in a soldier's boot.

The angry water buffalo that stomped into a tent and gored a soldier to death.

Ducking back into a bush out of sight as far as possible, he waited and watched his back at all times and almost stumbled sideways while turning circles. Above, he saw a ledge that jutted out in his direction. Seeking to stand on it for a better view of his surroundings, he scrambled and crawled northward under tall branches. Thick, thorny bushes tore at his pant legs. Looking down, he noticed his ankle started swelling as the pain worsened.

The ledge gave him a feeling of his whereabouts as he had a 360 visibility, clear of banana trees and the thick thorny bushes that seemed to take over the countryside.

He shot his gun once, needing to be conservative.

No response.

Where were the other three? Squinting up toward the mountain from where he assumed they crashed, he saw no smoking plane. The numerous clouds and descending darkness were of no help.

Had he drifted so far away?

From his kit he took out his directional compass. South was where he needed to head, down towards a river bank where there is always an opening, where Search and Rescue flew through the canyons following the rivers and even landing small planes like the L-5 and Kaydet to rescue downed crews. This was constantly on his mind.

At his back he heard the loud noise again of small rocks and something scrambling toward him.

And there he was!

Immediately upon the same ledge within six yards in front was a native, a short square of a man staring with an angry frown and tall spear in hand pointing to the ground. His hair was a jagged cut and he wore a dao necklace of teeth and bones down from his shoulders to his waist. Bare chested with only a flap in front to cover, he stood barefooted on the cold rock and stared.

With a thumping heart, BOBBY stared back and tried not to show how startled he was. Surely the native had heard his gun when he signaled a few moments ago and knows its danger. Or does he? *What sign language can I use? What native words can I say for friendliness?*

The native's face was void of expression and eyes seemed to squint in anger as he slowly moved his hand to the shaft attached to a cord around his waist. Pulling out a twelve inch knife, he thrust it outward all in one super motion—two, three times. Acting pie-eyed, he swayed from some unknown substance and almost fell.

Stunned, BOBBY held his hands up as a form of peace sign and slowly opened his jacket for the native to see the leather piece sewn to the inside. Pictographs explained for those who couldn't read, that he is an Airman and needs help. Although there are words written in Chinese with drastic information, the native was not the least bit interested because he never looked at it—only keeping eyes on a strange white man—acting like he had never seen one before.

BOBBY felt the savageness of the place and had heard stories of local hill bandits who stole everything on sight and killed for entertainment. Or, if he is a head-hunter, as some of the Naga are, he knew he was in trouble. He had learned from his earlier briefings that some of the Naga are shifty characters, and greatly exploited by a number of illicit opium traders who use them to produce the opium in the hills. Although now prohibited in Assam, he had been warned it is still an existing problem. Where the major tea gardens of the world run up and down the mountain sides, the workers never seem to be without the dope.

The way this native teetered and could not stand still, was a reason to worry. And if he traveled down from the North East in the Margherita direction, he is one of the wilder natives. All the more reason to worry.

He remembered the lecture. *It is on the Manipur Road, the heart of Naga culture, where Naga's practice tribal customs and dances. These are the manly, cheerful fellows.* He remembered watching groups as they came close to bases with their tribal drums, hewn out of solid tree trunks. It was a thing of wonder.

He decided to talk to the native pretending that he could understand and used soothing tones. Why not? What else could he do? For sure, the native could out run him. This is his territory. He would not turn and try to escape—at least not yet.

BOBBY pointed to the sky many times and made child-like airplane motions and noises.

He motioned the native forward, opened his pack and offered a piece of chocolate to him after biting off a small piece for himself. Sort of a peace pipe offering—soldier to Indian—like in the Lone Ranger movies he had seen back home.

He noted eight chocolates left.

The native indicated he wanted the entire parachute and kit by thrusting forward a muscular, dark-tanned short arm with stubby thick fingers motioning like a spider. The other hand still gripped the knife.

Caught off guard, the young airman stepped back, shook his head negative and thumped his fist on his chest—indicating what? A foolish reaction necessary for survival didn't bother him but giving his necessary equipment to the native, did.

Quinine and Atabrine pills kept amoebic dysentery at bay. Extra matches, leggings and mosquito netting could also help keep him alive. Fishing lines, hooks, a morphene syringe and emergency D rations with chocolate, were part of the medical kit. Parting with the kit meant certain death.

He shook his head an emphatic NO and reached for his 45.

Just as the short, angry native thrust forward with knife in one hand and spear in the other, a loud noise occurred from behind and BOBBY fell over while stepping back on a slippery moss fed rock. The spear flew by his head inches away and landed in mud.

On his knees he rolled to the side as a force of three fierce looking natives shouted and thumped their spears at the lone native in front.

"Jakeet! Jakeet!"

Words were yelled and the angry Naga native turned and disappeared.

BOBBY saw the flash of hate in his eyes just before he rushed through thick brush ahead still ranting and shouting. Occasionally he stopped, looked back and aimed his spear upward with angry jabbering.

He knew that the fierce native would be back.

CHAPTER TEN—June 1944

Using any kind of old fashion sign language, BOBBY thanked them as best he could. Than he opened his pack and offered each a small piece of chocolate. They nodded and smiled in gratitude.

Five pieces remaining.

Also, he noticed the three were pulling a solid tree trunk about four feet long and guessed an enormous drum would be carved from it. This was a good sign because he knew this trio was the friendly group. He started pounding on the tree trunk in a make believe drum beat and the natives laughed and shook their heads. Since they were barefoot, they made a big fuss about his shoes with the screw-in studs.

He lifted his foot showing how they worked. Each of the trio laughed again waving hands and arms around indicating swiftness and speed.

These were the good guys, the innocent natives of the hills and valleys. Surely the natives heard the loud planes, the C-46 and C-47 constantly flying above them. Planes of all types and purposes flew the sky day and night and the young Airman wondered how this group perceived the intruders.

Natives in the small villages must have been awed by all the activities—never having seen big planes before.

And the crashes like his. Loud booms must have awakened the curiosity of everyone.

Previous lectures about the different hill tribes came to mind while he decided the need to communicate with the trio. The leather 12 X 12 emblem sewn in the interior of jackets explained by picto-graph and Chinese language who the Americans and Allies are, relying on all those who looked at the leather piece, to be able to understand its meaning. Pictured were the flags of China, Burma and India.

So, he opened his jacket again and expected them to understand the pictures and graphs even if they could not read the language. Some crew men who didn't wear the emblem, carried it in a separate pack. During the extreme humidity of the monsoons in the lower regions, no one ever wore heavy clothing. Americans wore khaki pants and while the Brits and Aussies wore knickers, the leather flag was carried by all.

The trio pointed at the pictures, touching them and chatting. The picto-dictionary showed a plane and pilot parachuting down out of the sky. It showed natives helping the pilot and more words stating they are to assist the crew and take them to safety. Next, they pointed to the sky and then to Bobby. More arm waving and head shaking evolved with much animation. They pointed to his cuts and scratches in a concerned manner than motioned for him to follow. Luckily, this group was interested in the leather square unlike the angry lone native who refused to even try to understand.

As he limped along, he figured the politics of all these hill tribes must have originated centuries ago and wondered how they communicate with one another. Also, they each had a dangerous, crazy culture that was unique.

He knew that some are friendly and some are dangerous. The Brits had explained this well.

The Abors who are extremely well built--short and stocky--are friendly and quite a lively group. They despise the Mishmi natives who inhabit these hills as far as the Northern Frontier of Burma.

He shook his head thinking about the lectures and how the Mishmi cut off the ears of dead people and kept them as souvenirs. Fortunately they are a friendly group, even though they collect this macabre trophy.

The fast pace of the trio worried him as his ankle began to throb. Feeling both tired and hungry he tried to keep up with them. It seemed like hours as they plodded through the thick underbrush and he lost all sense of direction in the early darkness. Meandering pathways worn by local tribesmen traversed up, down and around in no sense of direction.

Yet, the trio knew where they were going and occasionally, turned and waited for him to catch up. He knew they were descending down towards a river. The weather was getting warmer, the foliage thicker, and the roar of water was somewhere in the distance.

Again he asked the natives if they had seen the three crew men who bailed out before him. They understood as he held up three fingers and pointed to the picture of a pilot parachuting down from a plane. They shook their heads and shrugged shoulders a negative.

His new and immediate concern is the leeches that are in abundance everywhere and a serious jungle infestation. Their thin brown-hair like features loop slowly over the ground looking for victims with one end waving in the air searching. *"The attack of the brown jungle leech is inevitable. They work their way through socks and lace-holes of boots,"* he had been advised during briefings on Jungle conditions. For this reason, all kits contained a sock of salt to rub on the infected area. Or better yet, as a deterrent if a brown thread-looking-leech tries to attach on an ankle or foot. At this time, he wondered what the heck the natives worried about as they scrambled ahead barefoot and leg free. Definitely, it isn't leeches. They are immune to rough conditions. This is their home territory; thick jungle vines and matted vegetation are everywhere. Currently, the well-worn trail had a bit of a width and BOBBY could see in the twilight the brown foot trail before him. He hated snakes and didn't want to step on one. This is another worry because he had been told, *"There's plenty of them everywhere you step."*

The three young natives stopped, jabbered and pointed ahead at a river. Next, they pointed to his swollen ankle in some kind of decisive manner. One of them walked off the trail and chopped aggressively at a thick branch. After cleaning it of leaves and thin stalks, handed it to the young Airman. This is now his new crutch enabling him to take some weight off his sore ankle. And since they had stopped, it gave him the chance to open his survival kit and offer each a few raisins and nuts. They smiled and jabbered in gratitude and humbleness.

They were now at the edge of a small river. It was a rare moonlit night and the shiny rocks strewn everywhere on the wide sandy banks, glistened a beckoning for all to follow. The rocks were slippery, but the sand patches offered relief for them. The natives continued dragging the small log behind them effortlessly, pulling and lifting when necessary. They stayed next to the river and followed it for too long of a time, he thought. Had they been walking for two hours? Their hardiness exceeded his strength and he began to falter. His ankle throbbed, his stomach growled and a light dizziness worried him. Where were they heading?

Occasionally they stopped so he could fire his gun and shout.

Nothing but stillness. Where were the others? The wind must have blown all of them a great distance off course. He knew that they could not go back up to where the plane crashed. The elevation and cold were killers.

Were the three injured? Had they descended into a Jap camp? He knew for sure there was one about ten miles to the south according to the map. Thinking about all this, he remembered seeing the three float away in the high wind. The stitching on his own parachute harness had come loose due to the extreme windiness and he worried that the crew could have met the same fate, only tragically.

The three friendly Naga hurried ahead with a purpose. Sensing the darkness, they used their long spears as balancing poles while side stepping slippery rocks and boulders.

BOBBY fell behind overcome with tiredness. After all, he had been awakened at four this morning for flight preparations. How many hours ago? He lost track of time.

They turned to check on him. Because planes had been flying over-head and crashing periodically for the last two years, they learned to be wary of the Japs, the group their country was fighting. Or so they had been told. How this related to them, they really didn't care. Being jungle hill people who lived off the land for eons, this circus in the air amazed them. They scavenged old wrecks on the hill sides and improvised special living quarters out of the large intact fuselages from the giant planes. These were shelters in the rough country of tribal warfare and survival.

Soon old fires and burned down shacks along the river meant they were near people.

Rounding a bend in the river, they could see a roof of a hut with smoke from a fire inside.

Now there was yelling.

CHAPTER ELEVEN—June 1944

Three small boys came running toward them yelling, "Ok Joe! Ok Joe!" They held their hands out for a treat. The natives jabbered to the small boys as BOBBY handed each a small piece of chocolate from his kit. His stomach growled a knarly sound as he tightened his belt again around his loose-bagging pants while leaning more heavily on the makeshift cane.

The shack was built on tall stilts. An old man, grey, balding, but heavily bearded, came down from a ladder slowly and offered them some cooked rice wrapped in a palm leaf which he opened to a flat surface. They fingered the rice and ate, talking all the while. But first, they offered food to the young Airman which he found most comforting along with the warm rice. Each had a small handful.

The old man motioned for them to follow him back up the ladder and pointed to a special surface on the ground where the Naga could leave their tree-limb-future-drum. The three natives jabbered something and hurriedly turned to leave. Bobby thanked them as best he could while shaking their hands in gratitude. They seemed to understand the custom.

The three small boys were eager to make friends with the stranger and offered him a limey cigarette. Though this was no Lucky Strike or Camel, BOBBY was thrilled to have the cheap Brit smoke but put it away in his pack for the moment. Thankful for the security of sitting in a hut, strange as it was, he knew he would have a tale to entertain the group at the next dance in the Swing Canteen Bar in Sookerating where most allies partied....provided he makes it back!

Although he was a healthy, strong twenty-year old with an entourage of sports played in his youth, he now felt weak and vulnerable to all the strange surroundings.

Trying to be brave, he rubbed his swollen, throbbing ankle with both hands. Moaning from pain and hunger, he gently tried removing his one boot but fell back on an elbow. He knew that it had to come off due to the swelling. He hissed through his teeth with pain.

The old man said something to the young boys and they became helpful, untying the shoelace and slipping the boot off. This all took great effort because the boot was tightly secured to the now swollen foot. Finally, after slowly rocking the boot with toe and heel motion, it slipped off.

One boy examined the studs on the bottom of the boot and began to clean away the mud and debris. The other two started massaging the swollen ankle while the old man watched jabbering instructions. Although BOBBY had heard stories of gratitude displayed by the natives and others, this was his first experience. He wanted to give them what he had to give without sacrificing survival. He remembered HOLT'S story.

Once after a hard C-46 landing in Kunming with an abundance of medical and food supplies, a Chinese officer entered our tent where we were resting and after seeing my boots off, began to rub my feet. Tears swelled in my eyes.

After noticing the insect bites on the hands of the boys, he decided what he could do to be helpful. He took the sock full of salt slowly out of his kit to show its worthiness, and after spilling a small amount in his palm, began to rub a few grains on the boys' bites. They jabbered in awe and amazement. The old man swayed back and forth and reached for his pipe. Though never smiling, there seemed to be a sparkle of grandeur in his eyes, perhaps from one who has seen too much.

Although BOBBY knew he was deep in the jungle of northern India, his confidence, along with innate positive thinking, kept him going. Above, there were noisy planes. Lots of them. The Japs were everywhere and knew how to take down an American plane with trickery. Located among the hundreds of hills, valleys and crested mountains were dummy stations with fake call letters trying to entice a limping plane which had lost an engine, into a mountain. For this reason, pilots had to learn call letters and identification of FRIEND OR FOE. Always, the F/F signal was important.

Since the Japs popularized the air spaces of low valleys between mountains and along low canyons of rivers, the Himalayas became the safest and only route for the large cargo planes C-46 and C-47. Safest from the enemy, but they crashed often from other problems… Just like he did.

And he thought about how the Americans and Allies flew fighter planes, bombers, and the popular night time Black Widow to assist the huge Dumbo ships C-47 and C-46 Commandos to safety as the planes flew long ranges from India to China with supplies. It was all very dangerous.

With all the above in mind, he feared that the villagers here in Naga land might be sympathetic to the opposing team. That is why he elaborated with sign language that he was the good guy helping this country. Showing the picto-map was the key. The Chino-American dictionary was no help. This group spoke their own tongue. Forget about what he had learned in camp. These people were in raw environmental conditions. He knew that he would soon learn more as the old man began putting a small black pot on a little fire he had started among a neatly placed flat pile of rocks in the center of the small hut.

Realizing again that the friendly three natives who brought him here were gone, he became leery. Facing him were the old man now smoking something in a pipe and the three young boys staring and jabbering to each other in amazement and excitement pointing at his 45 which was in its holster but noticeable under his unzipped jacket. He heard a noise near the ladder and the old man moved frantically, motioning for all of them to look below. Facing them and looking up was a huge cat, one paw on the ladder, hungry for something to eat. No wonder the houses were on stilts—above the cats, snakes, and leeches. The old man took a rock from a pile near the opening in the hut and threw it at the cat with lots of jabbering. This was his territory and he knew just what to do. The cat turned and ran. With instructions from the elder, the boys unraveled a bamboo mat that was tied in a roll with vines. Gingerly laying it down next to the small pot near the fire, they motioned for him to sit there. He wondered how in the heck they didn't burn everything down. But he remembered all the burned out huts along the river and hoped that this small group knew what they were doing. A comforting thought were the rocks under the pot as a support. Small twigs used for the burn, stacked far from the area.

This is tea country! Thanks to the Brits for their efforts from years past, and Bobby was not surprised when the old man took a handful of green leaves and threw them into a now boiling tea pot. Soon, a larger pot was added to the fire and rice scooped off a banana leaf and thrown into the boiling water turned it foaming an ugly color.

The boys left but soon came back scurrying up the ladder quickly with a five inch fish they swiftly threw on the floor of piled leaves.

Suddenly, the hut shook!

Below, an angry voice in an unfamiliar language, yelled in staccato fragments.

CHAPTER TWELVE—June 1944

The old man rose quickly from his squat position facing the fire, grabbed a spear near the hut opening and thrust it out the door in small jabs. With loud shouting and great force, he hurled it below. A crack, and the spear broke instantly by the intruder who lingered there. More words from below. BOBBY grabbed his gun and in two steps rushed near the entrance ready to shoot.

The Naga he encountered earlier on the trail, now wearing a huge monkey skull on a rope around his neck, starred at him and stepped down two rungs of the ladder. Reeling unbalanced due to opium or whatever substance he had taken, he fell back but never lost hold of the fresh cut head he held by its long hair spinning it around grotesquely with blood splattering everywhere.

The ground was red.

Seeing the gun, he mumbled and stumbled off toting his prize in one hand and a spear in the other. His Gurkha knife tied to the belt around his waist, shifted side to side as he hurriedly stumbled away. Turning and facing them as they stood in the opening, he raised his spear and shouted.

The old man, not to be reckoned with, shouted back.

Crouching at the entrance and unable to move, BOBBY watched the native walk away. Now he shivered from cold, hunger and a new one—FEAR. He looked at the four occupants in the hut and said, "I know you can't understand me, but I can hardly wait to tell the guys back at the camp about all of this."

"Ok, Joe! Ok, Joe!" The small boys rhymed. "Not in their wildest dreams could Hollywood make a movie of this!"

Hearing a scraping noise and feverish with trauma from his experience, he turned and fell back on his haunches.

Unbelievable! The old man and three boys laughed. BOBBY shook his head with amazement and offered all four a small piece of chocolate.

The cleaned and gutted fish swam in the pot of rice, and the young Airman hoped that if it's boiled to death, he wouldn't get the dreaded amoebic dysentery like so many other crew members who filled the hospital in Ledo with this problem.

Nevertheless, the smell wetted his appetite to the extreme. How long ago had he eaten? It seemed a blur. It was late. He was tired and his ribs began to throb, along with his ankle—or foot? The limb ached as one.

Somehow, when he jumped from the C-46—seems like hours ago—the lines jammed his holster in his ribs. He rubbed his side.

The cooked rice with the small pieces of fish, and other stuff tasted so good that he licked the broad leaf plate he ate from. Yes, he had seen the old man grind a few bugs with his fingers and throw them in the boiling pot. So, this was their territory, and how they ate for survival was their business. The protein tasted delicious.

The steaming pot of tea was passed around but to him first. From the side of the hut, the boys gathered empty soup cans for cups of tea. Brands on the sides were British.

Remembering his unique aluminum cup that folded up from a flat one inch to four, than back down again to be stowed, he entertained the small group with its magic after he drank it empty. Up, then down. He gave it as a gift to the old man who in turn handed it to the boys to use.

"Ok, Joe!" They shook their heads in excitement. Mats put down around the fire awaited his eagerness. He plopped down ready to crash not believing his tiredness. Although he shook from the cold which came creeping down the mountain into the valley near the river, the old man sat bare except for a small flap of leather secured in front by a rope tied around his thin middle. He filled his pipe with dried leaves and began to smoke in contentment.

Before sleeping, BOBBY looked around in the semi-darkness and discovered a small wall of shrunken head trophies staring down at him, blinking by the fire as it spewed waves of smoke when the old man sitting there, placed small twigs below the pot of tea.

His startled movement caused the old man to chuckle and jabber. In a reassuring movement, he took a spear from the floor and placed it over his lap where he was sitting cross legged content with his pipe.

Submitting to exhaustion, BOBBY closed his eyes and re-adjusted his chute, wrapping the silk around him for softness and warmth. He used his pack as a pillow and kept a hand on his 45. Although his body shut down, his mind wouldn't.

Where were the other three crew members? Did they climb back up in the snow to the explosion or down to the river near here?

In the morning he would take out his compass and try to establish his position. Again, he would shoot his 45. Luckily, he had extra clips of bullets. Shivering from cold and fear, thoughts again about the board of twenty heads on display in a small village riled him for the moment. He wondered why he had stared for so long. Buddies took photos which he found appalling.

"Don't be sore." They had said before adding, "This is a wild county and this is what they do here for whatever reason."

Wild country….his mind shifted. He remembers seeing the leaflets dropped by the thousands along flight routes over Burma and China. Leaflets depicting a downed pilot needing help, and sketches of pilots showing the leather flag sewn on the inside of jackets to Chinese people, were indicators of identification. This alone separated them from the Jap intruders.

Yet, the old man and three boys seemed so foreign that he worried about his safety. In his mind, he re-traced his route over the Hump of the Himalayas to Kunming, China. All good pilots who flew the dangerous upper route into China, memorized the different mountain ranges and valleys to necessitate use of the oxygen mask and suit heaters.

Flying west to east from Brahmaputra Valley, the first rise is Patkai Mountains. Naga Hills south of Patkai were next. Upper Chaldwin River Valley the first ridge at 14,000 was the group of Kumen Mountains. Than east over Irrawady River at Fort Hertz to the next ridges of 14,000 to 16,000 separated by the Irrawaddy, Salween and Mekong Rivers. Main "Hump" is the 15,000 foot range between Salween and Mekong, the Santsung Mountains. The mountains blurred while thinking about them. He shook his head.

What was in the tea?

It was only tiredness.

The other four in the hut slept in silence, the boys on mats and the old native leaning on a bag of rice. Again he thought of the fortunate circumstances--his plane empty of Chinese workers, soldiers, mules and abundance of 'difficult-to-find' plane parts for fixes. He thought of LUCKY LARRY and his maintenance expertise. All parts are usable to him.

Cargo lists that exploded with the plane included ammunition, food, supplies, and much needed 55 gallon drums of 130 Octane fuel for the allies. He and his crew had thrown out about five barrels of fuel when the plane began to lose altitude. This was an unfortunate practice when flying high over the Hump. The loss of much needed fuel for the hundreds of planes was as tragic as the many downed flights trying to get the octane to China. Without fuel the war would shut down. *Not a bad idea,* he thought. As he lay there half asleep smelling the sweet smoke from the old native's pipe, his thoughts drifted back and forth to his lost crew. Should he head back to the remnants of the plane and follow the book of rules *stay with the plane so we can find you* or keep going down the river. Thoughts were of his tent buddies, guys he knew who had survived a couple bailouts and lived to tell about it.

He wished he could talk to them now. However, the wide range of miles through different airports all over India, Burma and China, plus the diversity of terrain from Mt. Everest to the lower swampy southern jungles of India and Burma, allowed each Bail Out a lone uniqueness.

He just knew that he was somewhere between cold and swamp. And for June, the temperature varied.

In his parachute again he is drifting down, down out of the icy cold of the summits—down, down to greenery of thick bushes, trees and palms. Strong currents of wind kept him twirling, moving sideways—down towards the Burmese River Valleys. So vulnerable in the sky, drifting slow motion, causing anxiety, fearing a Jap Betty could come swooping in and wipe all four of them out of the sky.

Moaning and jerking movements awakened the old man leaning on the gunny sack of rice, and he gingerly covered the young pilot with his jacket that had fallen sideways. He leaned again on his sack, clutched his pipe firmly and stared around the hut for any unknown problem.

Japs flew in clear weather under the turbulence caused by winds among the "Rock Pile" and only the CBI Hump boys flew the "Soup", the vicious weather's nickname.

Now turbulent winds thrust his chute upward violently during descent, followed by a swift downward thrust. This is typical of the entire Himalayas during all seasons. This being June, directives noted the icing level usually averaged 18,000 feet over the ridges BUT could fluctuate to as low as 8,000 feet brief periods of time. While searching for a clear flight path, this is what brought Bobby's plane down. He tried a 180 half circle out of the ice build-up to find clouds clear of the storm he had now run into—all to no avail. What happened to the C-46 was not that unusual. As the wings iced, they lost altitude. By throwing out about 10 of the 50 gallon drums of high octane gas bound for Kunming, they thought they could buy back some altitude.

The plane dropped lower and lower in the clouds. With peaks of mountains surrounding them, he yelled 'BAIL OUT' just in time to save them.

Fortunately, the crew members were buckled in their chutes and ready to jump. During earlier discussions, Bobby had learned that both Walt the engineer and Chuck at the radio were survivors of at least one other bail-out.

"If we have to bail, find the plane so Palooka with Search and Rescue can find us."

Harry the co-pilot and BOBBY were the newcomers to this survival ordeal. Although all four of the crew had many air miles under their belts--flying since age nineteen-only Chuck and Walt had experienced a bail-out—walk-out—and live to talk about it.

Earlier, this was not part of their discussion when they took off from Tezpur. It was of painted dames on the noses of planes. His friend's art work.

The sleeping young pilot's frowning face turned to a smile as he dreamed about dancing at the Swing Canteen in Sookerating.

"Party! We're ready always." Walt had mentioned their interest in Bobby's twenty-first birthday party.

"Get the nurses there by spreading a bulletin around at the different airfields." Harry the co-pilot mentioned that this worked for him six months ago for his 21st.

"And the musicians in Sook are always ready to volunteer—especially the sax. We need a sax."

THAT was when they hit the thundercloud that they had been warned about. *"Thunderclouds can be completely hidden by other clouds associated with them!"*

This one was too high to fly over—too big to fly around—so they headed into it.

BOBBY was awakened by the old native shaking him as the loud ROAR of a plane flew overhead.

CHAPTER THIRTEEN—June 1944

The roar of a plane flying through the canyon and above the river was loud and quick. Was it routine or a search party?

Climbing down the ladder he almost fell as he rushed to the middle of the river out of trees and bushes to wave. He waded in mud and swift debris frantically needing to be seen. He waved and yelled. Realizing there was a wide sandy bank where a rescue plane could land he knew that he could be saved. If only—

The B-25 was gone as fast as it had arrived, but he felt good. He said aloud, "They could be looking for me."

His ribs hurt and his stomach ached. Last night he was cautious about drinking the fish soup until it had been boiled for a long, long while. Therefore, the ache was attributed to hunger, he thought.

Looking around this early morning, he decided that he had never seen such a foreign country and needed a plan to get out of here.

He shot his gun and yelled. Why not? His crew could be nearby.

 Nothing.

Soon, he pulled his body with aching foot back up the ladder to the three boys and old man who was now boiling eggs in a pot while the boys hurriedly sifted through Bobby's chute kit.

"Hey!"

They quit instantly but indicated a need for the salt rub on insect bites. This is what they wanted, so BOBBY carefully accommodated as each held out a skinny little arm.

The old man sat near the pot smoking again from his pipe, stirring the boiled eggs slowly, jabbering away with squinting eyes and grunting with pleasure as he watched the salt rub.

Motioning everyone to sit on the bamboo mats, he slowly took out an egg one at a time and placed each in front of his folded legs on a group of wide banana leaves.

There were four.

In the same pot, he now threw in a handful of tea leaves which he took from a small rusted tin can. BOBBY noticed in the morning light that tin cans were everywhere in the hut, all useful for drinks and bailing water from the river. He was grateful when handed a can of hot soothing tea and silently saluted the Brits for planting fields of tea bushes long ago. The four eggs were divided among Bobby and the three boys. He attempted to share his with the old native after peeling it but was waved away. It was better than a steak. Nothing tasted so good! He packed his gear and prepared to leave when the old native yelled "Stop". Than he motioned for two of the boys to accompany him with waves of "Go-Go."

Hah! He knew a few words from other soldiers. They shook hands and nodded as he added, "Ok, Joe!" One of the boys, perhaps the youngest, stayed behind.

After climbing down the ladder, the old native jabbered while pointing west along the river. This was the route they were to take. He pointed to the .45 on Bobby's hip and did a two-thumbs-up referencing the importance of this weapon.

Time—6 a.m.

Temperature—cold.

CHAPTER FOURTEEN—June 1944

Sookerating—Assam, India

"Hey Mitch, this is a pretty big tent." Loud and friendly Nurse Milly entered in the flapped entrance of the canvas marine green compound.

Four cots were in groups of three spread out in an easy arrangement with a narrow lane of access between. Twelve soldiers grouped as one unit of comradeship. A four drawer tall bamboo chest accompanied each grouping for placement of personal items. Metal plates with handles used individually for the chow line stacked a short one on top of each chest.

Crew members' personal drawers contained letters from home and other memorabilia. Chests were wide enough on top to hold small framed photos of home.

Mitch admirably noted Milly's short sleeve khaki shirt, full at the bosom with two buttons un-done at the neck and neatly tucked tightly in a belted pair of loose slacks. She addressed HIM first—duly noted. She walked in smiling, put her hands on fully shaped hips and looked around. Fluffy brown curls backed behind one ear with a barrette, poofed each time she talked and moved her head.

"Phew, it's hot and sticky!" She fanned her face with lily white fingers.

Men in the compound, all dressed alike in marine colored under shirts and loose baggy shorts stopped what they were doing and gaped.

Pushing back his canvas chair where he had been playing penny poker with three others he asked, "How long you been here?"

"One week!"

"You ain't seen nothin' yet!" Taking the liberty to react with slang, Mitch continued. "This is your problem." He feathered out her collar a bit and pulled her shirt up from the tightly belted slacks. "You're in Northern India, akin with

Burma Provence and immersed in a dense jungle of Bamboo and wild Banana trees. This is not Seattle!"

Mitch began to fan her with a piece of manila file as the other men came forward with fans of their own to also be accommodating and helpful with phrases of "It's sweltering."

"It's June."

"And it's muddy and wet—forever!"

Mitch gave them the meanest squinty-eyed look he could muster and they all went back to their card game.

Mitch said, "But good for the skin and tea plantations everywhere. What you doin' here anyways?"

"I'm just the messenger. Red Cross is coming tomorrow with doughnuts."

"DOUGHNUTS?" It was a simultaneous eruption.

"True, true." Millie sauntered around the tent looking at framed pictures, picking them up gently.

"I'm first in line," said Ears.

"I'll believe it when I get a taste," said the one called Snake.

Mitch put a damper on everything. "Forget it. We'll be up at 4 A.M. and fly out at 6."

"Who's we?" She asked.

"All of us. We have three crews in here ready at 4 A.M. Makes it easier for headquarters if we're all together." Mitch moved as close as he dared to stare. Her eyes were round swamps of green. Greener than green above red cheeks rosy from the heat. He sighed.

The other three men paused with cards in hands, sighed and gawked.

"A few more tours on old Dumbo and I'm headin' to stateside," said Ears putting out his cigarette as a final gesture.

"Ears. How many hours you have now?" Snake asked.

"450."

"300 more and you get an automatic transfer." Snake put down his cards and yelled—"Snake, not again!" He pointed down below a table.

All three bolted from chairs, dumping the card game and ran a short distance jumping over cots. Millie screeched and reached for Mitch who was quick to scoop her in his arms.

"Something crawled across my feet," Snake wailed.

Millie pointed to an innocent looking, small green lizard tucking away and soon to be out of sight in a corner. "What was that all about?" She stared from Mitch to Snake who was sweating real adrenalin of anxiety. "You can put me down now." He slowly complied. "We call our Navigator 'Snake' because a cobra came visiting him—not once but twice."

"And I found the second one all cuddled in my boot, curled in there like it owned the place." Snake shook.

The mood changed when a small plane came in low above the tents for a landing on the short strip nearby. Millie ducked down in surprise noting the rattling of tables and small lamps. "Japs," she screamed.

"Nah. You've only been here a week. You'll soon distinguish sounds of different planes. That was an L-6, part of PALOOKA'S Search and Rescue Team, in for a landing."

"Do Japs ever get in here close?" Her fright was real. "Aren't you afraid of running into one when flying?"

They walked outside to the open air laundry room where men were hanging clothes on a makeshift clothesline and young topless Burmese girls were busy helping.

"Nah! The weather will bring us down before a Jap Zero has the chance."

"Weather?" Millie held up her hands as if feeling the dangers of the warm humidity. Mitch grabbed a few undershirts off the line and flung them to her out stretched hands.

He continued. "We fly over the Himalayas extremely high—too high for the Jap Bettys. They stay down on the mountain sides and near the river valleys."

"Himalayas?"

"We fly with heaters in the cockpit. And air is so thin we wear oxygen masks. If we bail out, we freeze at 50 degrees below, before we hit the ground." She was so close he counted the blinking eyelashes. He continued. "Of the two routes, Upper ABLE and Lower CHARLIE, ABLE is the dangerous one. Too high up and too cold. One time when hauling Chinese Nationals we had to fly as high as possible to escape Japs. Without proper oxygen masks, the laborers vomited in the plane and passed out." He shook his head in remorse while recounting the story. "We all made it down alive." They went back in the tent with armfuls of dry clothing and flung them on Mitch's cot.

Serious tones of quietness were broken as PALOOKA came bouncing in.

CHAPTER FIFTEEN—June 1944

Sookerating

"Hell-of-a-Note!" PALOOKA always walked with a pounce—giant steps in a hurry for a reason or not. Tanned, broad shoulders as square as his jawline always made an entrance phenomenal.

All smiled, shook hands and patted backs.

"Hey buddy, what's up? Cards?"

Mitch started to bring a canvas chair close to the cot filled with cards and dice.

"Shot of whiskey? Cigar, cigarette?" All ringed around anxious to keep PALOOKA near.

PALOOKA said, "I'll take a shot. I'm here to gather my laundry and get things together for the big birthday party tomorrow night for BOBBY JOHNSON here in Sook!" Than he added on a serious note—"I'll find him."

"Party?" Millie came forward.

After introductions PALOOKA said, "In the words of LUCKY LARRY— Hubba-hubba and Ring-a-Ding Ding!" He kissed her hand and kept a broad smile.

Millie blushed and pulled away.

PALOOKA continued, "Any excuse for a party works. Hey, you're a nurse. Bring all the friends you can. We need girls." Taking off his cap, he wiped sweat from his bright red hair.

"And don't be too loud about it," offered Snake.

"We don't want to fight off the Brits."

"Don't worry," interrupted Ears. "Just make sure you wear the shirts with the C.B.I. shoulder patch." "Ears is right," said PALOOKA downing a second shot.

"What's a C.B.I. patch and why do they call you 'Ears'?" Millie sat with arms folded on the closest cot, sort of in the middle of the airmen. Not her intention but theirs.

"Put your cap on and show her," someone teased. Ears grinned widely. "They're from my Dad!" His ears stuck out a mile.

"And best damn Engineer in the whole of C.B.I." said PALOOKA.

"We'll drink to that." Another round of shots.

"Ok, ok. One of three. Now explain the patch and C.B.I." Millie was melting from the heat and losing patience.

Mitch pulled her close and began fanning her again with the manila folder.

"China, Burma, India Theater is why we're here," said Mitch. "We're all fighting the Japs who are trying to take over the territories. Our particular job as Hump Pilots is to haul cargo to the Allies based in Kunming, China. We haul supplies for the B-17 and the B-29."

Snake interrupted, "We Hump Pilots fly the Himalaya route at such high altitudes that the Japs can't get us—usually."

"Why?" She asked and wished she hadn't.

Everyone talked in spurts.

"The Jap Betty is a G4M used for bombing and very susceptible to a fiery doom if its fuel is ignited. We call it the flying cigarette lighter."

"The B5N, code name 'Kate', is the bomber that attacked Pearl Harbor three years ago in '41. A dangerous torpedo bomber to Naval ships."

"But the A6M Zero is the dangerous one we face. It dominates."

"Why?" She asked, trying to look involved.

"It's light weight. Lots of power, and flaps fitted on backs of wings give it phenomenal maneuverability."

Millie started to get up from where she was sitting when PALOOKA subconsciously grabbed her arm and pulled her back down for some more lessons. "That was the old Zero." Taking charge, he got up from where he was sitting, took a half smoked cigar out of his pocket, un-wrapped it from wax paper and lit it. Leaning against a tent pole, he continued. "As of now, new American fighters are outfighting the original Zero. The Japs can't keep up with all our improvements." Again he took his sweaty cap off, threw it on an adjoining cot and swiped a thick glob of red hair off his forehead.

"For example?" asked Ears. Like the others, attention was riveted toward PALOOKA, whose uniqueness and knowledge commanded it. "The F6F Hellcat, an outstanding dog fighter is right now 'King of the Carrier Fighters'."

"But", interrupted Ears, "It's the Mustang that's winning the War in Europe—750 mile range, speeds of 445 MPH."

Millie shook her head and yawned.

"And then there are the Hawks. Tomahawk, Kittyhawk, Warhawk—all P-40's."

Excitement escalated as PALOOKA mentioned his best flight buddy LUCKY LARRY. "I believe he was part of the group who initiated the Shark Mouth paint job for the Flying Tigers of the American Volunteer Group used in China."

"Ok, ok. What's with the patch? You haven't explained its use. Do I need one for the party?" "Oh yeah! Two of them," said Snake.

Mitch gave him a swat on the shoulder and began the explanation. "The shoulder patch is worn to distinguish Americans from other Allies. Especially the British. It's called 'saving heads' and was designed two years ago."

"What?" She was losing patience. On the other hand, the crew enjoyed the way she turned her head from one to the other, sort of lost.

They snuggled in closer.

"It means," offered PALOOKA, "when the Military Police arrive at bars swinging their night sticks indiscriminately to break up fights, they avoid hitting Americans."

"Huh?"

"Our uniforms look alike otherwise."

"What does the patch look like? Show me one." About this time, Mitch figured that she was really an inquisitive girl or a lonely one. Probably the latter.

Mitch pulled out a shirt from his cabinet and described the patch. "It's a simplified U.S. shield. At the top is a blue field with the Kuomintang Sun of China and the Star of India next to it. The vertical red and white stripes pertain to us. The patch is worn by all the C.B.I. military."

"Pretty." She had to touch it fingering its outline. "So glad you approve." They laughed in unison and sighed at the same time.

She got up from the cot and casually began weaving around inside the big tent checking out things.

PALOOKA joined the crew at cards as Mitch followed Millie around a little too anxiously.

"How many in a crew?" She seemed to be wondering aloud wiling away the time.

"Four…Flight Officer, Co-Pilot, Navigator and Engineer."

"And what's your job," she asked quietly.

"I'm the Flight Officer or better known as an F/O."

They were close. So close that he wondered whose heart was pounding.

"Do crews alternate?"

"Not really. We fly when we get the order from HOLT our Deputy Base Commander." He put his arm around her and led her outside to a bench near the laundry action.

She sat.

He straddled.

She took a rag from a nearby bamboo woven basket and whipped it over the surface of the bench removing minute debris.

"And what are your jobs?" It was his turn to ask. "I'm a medical assistant and spend most of my time out on the field helping the injured." Her tone was slow and depressed.

She was far from home.

She was lonely.

She was only nineteen.

CHAPTER SIXTEEN—1944

Jorhat Area

HOLT rushed the Willys Jeep full speed down the dirt runway knowing full well a Jap Betty coming in for an attack raced right behind him. He ducked low knowing it wouldn't help and swung the Willys to the edge of the too short, pothole-peppered-runway.

WEN WU in the side seat yelled, "Pull off NOW."

The swooping Jap A610 spraying bullets low on the tarmac aimed for maximum damage. Gas cans exploded far to the left of the runway where a dummy shed facility loaded with worthless straw burst in flames. The burning fuel maximized the scene beyond its worth. The strategy worked.

Sirens blaring in advance warned all the War weary people on the ground to get ready for an attack. Diligent Chinese workers rushed elephants and mules to the tall greenery of banana trees and heavy brush where War supplies carted there minutes ago were saved—this time.

Staff slid belly down into the ditches next to the sides of the runway dug for this safety purpose. Simultaneously, trenches were always formed with the runways, a handy way to save lives.

"Saves lives" HOLT demanded during inspections of new ATC fields. Base Navigator and Briefing Officer in Operations—were also two of HOLT'S many titles. Today he was here as Base Operations Officer, he and his constant companion WEN WU, to make sure the truck to be loaded on the C-46 was properly blow torched apart. It was to be flown to Ledo for General Stillwell's crew out on the Ledo Road, heavily under construction, where it would be welded together again.

Now, the Willys flew sideways into a ditch as HOLT and WEN WU narrowly missed bullets while escaping out the Jeep's open cockpit.

"Son-of-a-bitch!" HOLT rubbed his left shoulder, always enflamed from previous episodes.

"WU, you ok?"

"Too close for comfort." WEN WU flipped pieces of mud and twigs from his American uniform, khakis and all, clothes HOLT insisted WU have available as one of them. Chinese born, but British reared as an orphan, his lingo was a vital piece of the many parts needed for the War effort.

Efforts more hurried than usual began again as carts pulled by Water Buffalo, hidden previously from view, rushed about.

"Bad timing for an attack," mumbled HOLT knowing full well that there was never a good time.

WEN WU, speaking Mandarin, waved over some laborers ordering help to get the Willys out of the ditch and back on track. Efforts were minimal since there were many people available to lift it out like it was a toy.

Large groups of Chinese and Burmese laborers were here working together to repair the runway which had become a muddy quagmire due to last night's heavy rain. This explains the Water Buffalo carts filled with crushed rock to be dumped in holes and crevices. Previously, and for days, many laborers pulled a five ton roller to crush rocks for this landing strip, a vital supply route for the building of the Ledo Road which eventually will reach the Burma Road coming out of China.

Most of the time, landing strips had to be hewn by hand and machine along mountain sides. These impromptu bases made landing strips too treacherous for the large cargo planes. Always, they were too short.

HOLT and WEN WU are on the strip to check out construction and the multiple needs of the men. The importance of chocolate, raisins, cigarettes and whiskey, can't be underestimated. Since most of the bases are in India, the two face a stockpile of problems at every one.

Of the tents along one side of the strip, there needs to be one large enough to house the multitude of supplies prepared for MAETS, PALOOKA'S Medical Air Transport Squadron. These small support groups, consisting of one flight surgeon, six nurses and six technicians, are transported out of Ledo, Assam. Numerous casualties are then flown in for mending before lifted to hospitals.

HOLT and WEN WU loaded up again and took off frantically looking for casualties.

"No blood this time, just trauma among the animals," HOLT noticed. Elephants were bellowing, and carts of heavy crushed rock were being up-righted by mules and re-attached to the Water Buffalos. He knew the dummy base station had worked.

"That siren came almost too late. What's going on with Bed Post on the ground?" WEN WU wondered aloud.

"Somehow the F/F call letters got confused at the radio base. The Japs must have infiltrated the airways by tapping into the system of Friend or Foe." HOLT sped down the strip missing the pot holes and debris while waving at the busy working crews filling the small craters on the tarmac. "We need to diligently re-word call letters to out trick them."

"And," he continued, "the Army Airways Communication Services is down half of the time and the other half can't be trusted." HOLT shouted to WU due to all the racket on the runway.

"You mean the AACS?" WEN WU knew all the military services by acronyms as he was trained. "Yes. Be sure to group together a new crew of wire sweepers after explaining the importance of their job." HOLT'S many responsibilities included keeping spiders away from the coaxial cable system that was constantly being re-wired along the new Burma Road under construction. Dew covered webs and fungus lined the brown cable wires, and they needed to be swept before problems of shorting out.

"And would you spread the word to all the workers that these are not snakes but wires and to quit cutting them with knives!"

PALOOKA'S frustration weeks ago was a loud tempo, explaining a major problem the ATC incurred.

Now, HOLT and WEN WU revamped the command and ordered flyers to be dropped ASAP around the bases, tent camps, and everywhere along the flight path.

"If it's sabotage," questioned HOLT, "we are in trouble. The JAPS have been noted to offer big bucks to Chinese laborers who really don't know which side to support." Sirens again.

"Mayday. Mayday." Over the loud speakers came fear.

"Brakes failing! Coming in!"

The plane skidded and bounced. The pilot maneuvered the huge cargo plane as best he could as it slid sideways and skidded up and down before dropping off at the end of the runway into four feet of mud which helped to bring it to a halt.

All lookers thought that it would never stop. "Son-of-a-bitch," wailed HOLT accessing the calamity. "What a predicament this is."

"HOLT, this is a special plane." WEN WU yelled talking with his hands, his usual. "It's mail time so the ship's loaded with cookie tins, gallons of soft drink syrup and letters from home."

The crew hurried out of the plane through the cargo door ready for an explosion which didn't happen. HOLT and WU scooped them into their Willys as fast as possible, and drove a safe distance away before assessing the damage. Chinese laborers and other crews rushed to unload all the precious cargo, including four mules.

"Damned mules kept shifting and one came untied," said F/O Mel. "We brought the ship down the best we could." He and the other three were stomping and shifting around while shaking their heads thankful to be alive.

HOLT took his empty pipe out of his front shirt pocket and thumped it vigorously in the palm of his left hand. "Ok. You did an ok landing due to the circumstances. The incomplete runway that's washed out at the end created this problem."

WEN WU scooped the crew into the Willys for a quick ride to a check tent for injuries and the customary round of whiskey.

"What gets me," said F/O Mel, "is how the hell did the mules come untied? All of us double-double checked the tie downs as extremely secure. We know the trouble these big mules can cause."

"Did any person enter the cargo area again before take-off?" WEN WU asked.

"Yeah," said the co-pilot Jones. "I looked back and saw a couple of bare chested natives with Gurkha knives tied to their belts. I assumed that they were part of the dispatch crew bringing in more supplies." "We have problems," said WU. "And it's not with the Gurkha Warriors from Nepal. They're on our side."

"All types of native tribesmen carry the Gurkha knife," HOLT added.

"Jones, could you identify them again if you saw them?" HOLT was quick to ask.

"Are you kidding? They all look alike to me!" He was still shaking from the traumatic landing. "Give me all the descriptive details and I bet I can figure out the tribesmen," said WEN WU anxiously.

"I know you can," said HOLT.

They all stood looking at the huge C-46 stuck in the mud at the end of the too short runway, knowing full well this was their immediate dilemma, and a tough one.

CHAPTER SEVENTEEN—June 1944

BOBBY'S goal is to stay as close to the river as possible because of the open skies above and the possibility of Search and Rescue flying in the area. Rescues were made from these open river sightings by specially trained crews anxious to save the lives of the downed pilots and crews. This is his only hope.

Leaning heavily now on his thick make-shift crutch given to him previously by one of the boys, his goal is to stay near the wide sandy banks. Here he could be seen and indicated to the two boys the importance of the area.

Knowing that most rescue crews worked out of the U.S. Army Air Corps in Mohambari, his confidence of a rescue soared. Chuck, the Radio Engineer, had given their bearing to the tower at Mohambari before the crash.

From there, the AAFBU – Army Air Force Base Unit flew the small aircraft that is capable of landing in tight places. The L-1 Stinson had limited range capabilities until its fuel tank had been modified to hold a thirty gallon fuel tank. Thanks to LUCKY LARRY who kept all this in motion.

BOBBY heard how it could fly a low level at 25 MPH saving quite a few desperately downed crews. However, the L-5 was the star of the rescue show. Its short field take-offs and landings with brakes set, were often required when maneuvering in mountain and jungle. It landed frequently on river sand bars and the Ledo Road for pick-ups of injured road crew. He kept his mind busy with positive thoughts of rescue. More importantly, thoughts of flying these rescue planes would be more to his liking. With flying the HUMP, he wondered how he could beat the rule of 750 hours or six months over the Himalayas, requirements necessary before sailing home, state-side.

Looking around at the extreme rawness of the jungle, he took out his compass and showed it to the boys as if they understood the necessity of direction. Noticing his shaking hands, he blew on them for warmth.

Believing to be east of the Patkai Range, he needed to follow the river up-hill towards Ledo where the new road was being built by Stilwell and hundreds of laborers. But, what if this river was the Mali which headed down to Jap territory and to Myitkyina (Mit-chee-NAH) Burma? Now, he worried. He heard that an attack was coming soon to clear the Japs out of Burma, and he didn't want to be in the middle of it.

After studying the compass, he decided they needed to go north-west from where they were. On the map he had reviewed back at the base in Tezpur, Assam, this area looked like inches. On foot, it could be days, maybe weeks. Nevertheless, he had met several who had bailed-out and made it back ok. *Most famous story was about the F/O and CoPilot who made it down from a snowy peak to be rescued after walking for about six weeks with a broken leg and crushed ankle. They engineered their plight with make-shift boards that propelled like sleds.*

Now, fortunately, here he was with only sore ribs and one bad left ankle. He leaned more heavily now on the short but thick-enough-stick of a cane.

He didn't like the loneliness and kept jabbering to the rag-tag young boys for comfort. He discovered by lines drawn in the sand, one was ten and the other fourteen. They felt important.

Making sounds like a jeep and drawing a design on the sand, he communicated to them that he needed to go in that direction. Finding the Ledo Road is a goal. He pointed up river and the importance of staying on it or as near as possible.

The boys jabbered then motioned for him to follow them on a path that led out of the river and up a hill. This was the only usable direction. As noted, paths went up and down in zig zags and not around mountains and hills. He worried about the variety of wild animals and native tribesmen he could face. Alert to every new sight and sound, he scrambled and hopped along the best he could to keep pace with the boys.

Soon, the path widened and he hoped for a clearing like a rice field or tea patch. The boys walked anxiously fast and the young Airman took note of their anxiety. Bushes surrounded the edges of the path as did Bamboo and Banana Plants. The boys turned their heads looking among the greenery for some kind of trouble. He saw it in their faces. Soon they stopped so abruptly, he crashed in to them losing his walking stick and landing face down in mud.

Fifteen feet ahead on the path stood NAGA man.

CHAPTER EIGHTEEN—June 1944
Sookerating—Assam, India

MITCH lit a cigarette. The loud drone of planes above prompted a continuation of their conversation. He needed to keep Millie occupied and interested. After all, he found her first.

"So far we have 13 bases in India and 6 in China. Of course, along the way we land in swampy quagmires or rocky strips cut out on the sides of mountains."

Silence for about five minutes as Mitch and Millie watched the action before them. Wet khaki clothes were hung as dry ones were taken down. It was a quick frenzy of arms shaking pants and shirts to get out the wrinkles. Bamboo baskets were nearby containing folded goods which were now piling high with undershirts, shorts and towels.

Millie elbowed him. "What's with the down mood?"

"Right now we're waiting for BOBBY JOHNSON'S crew to return. They're late. Haven't been heard from in twenty-four hours." He flicked his cigarette butt on the ground, got up and stomped it with his boot. "That's why PALOOKA is here from Search and Rescue."

Millie started to ask more questions when Mitch put his hand over her mouth and pulled her close.

"Hey Tokyo Rose. Time out!" Hearts pounded. Was it his? Was it hers?

"Hey steamers, look what I found." LUCKY LARRY interrupted with a gadget in hand. "A small motor for my ice cream machine."

Mitch stood. "Where did you come from?" They patted each other on backs briskly.

"I came in with PALOOKA." LUCKY LARRY's many titles included MAC—Maintenance Aircraft Command. Notoriously he concerned himself with recreational projects when not hunting down parts for plane repairs. His last project was putting together a digging crew for a swim pool behind some old housing barracks. When top brass got wind of the project, they had a backhoe flown over in pieces from Assam Valley where the LIDO ROAD is under construction.

"These boys who face hellish conditions flying THE HUMP need some R & R," they were overheard saying to HOLT the Deputy Base Commander. Hence forward, LUCKY LARRY's popularity soared.

They walked back in the tent.

Mitch said, "Put it under my bunk." He pointed, "over there."

"Guard this with your life." Tall and skinny LUCKY LARRY hurried out the open flap of a doorway, knees always bent in a hurry.

"Home-made ice cream for BOBBY'S birthday party Saturday night at the Swing-Canteen in Sook. You have to come," Mich ordered. He held her right hand in his and rubbed her arm smoothly, feeling the soft skin and tenderness beneath.

"How old?" She asked. Did she sway a little?

"Twenty-one."

"Oh my goodness! I just turned nineteen last week." Looking around the big tent she asked, "Who's the oldest here?"

"Of our three crews, I am," said a soldier throwing down cards on the cot. "Full House, pay up!"

Whistles, groans and moans followed as nickels flew into a cap turned upside down in the middle of the cot.

"Names Roy and I'm twenty-four." He scooped out the nickels, got up and placed them in a jar on the small table. On the list of names tacked on a bulletin board, he drew a star next to his.

While everyone was bustling about, Millie pointed to the four empty cots in the middle of the big tent and asked about the crew.

Silence.

Again someone repeated, "That's BOBBY JOHNSON'S crew that flew out of here twenty-four hours ago and haven't been heard from since." Silence.

With remorse, Roy softly stated "Either the weather or a Jap Betty brought them down." "That's such a disgusting name for a plane." Millie whined.

He continued. "Allies name the Jap planes for our identifications It's a Mitsubishi type-one medium-bomber." He was low key, repeating the info from before.

The tent group gathered around, clinked small glasses of whiskey and lit cigarettes. Roy threw down the cards and lay back on his cot, arms under his head and continued. "They also have bombers named Kate, Mary and Sally!" "Disgusting!" She said.

"But they don't have our nose art," added Mitch as he pulled Millie down from standing to sit next to him on his cot.

"When did you say that your crew flies out?" She whispered.

"Tomorrow morning."

The warm air and slight shots of whiskey enticed the youthful good humor of the crews from morose to nonchalance. They begin to sing.

"I have six pence, jolly, jolly six pence,

I have six pence to last me all my life.

I've got two pence to spend and…

Two pence to lend and…

Two pence to send home too my wife, poor wife

No cares have I to grieve me,

No pretty little girl to deceive me,

Happy as a king believe you me…

As we go rolling, rolling home dead drunk….

Rolling home, rolling home…."

"Hey." PALOOKA suddenly yelled into the tent. "There's radio contact from BOBBY'S crew. I'm off. Wish me luck!"

CHAPTER NINETEEN—June 1944

PALOOKA PENNY grabbed a handful of cigars from a cup he saw on top of a small bureau in the tent and waved goodbye.

"Wish me luck," he said again with the confidence that comes with experience and expertise. He, as well as all Search and Rescue crews, was hand picked by the Commander of Air Transport Command, Hastings Mill, Calcutta, India. All members were highly qualified with a number of assigned aircraft and fully familiar with the CBI area topography and weather.

Although PALOOKA was meticulous, well trained and in command of the unique group of personnel under the title of Intelligence and Rescue Coordinator, he still faced many obstacles. Natives and local laborers were not allowed in the area for fear of sabotage. Japs paid the hungry natives well if they could find the outcast members of the many groups. For this reason, guards watched over the set of planes, all fully ready to fly at little notice.

PALOOKA worked closely with LUCKY LARRY his assistant AMO-Aircraft Maintenance Officer, who kept nine different aircraft and models—single engines and twin engines in repair and fully functional on demand. Maintenance was completed at night at the main base in Assam.

Although he was a jump qualified flight surgeon and the para-medic team leader, he never had to chute-jump his way out of a plane on missions. "Jungle Wallas" they were called. He didn't consider himself to be a *"rough neck outdoorsman"* the description advertised for those who wanted to join the British trained Jungle Wallas. However, because of his tallness and boxing experience, he was one of the chosen few. Was it his square jaw? Red hair?

He swiped back long hair from his face and slammed on his sweat stained good luck cap, the jungle green that didn't wash out.

Of all the equipment assigned to him—the Douglas C-47, Mitchel B-25's models H. G. and J (stripped down), Nordsman UC-64, L-1, Piper L-4 and the Stinson L-5—he chose the Stinson.

This fine little aircraft is considered the workhorse of the small fleet. Instruments are few. Demands of short field take-offs and landings are the success of its maneuverability. Engine failures are rare, but if they did occur, it is due to water or foreign matter in the fuel tank. Thus, Sabotage is the main enemy of the fleet.

Once in the plane, his job is to check the supply of drop chutes containing food and medicine if needed. These emergency supplies saved lives. First on the agenda today, is the need to contact radio tower for communication with the lost crew members. Powerful radio beacons dot the HUMP air lines and are jammed to keep out unwanted Jap interference. The network inter-connects all bases in India, Burma and China. Lost crews knew to contact mobile or fixed units. PALOOKA needed both for proper location of his friend's downed crew. He was especially anxious to see him, the F/O he trained with back at the states. Born on the same day but two years apart, they celebrated their birthdays together. Word was out that a party is planned at the Swing Canteen two days away.

"Polly will be my date" he said to no one. And with this in mind he called the ground station for bearing.

Taking off, his goal was to find a glade to wedge plane under overhanging trees. Downed crew men were instructed time and time again to head toward an opening near a river bank so they could be seen, out and away from thick jungle foliage and trees. "PALOOKA to bed post! Did you get a name?" Static.

"John—sons—crew member," came across from a radio operator.

From an earlier briefing with HOLT, he learned that BOBBY JOHNSON'S crew flew out of Tezpur in the Assam Valley yesterday and last made radio contact with a radio compass reading to a terminal field near the Nagaland Hills and crashed into mountains in the Patkai Range. The Chindwin River was below the range and this is where PALOOKA headed.

Flying low in a canyon, he spotted a wide space of river bank suitable for a quick landing. Banking low, he decided to go for it. It would be a trial landing, a place he believed the lost crew could see.

Fearing that green shrubs and trees surrounding the area hid adversaries like wayward tribesmen and pockets of Japs close to the surrounding banks, he cautiously looked around before getting out but never turned off the engine.

Near him were food kits and medical supplies packed in chutes that he could jettison on the run if needed. Not sure what he had flown into, he could later drop supplies to a lost crew member if he was in a nest of Japs. Hopefully, the soldier had a gun for safety.

The area was so remote and the jungle so thick, PALOOKA squinted with the aid of binoculars looking for any kind of movement among the greens. Upward was the beginning of the rock pile and majestic mountains. He looked for white chutes stuck in tree tops which happened occasionally. This meant that a person was now on foot nearby.

He opened his door to listen.

The flow of the wide river cut the quietness like a knife and the beat of his heart threatened the stillness.

Something was wrong.

Innate fear set in.

Contacting mobile radio base again was his immediate action.

No response.

Looking east down the river he saw them coming.

"What the—?" He didn't finish.

CHAPTER TWENTY—June 1944

"Hell-of-a-note" PALOOKA heard himself yell as he quickly climbed back in for take-off. "LO LO'S".

Grabbing the controls of the mighty Stinson L Bird, he sped full ahead on the crooked, wet, slippery river-bank heading toward the on-coming Warriors riding full force who were yelling all the way.

He recognized their small stocky horses as they galloped the river bank, both sides, bows, arrows and spears ready in one hand and reins in the other. Mud splattered everywhere as horses and riders flew full speed ferociously.

They are the most dangerous group the ATC warned about. *"They're deadly superior attitude is uncompromising. This and their expert aim with bow and arrow make them the most accomplished terror group in the mountains."* PALOOKA memorized this lecture.

Although there is also a small group of renegade NAGA'S to avoid, most NAGA'S are harmless. However, the LO LO'S ruled the lands where they are camped in huts and make-shift grass Bashes.

They are their own rule and respect non others.

PALOOKA heard the points of spears and arrows "ping" on the sides of his little L Bird as it lifted quickly up and away over the heads of Warriors and steads.

Relieved that he had previously lightened the load by removing back seat, cases, and everything removable from the rear compartment in anticipation of a quick pick-up and take –off, he let out a deep sigh as he flew up and away.

Harvesting past experiences of quick get-aways had saved his life many times. Like this one.

How had communications gone wrong? Who transmitted the important message of signals from BOBBY JOHNSON'S group?

Someone was out there lost and sent a signal via the radio frequency board. Since the field radio equipment provided communication service among air bases and land telephones, accuracy is of the utmost importance and these officers are the best. Jamming and over-loading are constant problems the Japs cause.

However, PALOOKA had absolute information from a radio frequency that a crew member was out there communicating. Confidence set in. And the fact that his fist full of cigars were still stationed on the seat next to him, added new incentives of search and find. "Hah! I can do this!"

He flew the L-5 low following the Chindwin River Canyon looking for white parachutes anywhere, on ground or in tree tops. "Take that you jerks" he yelled to the Lo Lo's as he circled back around flying low over them. The horses spooked and a few of the mighty Warriors went flying off their saddle pads. He heard the "pings" of multiple spears and laughed.

Crew members knew to hide after safely coming down and folding chutes away out of sight, sometimes wrapping them around waists. Unfortunately, a chute in a tree could mean a devastating broken neck landing, or a quick escape out of a treetop and a run for your life.

Using call letters 860 "King Charlie", he tried the direction finder out of Mohambari Tower 290. Anything might work.

No connection. Only static.

After trying multiple frequencies he connected with call letters 770 "Fox Charlie" out of Myitkyina (Mit-chee-NAH).

"Crew member on mobile frequency"—static—"near Chindwin River bank"—"sees L-5—come in."

PALOOKA made several passes through the steep canyon following the Chindwin before spotting a lone figure waving a white silk chute near a landing bank close to where he had been before. Coming in too quickly he decided not to land but tilted the plane's wings signaling the crew member before circling around finding a good position for putting the L-5 down.

Landing fast and hard, the nose almost tipped to the sand due to the light tail end. Knowing the Lo-Lo's were nearby and furious over their loss, he hastily shot his gun in the air hoping the crew member could come quickly. The Lo-Lo's were about a mile away and traveling fast. Jap Zeros regularly patrolled low in the canyons also.

Hobbling as quickly as possible, and sometimes falling, the crew member came closer while yelling, "Chuck, radio engineer from BOBBY JOHNSON'S group." Explaining his identity added enthusiasm to the dangerous pick-up. "I think I broke my right foot." He continued coming closer leaning on a crooked stick for a cane.

PALOOKA jumped out of the L-5 and assisted Chuck to the plane while listening for dangerous sounds.

They heard the Zero before they saw the blunt nose. Ducking quickly behind a bush on the bank, they hoped the pilot wouldn't strafe the plane blowing it up with them dangerously close by.

Luckily, the Jap decided not to fire as he was going too fast and decided against a turn around. Saving ammunition was important for all sides of the War.

After loading Chuck, PALOOKA ran to his side of the plane, scrambled in and rearranged his cap to tuck in loose red tangles of hair before grabbing controls and taking off.

"He could have totaled us," Chuck mumbled. "Low ammo and probably heading to damage our ammo depot at the landing strip up river," mumbled PALOOKA. Than looking at Chuck, "Lose your supply kit? In the first aid box is salt. Use it."

Covered with bug bites and attached leeches, Chuck rubbed his arms, neck and ankles with as much salt as possible while shaking uncontrollably. Flying back to Assam, Chuck gave a full account of what he could remember. "Wind and ice too much. Plane exploded on a mountain top after we all got out. Don't know where Bobby and Walt are. Came across Harry floating on the edge of the river. Heavy gear pulled him down and he drowned. I did my best to bury him out of sight from predators." His lips trembled as he spoke.

PALOOKA handed him a cigar from his cache now in a small wooden box. "Smoke?"

With trembling hands he lit up. "I'm lucky to be alive. With good fortune I floated down forever out of the cold conditions, wind in my favor."

PALOOKA added, "One month earlier and you would have been a frozen ice-cake floating down dead. Too cold for the Upper Able flight pattern." "You ain't kidding. This country is wild. Ran into a few huts on stilts along the river but stayed out of sight. Japs are paying the natives to be on their side. Don't know who to trust." Chuck smoothed the sweet end of the cigar gratefully with his lips. "Sabotage is what we fear. We pay the Chinese Nationals plenty to guard our planes. They're happy with the basics like shelter, food, cigarettes." PALOOKA talked with the unlit cigar waving up and down from his lips which was his custom when flying for fear of dropping a lit one in his lap. "You have no clue where BOBBY JOHNSON and Walt could be? Did you shoot your gun for a signal?" "Only a few times. Decided to save my ammo for a life threatening situation."

"We have plans for a big birthday bash for BOBBY'S twenty-first at the Swing Canteen. We just need to find him. When we get back, let's study the area map."

PALOOKA called in for a landing as he circled low above Assam Valley. He could see Ledo and then Sookerating in the far distance.

"When?" asked Chuck.

"Tomorrow night at Sookerating. Lots of girls—nurses. Hate to postpone it."

"I bet he's somewhere in the Naga Hills," said Chuck.

CHAPTER TWENTY-ONE—June 1944

BOBBY JOHNSON ran as fast as he could to save his life. Through the dark tunnel trails, bramble bushes of thorny edges struck sleeves and legs tearing pieces of khaki from elbows and knees. Now leaning heavily on his short wooden crutch, he ran a swinging gait for fear of coming down on his aching, swollen, left ankle. His life preserving pack on his back slung tightly over his right shoulder helping him lean in that direction and off the throbbing ankle. Naga Man, short and stumpy, raced low to the ground skirting between short bushes and under branches. This is his native territory. He ran close behind, chopping at twigs in his way; the glint of his metal Gherka knife sparked off the razor sharp edge when it hit a stone. Toned for its main occupation, he, a Naga Headhunter out for a prize, wielded it well.

The pace of the short stocky native threatened BOBBY. His 45 pistol sat almost empty in its holster at his side. Maybe he could use it as a bluff? Save bullets for the real survival.

With the large monkey skull hanging from a rope around his neck, the renegade Naga Man raised his other weapon, a long spear, and jabbered at the two boys leading ahead of them.

They shouted in fright as BOBBY shot his gun in the air.

Naga Man, totally unfazed, pulled his own hair up in pantomime indicating he wanted BOBBY'S head.

"Nah—Nah!" The boys shouted and jabbered something while pointing to the sky indicating planes.

BOBBY screamed at the native hoping to startle him and pulled out his next best weapon, an idea that could save his life. The harmonica he kept in his inside jacket pocket was a keepsake, a memory from home. He played Jingle Bells, the only tune he could muster as loud and clear as possible.

Naga Man, never having seen a white man before, nor a musical instrument, stopped a few feet away and stared.

The traumatized young Airman finished the tune before offering the harmonica to the native. He held it out front of him; then tossing it in a nearby bush, turned and ran hoping this new toy would suspend the spirit of the renegade.

Next, he stumbled and fell. "Damned crutch!" The terror of escape and the wild eyes of the native had been too much considering he was weak, hungry and exhausted.

The Native looked at the bush where the harmonica lay hidden, took two steps toward BOBBY with his knife in the air, closed his eyes and fell sideways.

Behind him came the two boys, one with the Naga's long spear using it as a walking stick, the other with the native's Gurkha knife in his hand. They grinned and helped BOBBY stand. Though somewhat frightened, the young native boys were fascinated by all the excitement.

Opium had been the culprit. The primitive Natives in the entire area had access to the dope. Naga Man was probably asleep but would continue the chase. They were a relentless group.

The three hurried down a path that led to a short sandy bank ahead where possibly PALOOKA with Search and Rescue could land his L-6 and scrape him off. The two boys realized the plan having seen rescues along the river banks many times before.

Looking at his watch, BOBBY realized they had been walking for four hours. All three stared at the compass for direction as if the boys were knowledgeable. They decided to walk in a northerly direction up and down paths near the river canyon where planes flew and they would be in sight. Also, chances of a lone hut or small village near the river would be extremely helpful, so they decided not to go too high in the hills.

Hunger now troubled them. They stopped, sat on a boulder—an outcropping near the river—and BOBBY searched his pack of snacks that remained. He gave each boy raisins, nuts and pieces of chocolate. He thought it was crazy that he had to meticulously count each piece. Never had he been in such a predicament. His stomach growled noisily with each bite.

Abruptly, a B-25 flew overhead and they waved as best they could.

"Damn!" Realizing the lateness of unraveling his parachute, he now hurried and fumbled as he cut the silk from the lines. This is his treasure for survival. Wrapping the shroud around his waist and over his shoulders loosely, he decided to wave the piece like a floating sheet when the next plane flew through. He knew they were looking for him and his crew.

He showed the boys how they would be helpful as each grabbed an end and floated it billowing the best they could to attract attention. Good to know. He wrapped it back loosely.

Distant roars of planes were everywhere above and through the canyons when they stopped to listen. Constantly, BOBBY worried about the other three crew members, Chuck, Walt and Harry. Where did they land? Why didn't they shout or shoot for attention? And the C-46 Commando--did the pieces attract Search and Rescue? Maybe the snow had covered all traces of its remnants. On the upper "Able" route, he knew that it was part of the Aluminum Highway. On a sunny day and a cloudless sky, the plane pieces would sparkle.

He felt that he had floated miles and miles down and away from the treacherous Himalayas. Thinking back, it seemed a gust of wind swept him away for at least an hour. Was this possible, or had he simply lost all track of time?

CHAPTER TWENTY-TWO—June 1944

Somewhere in the Patkai Range

They called him BOBBY. Not Bob Johnson, but BOBBY. He was twenty and his blond-blond hair had not darkened yet to a light sandy color. Light blue eyes like his dad's added to his attractiveness and all the ladies noticed him. They all teased each other when he walked by. To the nurses, their aides, the cooks, the military dames, Salvation Army workers and everyone else who wore a khaki skirt--he was the one! The catch!

Literally, his heart and mind were in the clouds and flying over the dangerous, icy, wind-swept Himalayas again, added anxiety to his days of each mission.

The only female who kept his attention was the young girl from Missouri who awakened him and his crew very early, before day break, on flight days. Agony of another—"Sir, it's time to fly," was now on his mind. Picturing the dark blond wavy curls and red-red lips inspired his movements.

Bonnie, is her name. The dangerous flight seemed somewhat honey-buttered, unintentionally, by her as he and his crew left their bashas to be driven by Jeep to the pre-warmed C-46 a half mile away. Distance was necessary in case of a Jap invasion.

Studying the compass every few minutes as they walked up and down trails through the thick brush, he decided they must keep heading north-west because Ledo was close, just over the Patkai Range, and he was south of it. How far? He had no idea. He knew that the Japs had taken over Myitkyina (Mit-cheeNAH) and their Zeros were in all the surrounding canyons. If one flew by, would he know how to duck in time? Also, Search and Rescue could easily be in harm's way unless tailed by a fighting Black Widow or other fighter planes as back-up. The P-61 was basically a night fighter, extremely maneuverable with powerful R-2800 engines. Painted glossy black helped conceal it in glare of searchlights. With a top speed of 375 mph, BOBBY wished he could fly it instead of the dangerous missions over the HUMP in the huge cargo planes.

Briefings had taught him that searching for downed pilots was number one priority for small planes. This added to greatly needed positive thoughts. His crew of friends, the ones from the beginning of his career two years ago, were here in this part of the world, flying cargo or fighting Japs, knowing that rescues were highly possible.

Back to Bonnie. Picturing her as an image of nose art on the next plane he flew, he would be sure to tell his best pal LUCKY LARRY, the artist-maintenance man, what he wanted. He would describe her as a petite blond, a Veronica Lake nose, curvaceous body with a beautiful hip.

"Va Va Voom!" He said aloud as the two boys turned and stared back. They laughed. They were young. What did they know? For sure, he would teach them some fun phrases.

He was aware of all the girls who flocked around him more and more. And noticeably more so when they learned he was going overseas. They became strangely more interested.

His dad's last words of "don't get engaged and don't get anyone in 'the family way'" etched on his mind frequently.

In each of the barracks there is a Jade wall of young women's pictures—those who wrote "Dear John" letters to soldier boyfriends stating, *"I can wait no longer and have found someone else."* Jaded was a dirty word and Bobby did not want to be among the list.

Yet here in this trauma of life or instant death, he felt isolated, so alone. Thoughts of a girl his age that he barely knew gave him extra strength. "Bonnie." It made him feel good as he said her name aloud. As if he knew her.

The day was waning and it was getting colder. Worse, there was no sound of flight above, no chance of a rescue in the dark.

With open hands and a wave of both arms, he tried too pantomime "Where are we?" Hours had disappeared and they were nowhere.

The young boys turned in circles and pointed here and there with hunched shoulders. They were lost too.

He took out his pencil flash light. Six P.M. Time flies!

From his pack he pulled out his small sack of nuts and raisins. They each shared a teaspoon per palm.

The need to be frugal was on his mind in this hostile environment. The lurching of his stomach sounded like a bullet wanting more.

Aware that the British Scouting Columns were out and about as part of the rescue sequence, he hoped for a rescue soon.

Suddenly, the two boys became animated pointing toward a ledge ahead and waving a "come on" to him.

With the warmth of the chute wrapped around him, he followed, hopping slowly.

Ahead was an identical hut on stilts again with smoke above. Hoping they had not walked in circles, he hesitated remembering the awful sight of Naga Man waving insanely at the last hut. He knew Opium was a scary and dangerous drug and worried about the control it had over the man. Could he be following us?

Spry and agile was the best description of these stout little natives who wore callouses on their feet since birth.

The boys made a noise and a small group came out the open side of the hut to stare. Three men came down to talk. Shoulder length, loose shaggy hair jutted uncombed here and there around square faces. Again, sleeveless leather jerkins reached down to small loincloths above legs bare to the thigh.

Bobby noticed this group was different. Fur covered pouches hung over each left shoulder while sword-like knives were within reach of the right hand. Chains of coins and beads adorned necks along with the all so popular animal teeth entwined on a rope.

Unlike the last old man from the other hut, this group of natives was cheerful, childlike and interested in what the boys had to say.

BOBBY knew these were the MISHMI as described by HOLT when warning BOBBY one evening 'on the town' at a squalid little mud village where they and others had a few drinks. "The Dump" was the popular place in Chabua near Ledo. Good old stocky HOLT—his mentor—the go-to guy with all the right answers.

How he wished he was here now.

These people too had probably never seen a white man before by the way they looked closely at his skin and giggled when he let them touch his hair. Nodding yes as if they understood everything the two boys said, BOBBY realized it was all an act because the boys talked more loudly with greater elaboration in their explanation. One pointed to the sky. On seeing this, he himself mocked a plane flying and crashing. Next, he showed them his flight jacket with the pictographs inside.

"Ahhh!" One finally understood.

They all climbed into the hut where three old women and two children were sitting in front of a fire. They pointed to a place of comfort for the young Airman. Bamboo mats of soft twigs and leaves encircled the small fire.

Sitting now, he never realized his tiredness as he fought sleep. This meager comfort was paradise. Had he been walking for hours or days?

The women in charge offered boiled chicken meat, eggs, pieces of sweet potato and handfuls of rice to everyone. Plates consisting of broad leaves, filled to over flowing. They padded around and served with laughter and jibberish.

Food never tasted so good to the three hungry travelers!

After eating, each man and woman smoked a long bamboo pipe from which dark, stringy home cured tobacco hung. They offered him a smoke. He shook his head and took out the pack of limey cigarettes from his bag, and cut one in three pieces offering each small piece as a treasure. They giggled and popped the pieces into their mouths.

Remembering in his ration kit the small metal vial of whiskey allotted to each crew member for emergencies, he decided the timing was right for a hearty drink. He is especially hoping the alcohol would ward off problems of amoebic dysentery so prevalent among the soldiers he knew.

"Boil everything! Don't eat anything!"

Again he noted that the chicken and eggs were taken straight from the boiling water and handed to him on a leaf. Ok! This was good.

He became dizzy from both exhaustion and the heavy smoke inside the little hut. Wrapping his arms around his gear bag which contained his gun and extra magazine, he lay on top of it like a pillow. No one could wrestle it away during sleep. The two boys cuddled next to him, passed out from exhaustion, noises of the night and the warmth of the fire.

The old women jabbered softly as the fire popped and crackled into the late hours.

BOBBY'S thoughts were of home in the Missouri woods and comfortable three bedroom bungalow— flowers—mowed grass—neighbors baking pies and cakes. Just three years ago at his eighteenth birthday party he made the big announcement of joining the Army Air Corps and learning to fly. Dad, the dentist, was pleased—big pat on the back. Mom was in shock. June, 1941 was a far, far, away different time. Bringing his knees up in fetal position for comfort, he hugged his canvas supply bag tightly and briefly fell asleep to the drone of a nearby plane passing over in the dark night. Stirred by thoughts of a rescue tomorrow, he looked at his watch. One A.M.

Today is his birthday.

He is twenty-one.

CHAPTER TWENTY-THREE—June 1944
Sookerating

Millie left the tent slowly under the tender arm of Mitch as he followed her out with one hand on her shoulder and not wanting to let go.

"See you the minute you get back," she whispered. "I'll be here!"

Planes droned loudly above and a cool breeze suddenly blew her soft brown locks into her eyes. He fingered the hair from her face with both hands and gave her a short kiss on the mouth.

He was young.

She was younger.

"We're a couple of kids in a rough environment," he said, excusing the prompt sensitive kiss.

She smiled a ruby blush.

They held hands by fingers, only letting go as she slowly walked away toward the nurses' barracks, the Field Medical Compound.

He stood there flat footed watching her leave. She turned once and waved shyly.

Mitch walked back into his tent where the men were quietly playing cards, and lay down on his bunk with his hands cradling his head, his best thinking position.

Tomorrow was a big ordeal. He and crew were set to fly badly needed supplies to HOLT and WEN WU in Jorhat. A Commando, the huge C-46 air ambulance was stuck firmly in the mud and off the far end of the too short runway. It would be a difficult landing and an even more difficult task pulling the 29 thousand pound plane free of the quagmire. Mitch knew the plane would be unloaded of its full cargo to facilitate the difficult task.

A sudden thought crossed his mind as he lay there. "How much does that plane really weigh fully loaded?"

A crew member playing cards, sat up to light another Camel and answered, "Over 49 thousand pounds, close to fifty."

"I see this is weighing heavily on your mind," said Ears.

Canned laughter followed. Mood was low before a flight.

Mitch continued. "No wonder ice on the wings at 10 thousand feet can bring us down." Groans from everyone.

Next morning, 0100 India standard time, Mitch and crew were awakened by the "CQ", a standard procedure.

"China flight, sirs!"

After dressing, each of Mitch's crew checked individual parachute bags for all necessary items. *Oxygen mask, electric flying suit, flight cap, gloves, heavy winter flying boots, flight jacket with the CBI insignia on the shoulder and the American flag over the Chinese flag across the back, a 45 automatic, two extra clips of ammo, belt with trench knife and first aid kit. A canteen of water and small vial of whiskey completed the check list.*

With flashlight in hand, Mitch and crew headed out in the dark to meet shuttle bus filled with other crews, all heading toward the flight line a mile away. Mitch, the F/O of his crew, first proceeded to the briefing route to fill out his flight plan and gather up briefing folder with maps.

He checked his watch with the correct time from a navigator's chronograph on the counter and next studied the weather reports from the latest flights from China. Lastly, the weather officer had to sign a clearance.

"No rain, no wind, no sleet?" Mitch had to ask. "It's just a sunshiny day at the beach!" The weather officer had heard it all and was ready.

"I'll drink to that!" Mitch and crew lined up for coffee during the short wait before their plane is ready for take-off.

Finally notified the plane is ready, Mitch picked up his gear plus a money belt which might be necessary to buy his way out of China, and crawled into another truck which hauled him and others to the revetment area.

A crew chief and radio operator from inside the plane helped load Mitch's gear onto the flight deck. Mitch and co-pilot Ears inspected the exterior of the airplane calling out each area to one another; *"cowling fasteners:—'check', 'tires'—'check'"*, then *landing gear, struts, prop, turbos, hydraulic fittings, brakes—etc.*

Next, they crawled into the cargo compartment on the way to the flight deck to inspect cargo for leakages and proper tie downs.

"All's good," said Mitch. In the cockpit he read FORM ONE. The plane is OK.

The auxiliary power unit is connected and started. Mitch begins the process of starting the engines by turning on all master switches one by one until all engines flicker into life and remain steady in the green arc of the instruments.

He signals ground crew to disengage the auxiliary power unit, turns the radio on and listens to the taxi instructions from the tower.

After receiving ATC clearance and all instruments in the green, half the tensions of the heavy task of flight are released.

Now, Mitch has to hold the brakes on while heading straight down the runway. He moves the throttles carefully to 25 inches of manifold pressure, releases the brakes and eases the throttles on up rapidly to the 47 inch marking. The ponderous weight gathers momentum and speeds down the dark runway. Co-pilot Ears takes over and holds the throttles as Mitch needs both hands on the control wheel to pry the nose wheel off the runway and up to an angle for takeoff.

Finally, after a few light bounces, it's a successful lift off.

"Gear up," Mitch calls as he touches the brakes to stop the wheels from turning.

Mitch concentrates entirely on his instruments as Ears adjusts the four prop controls to synchronize the four roaring engines.

After more power adjustments, and at a safe altitude, Mitch can feel the entire tension of the crew relax. They have the over-loaded plane flying, after a terrific and mental physical effort.

Mitch is covered in perspiration and remembers the night those close friends of his did not get off in time and hit the trees. He can still see and hear the explosion.

Maybe this is why he is soaking wet.

Earlier before take off, while everyone was busy loading and inspecting the plane in the dark, flash lights in hand, no one noticed the two Chinese with Gherka knives, dressed as personnel, walking around with a tool box in hand.

CHAPTER TWENTY-FOUR—June 1944

At 8,000 feet, Mitch turned the controls over to his co-pilot Ears, and stepped out of the seat to crawl into his electric flying suit. To his flight cap he fit his oxygen mask.

After crawling back into his seat wearing his heavy flight boots, he attached his electric suit to the plug in. The oxygen mask and its built in microphone were next. After testing his oxygen mask with the indicator, he did a thumbs up to Ears who would now go through the same procedure. Mitch does a huge sigh of relief and says, "HOLT, here we come!"

"To the rescue," added Ears.

They knew that the heavy ropes and other supplies needed by the big trucks to pull the C-46 out of the mud were fully loaded and ready for use. "We're heading south on the EASY route to Shingbwiyang," said Mitch as Ears studied the map. "Then we need to head west on CHARLIE to get to Jorhat," he added. "On the way, we contact two radio beacons."

"Roger that," said Ears.

Mitch added, "These short runways are a pain in the ass. I can only hope we never over run a landing!"

The arising sun shooting between the clouds in an array of false warmth sparked conversation. Chit chat with head-phones always seems to highlight the tense conditions, each member of crew well aware of the numbers of crashes and rising death toll.

"I hope PALOOKA finds BOBBY and crew."

"He's the best that Search and Rescue have."

"It's been 24 hours since the crash was sighted." "If they floated down to the Salween River, there are many huts with helpful villagers."

"You hope!"

"Can't trust some of the tribes."

An hour and a half after takeoff, the crew noticed that Number 4 engine was heating up.

"Not badly," said Mitch with a frown. "But it deserves watching."

Crosswinds of 80-100 miles per hour shook the plane and it weaved uncontrollably causing alarm.

The engine continued to heat.

The crew's tension mounted.

"It's not at a critical point yet," voiced Mitch anxiously.

Coming close to Jorhat, they encountered heavy fog. The more they let down, the heavier the fog.

Always feeling squirrely in this kind of situation, Ears blurted, "Can't see the wing tips!" Mitch made contact with the tower.

"Hang tight; we'll guide you in."

As Mitch let down attempting to land at Jorhat, the ceiling was zero.

Tension thick, the crew felt the critical situation. Stomachs rumbled and bowels cut loose.

"The runways 100 to 200 feet to our right," said Ears. "And we're barely 50 feet off the ground." Air speed was dropping fast and the flaps were full down.

Mitch shouted, "We go around."

They had to "pour the coal" to all engines and try to regain air speed. Each crew member knew a stall was a real danger and could be fatal.

During the second fly over, they briefly glance at the huge "ol' Dumbo" stuck in the mud and realize that they want no such dilemma, or even worse. This time they got the plane down and taxied to a stop.

Wobbly legs climb out of the plane.

Ears got down on his knees and kissed the ground.

"Kiss it twice for me," said Mitch.

A convoy of heavy trucks head toward them to gather the supplies.

HOLT and WEN WU lead in the Willys.

"Son of a bitch! What happened?" HOLT needed to know. "One plane down is enough!" He pointed his pipe stem toward the huge plane stuck some distance away.

Next, they all shook hands, a friendly companion gesture due after every tense mishap.

"Engine Number 4 froze." Mitch and Ears walked around the plane checking it out, shaking their heads all the while.

HOLT gruffly remarked, "We'll see what that's about!"

WEN WU was already checking it out. "Tool box is in the air intake scoop" he said with fury.

Shaking his head, HOLT yelled, "Another careless mechanic. LUCKY LARRY better check his staff".

"Wait a minute! In the dark I thought I saw a couple of Chinese staff walking about with a tool box." This is from a crew member.

WEN WU got out his note pad. "Description please as best you can."

HOLT lit his pipe and blew smoke angrily about. He would get the word out to every major brass unit in the ATC and its Allies to be aware of sabotage groups causing serious problems. From Executive Officers of the numerous branches down to Maintenance Squadron Command, all units were vulnerable.

Since the Air Traffic Command—the ATC, regulated aircraft radio equipment, HOLT would make sure that communication units, both fixed and mobile would help get the word out—the warnings sorely needed.

The network interconnected all bases in India and China. WEN WU hoped to send exact descriptions from information he has learned so far.

CHAPTER TWENTY-FIVE—June 1944
Jorhat

HOLT, WEN WU and about 1000 Chinese laborers got busy tying the 250 foot thick ropes to every part of the plane that would stay firm during the pull.

Everyone shouted orders as they all wanted to get involved, and like any emergency, everyone was an expert.

Since the center section of the wings was built into the fuselage, and this area could withstand a heave-ho best, two thick ropes were tied to each side of the plane. Loose ends were then attached to the rears of four U.S. Army tow trucks.

"Shovel more of the mud away from the plane as much as possible," HOLT yelled as he hurriedly walked around pointing with his pipe, inspecting every issue. "Don't pull yet."

Mud was cleared and tracks were leveled for the tires to grasp some dry land during the pull.

The last of the boxes were unloaded to lighten the plane. "Very important cargo," WEN WU blurted in both languages as he took on the task of watching the unloading of box after box. Mules, the first to leave the plane hours ago, stood by innocently now, tethered and munching hay.

"Letters from home and baked goods on their way to lonely fly-boys," WU continued to the laborers as they gingerly handled the supplies from the immobile C-46.

HOLT and the downed crew that had flown in with the plane of shifting mules, stood by in frustration as the Army trucks pulled again and again to no avail. Wheels spun spewing mud everywhere and the huge trucks rotated sideways with each pull.

After about 30 minutes of trying every kind of rope tie and much re-digging in the loose mud, HOLT said, "This is not going to work!" He took off his cap and replaced it several times during the process. Helped him think! Never letting go of his pipe, it was his pointer as he stuffed it over and over—tobacco flying around.

"Ok, I have an idea," remarked WEN WU enthusiastically waving his arms in a display of animation (from his mother who was a Brit).

Blurting to the Chinese runway workers who were standing by, he instructed them to try pushing and pulling in unison. After all, there were 1000 or more watching and wanting to be helpful.

Pushing and lifting of every piece of metal, and pulling from the thick ropes tied to the wings near the fuselage of the huge plane, they moved to a synchronized drum beat nearby and the wailing of WEN WU.

Mitch and crew joined them. Every sweat of manpower was welcome.

The big 16 ton monster began to move.

It was like a carnival, a festival of some sort with much singing and laughter.

The workers, realizing the possibility of success, pushed harder.

"I've never seen such participation," HOLT said as he positioned himself at the front end of a rope to help pull.

WEN WU went crazy with excitement as the huge BIRD became free of the mire and sat free and eager with tires back on the runway.

"Unbelievable!" HOLT took out his small vial of whiskey from his waist pack, drank a shot and offered some to WEN WU, Mitch and the two crews. "It's celebration time!" They all agreed after experiencing the astounding feat.

"Salute," said WEN WU. Then added "Another gem of a story for the Swing Canteen."

They groaned simultaneously. "Where's BOBBY?"

Loaded with new supplies, and with the overheated engine repaired, Mitch and crew took off for Sookerating near Assam.

The rescued plane and its crew need an overnight stay for report detailing of the Commando's plight and a de-stressing rest for the crew.

HOLT was in charge calling for a complete mechanical check of the plane and getting the crew in the air for the next flight.

Next, he got busy writing a directive to all the liaison Officers of Executive Headquarters and Directors of Operations the warning of sabotage by unknown Chinese workers paid by the Japs. Word was, "Pass it on!"

On the runway and left behind from the Commando that took off, stood two large crates of soda-pop syrup ready to be mixed with gallons of water and distributed among the entire ground crew--all thousand of them.

CHAPTER TWENTY-SIX—June 1944
Patkai Range

After much needed medical help and his broken foot in a cast, Chuck was ready to study maps with PALOOKA and ride along as an assistant. "Two searchers are better than one!"

"Plus, you've been scouting the range since you floated down," PALOOKA said with a half-smile. "Very funny! I should do it again." Chuck lifted his knee with the broken foot and cast of many signatures.

LUCKY LARRY'S art piece included a dame in distress, a red headed girl with skirt a-float. "This cast is going on my wall," Chuck bragged. They laid all maps available from the ATC on a table and penciled in areas of interest.

"About here is where I found you."

They put an (X) south of the Brahmaputra River but above the Naga Hills. An abundance of rivers flow south, down from the Himalayas, and they tried marking one.

"The rivers break into others and the names change," said PALOOKA. "The Chindwin starts here and descends down to the Manipur." He was now mumbling to himself as he penciled the map with precision.

"Word is out for the British Scouting parties to help look for them," Chuck said.

"They're good," declared PALOOKA. "They know the trails. The Jungle Wallas never give up."

"That would be you."

PALOOKA breathed a sigh at the compliment. "We are all doomed if we don't pay attention. The wild natives are everywhere." He thumped his pencil on the brim of his cap thinking.

Radio Engineer Chuck began to list them as he read the maps. "The Abors in the Abor Hills; The Mishmi natives in the upper hills." His fingers slid from place to place pointing. "Those two are not far apart land wise, but the Abhors despise the Mishmi who are cheerful pipe smokers."

PALOOKA added, "But the Abors helped train all of us on surviving from stream fishing."

"And the Kachins are around here somewhere." Chuck was looking for them as he tapped on the map.

PALOOKA added coolie, "They cut off the ears of dead people."

"But they're friendly," said Chuck. This brought on a nervous laugh from the two of them.

"And they love to sing and dance." PALOOKA didn't stop there. "Keep in mind they have joined forces with the Chinese and Americans and have proven to be an excellent source of combat troops."

"Ok, let's drink to that!"

They each had a short shot of whiskey and continued.

PALOOKA thumped his pencil up and down now on a map eager to go. "Since I picked you up here along the Chindwin, we need to work this area." "And stay away from the Irrawady which is too far south of our search."

"Incidentally, you know that I ran into a herd of Lo Lo's at about here." He indicated on the map where the dangerous warriors chased him. "I barely flew out of the area."

"So, we need to be on the lookout for Lo Lo's and perhaps the bad Nagas."

"Most of the Nagas are good and try to be helpful. But it only takes a couple to ruin your day." PALOOKA began to fold the maps as he handed them to Chuck. "I'm happy to have you aboard as lookout!"

"The most important part of the search will be buzzing over the stilt houses along the river a number of times in case one of them is injured and has trouble getting out."

PALOOKA next inspected the "drop chute" supplies for an emergency drop. "Plenty of food and medicines to survive for a week."

"Are we taking the air drop propaganda leaflets that explain to all the natives how we need assistance in the War effort?" Chuck had to ask as he helped bundle a pack of tied papers.

"Absolutely! They all need to be on our side. I'm worried about HOLT'S memo concerning sabotage. But I'm convinced WEN WU will weed them out. It's got to be a string led by a lone leader." PALOOKA continued, "They cause havoc in a number of ways and hide out of danger. For example, they loosely tie horses and mules so the animals will shift around and bring down a plane."

"Like the one on the too short runway that ended stuck in the mud," said Chuck.

"And watch who puts propane in the barrels. They sometimes add water the last minute when no one is looking. Or, they will cut short the needed amount of fuel to make it over the HUMP. This is my measuring stick for this little 'Flying Jeep' I use for search and rescue. Safety measures tell me to recheck everything." PALOOKA took the stick and double checked the fuel as he spoke.

Chuck hobbled around inspecting the Kaydet. "So this is basically a liaison aircraft used for spotting casualties?"

"That and communication work among other things." He inspected the large rear door that folded down.

"You need to tell top brass the importance of a ride-along spotter. That would be me!"

"The river jungle is dangerous but a lot less than the HUMP!"

The wind was whipping and rain was pouring down as they worked getting ready for the flight.

"Let's do it," said PALOOKA. As he and Chuck buckled in, he tuned to the control tower telling them his route.

"You're braving the weather," was the report back. "Good luck!"

As part of the routine, PALOOKA was used to drenching rain and heavy winds and took off in command of the little L-5 heading down towards the river following Chuck's directions.

Within an hour they flew low over the tree tops, buzzing huts on stilts in the low sweeps near river banks. Chuck was directing and spotting.

PALOOKA made radio contact when possible and very thankful that the usable radio frequencies were not jammed. Radio operators knew PALOOKA well and were in constant contact with him and the British Scouts out and about. They tried their best to correlate efforts. Search parties were on going when word was out that flight crews were down and contact made over the frequencies.

The two searchers learned that natives and soldiers, on elephants and in canoes, had been searching south of Ledo all night. The area was below the

HUMP flights but thick with jungle plants of all kinds. Because visibility of trail patterns from air is impossible, ground search is necessary.

Information reported that parachutes were seen floating down two days ago and also gun shots were fired.

The men also learned that a B-25 pilot swooped down through the trees yesterday seeing a white parachute stuck in a tree near a river bank. Notes were then dropped down to search parties along the river giving information and directions.

"I wonder if this could be Walt's or BOBBY'S chute?" PALOOKA asked.

"Let's check the vicinity!" Chuck, in determination, never took the binoculars from his face.

After swooping down low for a view, they each saw two small boys running up and down a wide sandy river bank, hands waving violently for them to land.

CHAPTER TWENTY-SEVEN—June 1944

Millie missed Mitch more than she needed to. She didn't need to fall in love so far away from home. She didn't need another problem—like another injured person to worry about. Most importantly, she didn't need another casualty beyond repair. Yet, these were the things that rattled her thoughts as she helped care for the injured out here today on the field so far away from Assam, the home base.

Flown here too early this morning with ten other nurses and staff, she barely had time to adjust to the trauma of the awful sight. Patients were tended to on an emergency field set up with cots and tents. Canvas ground cover was sporadic with wounded men too injured to be moved.

"Two Jap Zeroes flew in fast and low, spraying bullets at everything in sight." She had overheard. "They made two trips before chased out by a P-40 Warhawk that came diving in vertically from a high altitude to near ground level its six, fifty caliber machine guns blazing away!" "Wow," she whispered.

Now, blood and broken bones consumed each patient. This was the gathering point, the emergency stop, the drop off between life and death before air lifts to hospitals. Others had been flown here by emergency rescue crews only compounding the crowd of injured.

She and the crew worked quietly to stop bleeding wounds and to administer needles and liquids when necessary for shock patients.

Fortunately, landings and take offs were frequent and patients loaded as soon as possible, thanks to the establishment of the 803rd MAETS at the start of the War. Millie had signed with the Medical Air Evacuation Transport Squadron back at the states, but really had no idea of the severity of the injured. "Another load," she whispered as planes landed with the newly injured from nearby fighting.

"Sometimes, two to three planes land per day with trauma patients." She had been schooled earlier. "Our job is to administer first aid on the field quickly in order to save them for transport to hospitals in India and China."

This was her second field trip and the bloodiest. Patients were mixed. Most were young Chinese laborers who were in harm's way while performing their difficult tasks of loading and unloading planes on the tarmac. The dangerous task of building runways in the thick foliage of sweltering jungles and on the rocky terrain also took its toll on the men. Because the wind was howling and the rain coming down in torrents, "Mayday, Mayday," sounded on the loud speakers everywhere of another emergency flight trying to land, brought down by the weather.

Millie knew she would be spending most of the night out here until all the patients were evacuated. Beacons of light spread out in the area by mobile generators determined this operation to be a long, long one.

She missed Mitch and re-played over and over their contact, their conversation, their quick kiss. Where is he now? Did he make it back from his early morning flight?

Word was out that his plane crash landed somewhere. What were the details? Was this true? She knew that Mitch and crew were headed to the field in Jorhat where HOLT and WEN WU worked heartily to remove the large C-46 from the mud. Mitch explained it well.

Since crash landings were frequent and she knew that many crews walked away unharmed, her gut feeling was—"he's safe." Talking aloud gave her confidence.

A plane was loading and ready to take off. Nurse friends waved at her to "come-on" as they boarded the old Dumbo C-46. There were about thirty nurses and staff packed in the belly of the old plane. A few of the injured were loaded. These were not so severe and could be taken care of at the Assam camp.

Tired and drained, she decided to wait for the next flight. Injuries were too devastating and she felt compelled to stay with the small crew of one surgeon, one technician and five other nurses. Besides, a very young soldier similar in age was gripping her hand mercilessly. She knew that her soothing words and sips of water helped to keep him alive.

"Much too dangerous," said the surgeon under his breath watching old Dumbo take off. "Too many valuable people on that flight."

Like an omen, this put fear in Millie's heart.

CHAPTER TWENTY-EIGHT—June 1944
Somewhere in Patkai Range

PALOOKA and Chuck knew the two boys must be an important key to their search as PALOOKA swooped the plane low back and forth twice over the river bank.

The boys never quit running and waving frantically as they tried to follow the swooping plane.

"Hell-of-a-Note!" Ranted PALOOKA as he cautiously searched for a piece of ground to set the L-5.

"There's no place to land!"

They were in a heavily forested river basin between two steep sides. It was a dangerous area. They both felt the fear of Jap Zeros flying through in a military strategy of attack ready to fire on any obstacles in their paths. Frequently they flew fast and low over the rivers, wheels almost touching water.

PALOOKA decided to wave both wings indicating he saw the boys. He swooped low and waved a couple of times before flying off to search for a landing spot.

"The boys must know something," said Chuck staring anxiously through his binoculars. "But I see no huts nearby."

About a half mile from the boys, PALOOKA landed on a wider than usual bank. The little Kaydet set down clean and stopped short of a separate tributary that split the river channel. The broader than usual area encouraged PALOOKA to steer the Kaydet closely to an outcropping of broad branches near the bank to remain partially hidden.

"Can't get any better than this!"

"Trouble is," worried Chuck, "how we going to get to the two boys?"

"Let's sit awhile and maybe they'll come to us. They can hear the plane running." PALOOKA was nervous. "This is never easy. They may call me tough and rough around the edges, but they will never call me stupid." He smoothed his red, slender mustache with his left fingers, keeping his right hand tense and ready for a quick escape.

"How fast can this thing take off? You need to turn it off so I can listen," said Chuck.

"On the dime." PALOOKA bragged snapping his fingers as he turned off the engine.

Chuck shot his pistol twice in the air and walked away from the plane to mount a small incline about twenty feet from the noisy river. Where were the two boys?

After ten minutes, the quietness became staggering. Only the far away drone of the many planes in the sky cut through.

PALOOKA stayed close to the Kaydet ready for a quick take off. Surely the boys understood the waving wings of the plane as a positive signal. They had to know something about BOBBY because this is the greater vicinity of his crash and hopefully, bail out. Chuck and he had studied the map.

Suddenly, a chilling sound broke the stillness. An harmonica played in the far distance. It was the sound of a non-player, a tuneless combo of in and out breaths moving along the harmonica spokes. Chuck immediately hobbled back to the plane. PALOOKA put his hand on the half opened cock pit door ready for departure.

The player stopped, didn't come any closer just as the two boys came running down a canyon path that emptied near the river about fifty feet away. They were panting.

PALOOKA whistled and waved for them to come near, knowing how most of the natives are so shy. They ran fast toward him, not stopping until a few feet away.

Scared, they looked wild eyed toward the upper crest of the hill and toward the sound of the harmonica which was becoming louder.

Alerted now by the boys' attitudes, PALOOKA and Chuck knew this was not BOBBY.

"He used to play the harmonica," whispered Chuck in a mumble.

The four stood staring toward the sound, up the hill, and now heard something else.

"Not good," said PALOOKA. "Running feet, crashing through bushes." Jumping in the L-5 he motioned for Chuck and the two boys to get in as he started the plane.

"Wait," yelled Chuck. "If it's a lone person, we could get information about BOBBY."

CHAPTER TWENTY-NINE—June 1944

Both men pulled their pistols ready to shoot as they scrambled to leave.

All synchronized with PALOOKA as he opened the large drop door in the rear of the little 'Flying Jeep' and waved an arm towards the two boys to jump in.

"Ok Joe!" They shouted loudly and loaded with a quick hop ready to get away from the danger to come. Extending their small arms towards Chuck who was hobbling on one foot now, they pulled him in.

It was a tight squeeze but PALOOKA took off just as Chuck was shutting the door.

"Safety first. I can swoop back down to have a look and throw out the drop chute of food and supplies if necessary." PALOOKA headed straight through the canyon, tires almost skimming the water. "You know," shouted Chuck over the roar, "BOBBY would have yelled knowing we were there."

"No good was coming down that trail," PALOOKA added. "Brits would have shouted and shot guns in return."

After a wide turn above the canyon, he headed back down again to the spot they had left.

NAGA MAN, short, square and angry, stood in the center of a small group that looked like cave men. Long stringy hair hung almost in clumps circling broad foreheads and wide-square faces.

When they saw the Kaydet, they flung spears toward it with great strength and accuracy. The four heard the 'ping' of a few steel heads.

The boys chatted nervously and Chuck said, "Good thing there's only a few!"

On his radio, PALOOKA made contact with the nearest base explaining the situation.—"and they have BOBBY'S harmonica, the one he used to play frequently." He gave a full account to the radio engineer on the other end, thankful for the powerful liaison receiver always in contact with Search and Rescue.

"We have your bearing! Jungle Wallas and British Scouting Columns are on their way to the area since they are in the vicinity."

PALOOKA, determined to stay near where BOBBY or Walt could possibly be, continued radio contact with some new ideas.

"We need someone who speaks the Chinese language now. We have the two young boys with us who know something. We need info' about BOBBY and Walt"

"Will do! Hang tight!"

Chuck said, "We're in Naga Land and east of the Naga Hills. We'll run into more natives before we're done." Binoculars never left his face while talking. "Those natives have never left these hills and run up and down trails like on roller skates."

"But," interspersed PALOOKA, "most of them are friendly and helpful. We just need to weed out the bad from the good." Looking down he commented, "Our two crew members have got to be close and down there somewhere. We have to stay where we first saw the boys."

Making a quick turn, up and around above the river and never losing sight of it, PALOOKA added, "Keep looking for the white parachute stuck in a tree."

The two boys rolled their eyes with a dizzy reaction to the quick turn.

PALOOKA landed quickly on a divide near the mouth of a small tributary that flowed rapidly south. "This flows into the Chindwin and the bank is close to where we first saw the boys. Hopefully, the Naga's left."

"I have the area specifically penciled in," said Chuck now studying the map since the landing.

Radio static alerted the four of them. "Ok, PALOOKA! I have an interpreter here who speaks Chinese and other dialects."

"Roger that. Put him on."

The dialogue began and the boys became overly animated with information. Not only did they feel important, but now realized that they could communicate their situation.

Communication began first from the radio contact. "They said that they hid a pilot in a huge pile of bushes because his left foot was so swollen, he could barely hobble. They know the NAGA MAN meant to kill the three of them, so they distracted him and hoped he would follow the two of them to the river and safely away from the pilot who was a nice man who gave them lots of chocolate."

"Ask them to describe the pilot."

After more garbled speech, they all determined that the injured pilot was BOBBY with the 'light shiny hair' and eyes the 'color of sky'.

"Tell the boys to be on the lookout for Walt, who has brown hair and brown eyes and is short and stout," said Chuck. "He's still out there somewhere." "I'll pass this info to the searchers," said the radio engineer. Static again… "Try to stay where you are as long as possible. Jungle Wallas now have your radio bearing."

More Mandarin came across the radio and the boys became even more excited.

They waved arms to Chuck and PALOOKA to follow them as they walked away.

"Ok Joe! Ok Joe!" They pointed up river and towards the thick foliage.

CHAPTER THIRTY—June 1944

BOBBY knew they were looking for him. The sky was a noisy racket of planes, some droning in the distance and a few closer. Planes flying nearby were his concern now. Jap Zeroes flew through the canyons regularly, slightly above the water, and he figured he was safely hidden within two hundred yards of the river's edge. Plus, he recognized the speed of their sound.

The two boys helped tuck him away hiding him in a small depression near the path the three previously stumbled through. Next, they made a loud commotion as they ran through the bushes and out to the river.

"Smart," BOBBY whispered as he heard the NAGA MAN blowing in and out on the harmonica while stumbling away after the two boys. "I'll know where you are." The noise was getting dimmer and dimmer which was a good sign.

Keeping a close view of the ground because of snakes, he decided to crawl slowly down to the river and make a mud pack for his left swollen ankle. The throbbing pain was getting worse. A wet, cold mud pack would help.

He had taken the last of his medicine four hours ago and now threw away an empty aspirin metal container. Searchers could possibly find it and keep on the trail.

Suddenly, loud native jabbering, the recognizable tongue of Nagas came down the path above him. He froze and clung motionless to the trunk of a nearby tree about twenty yards away.

The loud group joined NAGA MAN. Were they angry or joyful? He couldn't tell.

And just as quickly, almost at the same time, he heard the sound of the Search and Rescue Kaydet flying very closely. "PALOOKA", he sighed loudly.

"Holy Shit!" All hell broke loose.

The plane landed; the Nagas ran yelling loudly toward it; the plane took off.

Hoping they were some distance away, he decided to make his way toward the water, crawling hesitantly.

Luckily, there were thick bramble bushes close to the edge for a quick retreat if necessary. The natives seemed to be in a daze over the new noise maker that he had given to NAGA MAN and wouldn't come back.

Knowing that PALOOKA would circle around, he needed to be in a clearing. Surely the two boys had located the plane and boarded. They were an eager energetic pair and seemed to know what they were doing when they motioned for him to stay put and out of sight. This was their territory. They ran away purposefully noisy and loud to be followed by the native.

All these things were on his mind as he dipped his leg into the water up to his knee. He hoped to stay here as long as possible.

Also familiar with the L-5 that was now redesigned for use as an air ambulance and cargo work, he knew that the 'Flying Jeep' had room for the boys. A wider and deeper fuselage section and a large rear door that folded downward allowed for quick loading and boarding.

"That's why PALOOKA took off so quickly," he whispered. He knew that the boys were scooped away.

He scooted slowly at the river's edge, feverishly making a mud pack from the soft silt. The mush slid into his boot which had been widened by lost shoe laces hours ago. Noticing leeches around his swollen ankle, he shook as he grabbed salt from his pack to rub them away.

Realizing that thirst had been a major problem, he filled his flask with river water. Next, he added two decontamination pills and shook the container. Looking at his watch, he realized that twenty minutes was a long time to wait but absolutely necessary. The baggy pant leg was easy to pull up around his knee. He noted its looseness and knew his khakis were torn and dirty, but worried more about losing weight and energy. And, there was no more food in his pack. A growling stomach and watering mouth reminded him of the bits of chicken and rice served to him—where? When? Was he losing track of time? Has it been two or three days? He lost count but knew that he needed to move away from this danger zone.

Since this part of the river seemed to bend, a long sandy bar extended out and followed the edge. A trail headed both south and north. Noting footprints everywhere, he knew he needed to be on the move. But where? Which direction?

The decision was made for him as he heard the Kaydet again and determined PALOOKA landed south of him where the Naga group was heading. A large commotion of shouting and shooting began again to the south.

Crawling and scrambling fast up the bank to the bushes, he hid just in time as the noisy group of Nagas almost came upon him. They turned and ran back south again where they had come from a few minutes ago. They were determined to catch the Kaydet and cause trouble. For sure, PALOOKA had them confused.

"My whistle!" Realizing its magic, he put the cord over his head and whistled softly making sure dirt and water had not ruined it. Where was his crew?

He knew he saw them parachute out.

All alone now, he felt fear for the first time.

"Land PALOOKA, land!"

CHAPTER THIRTY-ONE—June 1944

PALOOKA had a new plan. Calling to the boys and using sign language the best he could, he indicated that he would fly away and land up-river but close. Also, he decided to send with them a small emergency kit of food and medicine.

They shook their heads in acknowledgment and took off, both grateful and excited. They knew they would find BOBBY and get some chocolate.

"What if they run into the Nagas?" Chuck shouted as PALOOKA started the engine and took off quickly.

"The boys are faster. The natives look like they are groggy with Opium and won't catch them. We have met a bad batch of renegades that's for sure." Chuck next mentioned, "Where are the good Nagas when we need them? What's your plan?" Chuck noticed that PALOOKA did a wide turn above the river but never lost sight of it.

"In the rear I have two para-drops. I never fly without these small chutes tied to bundles of food and supplies."

"I read you loud and clear," yelled Chuck over the roaring engine. "You want me to drop one or both near the Nagas?"

"Drop one. We still haven't found BOBBY and might need the other one if we see him."

Flying low between the banks, he saw the two boys wave and point up-river.

"They speak another language but they wave in American," PALOOKA stated as he waved the wings to indicate understanding.

Within a short distance they saw the Naga group, much larger than before.

"This is all a game to them," said Chuck as he opened the rear latch and jettisoned a bundle along the bank and as close to the group as possible.

"Wow, look at that! Change of plan. Let's continue another short distance in the opposite direction and get rid of the second one to keep them busy and out of our way as I land." PALOOKA was excited. "Good plan." Chuck got ready and sent another out the rear door within viewing of the natives on the ground.

In a heap, half the natives tore at the second package and would now be oblivious to the sound of the small L-5 landing a short distance away and towards the boys. They wouldn't care. They now had items that they had never seen before and pushed and shoved as they fought over them. It was like a game.

One held the round compass for all to see as the arrows seemed to gyrate making the natives giggle and dance about.

One took the thick woolen socks and put them on each hand like a glove. The medicines fell to the ground and got kicked around in the mud as they scuffled over the bits of food—nuts, raisins and chocolate bars. The pack of Lucky Strikes meant sharing as each took a cigarette. One man began chewing his.

The two boys rushed to where they had last hidden BOBBY and made as much noise as possible. They needed to find him now and felt important as PALOOKA flew close by searching for a landing bank while keeping the two boys in sight the best he could.

The task became difficult as the June rain came down in torrents. PALOOKA knew the dangers of a swollen river from normal to swift rapids. Having flown in these conditions before, and knowing the Chindwin River well from his many rescues, he knew how to play it safe.

"Look for a bank near the bushes as far away from the river as possible," he shouted.

"Radio the British Brigade that's out there searching," said Chuck, his binoculars held tightly to his face. "I see a bank but on the opposite side of the river!"

"I'm going for it before this torrent brings us down."

PALOOKA feared the steady downpour and knew its turmoil well. "On the bright side, the enemy is not out flying in this soup!"

He brought the light plane down in a hard landing. Turning it sideways buffering the foliage, he felt safe as he brought it to a stop on a higher piece of river bed and near a glade, a flat square empty of denseness.

Wind and rain pounded heavily on the side of the L-5, its tail tucked away under a tree facing the empty space.

"Swell, we landed," said Chuck sarcastically adding in one breath. "Now how do we get across the river?"

"We radio for help. The Air Service groups set up camps every few miles near these river beds and the British scouting groups work with Search and Rescue. They'll bring a boat." PALOOKA got busy contacting radio base again. He knew that the AACS—Army Airways Communication Service would immediately respond and send help. Before long a B-25 came roaring low above the tree tops buzzing loudly and dropping a note.

SCOUTING GROUPS AWARE…BE THERE SOON…STAY PUT.

"We wait," they said in unison shouting above the relentless, pounding rain.

CHAPTER THIRTY-TWO—June 1944

BOBBY now turned his attention to the continuous drone of planes and knew PALOOKA was up there, somewhere close by. The pounding rain threatened his security as he hovered fifty yards away and above the muddy banks of the loud roaring river.

He heard PALOOKA land a second time and take off confident it meant the unloading of the two boys to find him soon.

Knowing that his pal was the best at handling the little Wichita-built Boeing trainer gave him courage. Its maneuverability in heavy rain and high winds always meant successful rescues. With a renewed spirit, he paid no attention to his wrenching stomach and swollen ankle.

"Hah," he yelled as he held his whistle. "My rescue aid." His pistol of no use now due to spent bullets, he still kept it handy as a bargain tool against thieves if necessary. His best buddy HOLT warned him and his crews that there were numerous thieves around the area.

"Be extra aware during dangerous times." And this was a very dangerous time.

It now felt like hours since he started blowing on the whistle.

Time slows during pain.

The howling wind, the torrential rain pounding all around him drowned out the sounds from the whistle.

He kept at it nevertheless.

A short distance away he heard noise coming down the trail. Ducking away, he parted a few leaves from the branch he hid behind.

He heard their noise. Did they hear his whistle? Fair trade or danger? Friend or Foe?

Soon the two boys banging rocks together, one in each hand, came up the trail from the river's edge. All smiles and jabbering with feelings of importance, they handed BOBBY the bag of supplies from PALOOKA.

Shaking, he knew which medicine to take pertaining for survival. His canteen empty again, he handed it to the boys to fill with water from the river as he took two decontamination pills from the kit. They were like twins, both carrying the canteen back to him, so excited about participating. The three shared the raisins, nuts and chocolate like a feast of joy.

After bravely opening the parachute and hanging it on branches like a tent, the three hovered under it as the rain, now a cloudy wall, blew sideways. "We wait," the young twenty-one year old pilot said.

"Ok Joe! Ok Joe!"

CHAPTER THIRTY-THREE—June 1944

Meanwhile, HOLT and WEN WU, in touch with the AACS-Army Air Communication System, had orders to help participate in the glider and airborne assault into unprepared areas of central Burma. The assault titled "Broadway" began four months ago before March. Purpose of assault is to harass the Japanese who had taken over Ragoon, Burma, earlier and now needed to be driven out of Myitkyina (Mitchee-NAH).

"We need to help co-ordinate efforts along the upper Salween River," said HOLT to his crew.

They left the area of the C-46 that had been lifted out of the mud and were flying back toward Assam for recruits.

"Thousands of soldiers are fighting the enemy out of Myitkyina (Mit-chi-NAH) and in a matter of time, they'll be pushed out," added WEN WU sitting behind HOLT next to the radio engineer.

"Brits and every ally we have are fighting courageously. What a mess! They took over Mandalay along the Irrawaddy with no trouble," said the co-pilot.

"Secretly, 'Operation Grubworm' is about to take place in August incorporating masses of groups of allies." HOLT said. "And since it's in the higher elevation, closer to the HUMP, the Zeros have trouble flying that high."

"The Burma Road needs to be back in operation as the main supply route to China across Burma to relieve all these treacherous Himalaya trips." WEN WU, who is HOLT'S main helper with the communication of languages, is always in the know. "Stillwell's crew is working on it out of Ledo, and it's supposed to cut through Myitkyina."

The men realized all of a sudden that they were shouting to be heard above the wind and torrential rain rocking the plane around.

"Wow! Look at that," said the Radio Engineer as he retrieved the seat's belt buckle snapping it on.

Everyone did the same fearing the worst.

Towering cumulus clouds getting blacker, taller and meaner, meant heavy rain and visible lightening soon to endanger all of them.

The co-pilot turned on the cockpit lights.

The airplane was thrown around violently in quick gyrations. The loud noise of rain and hail hitting the fuselage in torrents sounding like bullets meant a great deal of shouting across the cockpit.

"The auto-pilot is still on," yelled HOLT. Co-pilot Bill was holding onto the controls with all his strength.

WEN WU desperately tried to disengage the auto-pilot underneath the control pedestal.

Bill shouted for help with the controls.

The rate of climb was going from stop to stop and the instrument panel was shaking badly enough to make it impossible to read.

The Radio Operator kept trying to make contact with the ground station.

"Hang on everybody, St Elmo's fire is about to visit," HOLT yelled as a huge fiery circle lit up the right prop and massive flashes of lightening lit the windows. "A few minutes of fire and it'll be gone," he yelled for comfort.

Finally, as they were caught in an up-drift, they were thrown out into the center of a clear area at about 13,000 feet.

HOLT said, "All power off, carb heat on, control wheel forward and rate-of-climb looks like 6000 FPM."

"Air speed above the red line," yelled the copilot.

"We just made it out of the HUMP'S famous tropical storms," Bill gasped.

"Not yet! All around us are towering cumulus black clouds we have to penetrate again to get out of here," said HOLT.

Nothing but static from the radio. As the navigator kept trying to establish contact, tension worsened.

Then, just as they were preparing to hit the wall of new cumulus clouds, Bed Post contacted them with *"Don't land! Everyone's calling in a Mayday."* Next, he contacted them with the necessary heading and distance from his station to allow them a bearing. "Ok, come and get us," roared HOLT flying into the driving rain, hailstones and wild lightening. "Thirty minutes we need," he added.

They went in, auto-pilot off, fuel cross-feed open, mixture rich, props high, and two men at the controls. The short thirty minutes seemed like hours. "Hey, there it is," said WU looking at a clearing of valleys below.

Beyond the ASSAM VALLEY was Ledo, and farther away, the lights of Sookerating. The lights were a heartening blur.

"Mayday, Mayday" from above them kept HOLT at the controls looking for a landing strip as close as possible. "We need out of this soup," HOLT blurted. "And before we have a collision with planes in trouble," WEN WU added.

"I'm heading for the strip closes to Ledo." As he made radio contact for landing, the copilot noticed that the hydraulic pressure gauge was fluctuating from 950 pounds down to zero.

Now the entire crew became upset.

"This C-46 Commando's landing gear and brakes, plus wing flaps and flight control boosters are extremely dependent on the hydraulic pressure," blurted HOLT.

WEN WU shouted, "Don't panic. LUCKY LARRY showed me what to do." He worked while explaining. "I'll use this Shepards's Hook to reach back into the tail cone and latch the retractable tail wheel in the down for landing position. Watch!" He opened a trap door located in the pilot's compartment and read the information that was printed for manually cranking the gear down. "The gear is down and locked."

"Let's land," said HOLT with relief. "I'll contact LUCKY LARRY and get him over here to find out why we had hydraulic failure."

After landing, HOLT and crew examined the area of the hydraulic failure.

WEN WU noticed a ruptured fitting and burst filter. "This looks like it was started with a knife. Someone purposely cut half way through the hose." They stared at each other with a question mark expression.

"I will find him," said WEN WU, gritting his teeth. He knew that contact with Chang, the Chinese Chief Communication's Officer, would be the right move. The two were close friends and worked together well. "Saboteurs are everywhere and being paid by the Japs. We'll find their leaders!" "This is getting much too dangerous," added HOLT.

CHAPTER THIRTY-FOUR—June 1944

LUCKY LARRY set aside the ice cream machine he was working on and jeeped over on a craggy rough road to gather HOLT and crew and take them back to the barracks near Ledo.

"Give me some skin," he said offering quick hand-shakes all around. "This damage was done manually," he noted. "We can by-pass the filter to the hydraulic system and you can fly back to base where I can find a replacement or make one." "We'll fly back. Night is setting in, so we need to hurry. Our barracks are much more comfortable than these bashas out here." HOLT was still in a gray mood from the letter he received a few days ago. Plus, the saboteurs vexed his missions like a witches curse.

LUCKY LARRY looked at him and sighed.

He knew that his friends did their best with cheery condolences if there is such a thing, realizing time was the best healer.

"Hey, have they found BOBBY JOHNSON yet? I thought there was some good news over the air waves. Keep me tuned in to his rescue."

LUCKY LARRY put his tool kit back in the Willys and jumped in, all in one swing. "I'm anxious for the birthday party at the Swing Canteen in Sook. I'm almost done with the ice cream machine!" "I have a recipe with powdered milk," said WEN WU.

"Swell. Bring a date that can boogie. I'm not sharing. Hubba hubba, ding ding!" He laughed as he waved goodbye. He was the king, the AMO— Aircraft Maintenance Officer everyone referenced as a 'go-to' person for help. After all, he survived two bailouts from crashes and now fixed planes instead of crashing them.

"We need powdered eggs too!" WEN WU laughed loudly. He grabbed every opportunity he could to tease HOLT having known him a long time. He read every mood of the pipe HOLT played around with. Today he was gray and dark and kept thumping the empty pipe in the palm of his left hand. "Shit," was HOLT'S only reply. Filling his pipe, he decided to have a quick smoke while the crew readied the plane.

"I miss my old crew from last year in MATS Military Air Transport Service." HOLT seemed to be talking to no one. "Me the F/O, BOBBY my copilot, PALOOKA as navigator, and LUCKY LARRY the radio operator." He looked over at his favorite Chinese consultant. "I'm lucky I have you."

"DING HAO," said WU.

CHAPTER THIRTY-FIVE—June 1944

The Chindwin River ran fast and deep, tumbling over large boulders, spraying waves six feet in the air. June nightly torrents of rain relentlessly pounded on both sides of the river adding to the drama. Six hundred inches of rain during this summer month is always a negative issue. River banks gyrate with each twist of the river and landing strips urgently require new maintenance.

PALOOKA and Chuck estimated that BOBBY and the two boys were down river at about a quarter mile from them.

"This was the only stable sand bar for a safe landing," stated PALOOKA.

"And, the boys took a survival kit with them which is all good," added Chuck.

"Let's hope they made a parachute for cover," mumbled PALOOKA watching the pounding rain. "For sure the Nagas shouldn't bother them! They had too many contraptions to play with from the survival kit."

"Chingmi is the capital village of the Naga head hunters. They're not all bad. I know a crew who got help from them and flew out of Mokochung on a soccer field in an L-5." Chuck reminisced.

"Be nice to have a soccer field right here," said PALOOKA. "This sand bar is wasting away. If this river gets any higher, we'll have to hoof it out!" The two rescuers shot their pistols a couple times in the air as they stood outside the cockpit to listen for a response. "A response!" "Or an echo!"

They stood silently in the rain waiting for a signal. A response sounded again up river, closer this time.

They jumped back into the cockpit to watch and wait.

Soon, a British scouting column led by Kachin native jungle fighters arrived on the opposite side. The Brits and the Kachins were riding small Tibetan ponies, animals highly sure-footed for the jungle terrain. The colorful parade of men, a welcoming sight, waved joyously.

"The AACS – Army Airways Communication Service has certainly been successful with this immediate response."

"I hope we meet with the B-25 pilot who dropped the note to us about this scouting group coming to the rescue."

After much shouting and pointing, it was decided that the rescue column would search for BOBBY and the two boys and take them to their camp in Shingbwiyang south of the Patkai Range. PALOOKA urgently needed to fly out and away from the swollen river, now rising higher by the minute.

Chuck studied the map.

"I've flown there before on rescue missions," said PALOOKA. "I hate to abandon BOBBY now that we've found him, but we'll get him later from the Brits."

"He'll need medical care for a while to recoup," added Chuck.

PALOOKA decided to fly up and down the river one mile each way searching for a parachute tarp that perhaps BOBBY and boys were under. With Chuck on the binoculars, they were easily found.

PALOOKA flew over the area twice and waved his wings when the L-5 was low to the river.

Only after the three waved back, did PALOOKA fly off.

The good news swept fast over the airways. Brisk optimism shook Sookerating again, the party town where preparations for the big twenty-first birthday party were re-started days later at the Swing-Canteen!

CHAPTER THIRTY-SIX—June 1944

"Unbelievable," blurted Mitch to his co-pilot Ears after receiving the news about BOBBY. "BOBBY boy has been found," yelled Ears as he joined Mitch with a solid thumbs-up.

"On with our party! We'll make our contacts when we get home." He sharpened his thoughts of Milly.

They were heading back from their drop off in China when the pounding rain hit. Aware that many planes had to forcibly land due to the "Maydays" over the air waves, worried the entire crew.

"We have another 250 miles to go and we are heading into the soup," announced the radio operator.

"This does not look good."

Hands trembling, entire crew worried about "unflyable" conditions so they double checked gear, seat belts and parachutes. Traps of turbulence in each cloud can pick up a fifteen ton airplane and hurl it around like a rag doll.

At 20,500 feet they were riding over thick overcast that was at 20,000, and each wore an oxygen mask. Soon after hitting a thick cloud, the left engine went crazy. Its RPM'S jumped from 2,500 to about 4,000. Mitch brought it back down to 'control' when it stopped entirely.

With extreme vibration and wings flopping uncontrollably, Mitch was unable to maintain altitude.

"MAYDAY! MAYDAY!" He called.

"I know a small landing space in a valley below if I can get over this next 18,000 foot ridge."

Breathing fast, saying prayers aloud, the crew crossed the ridge gear down, flaps down, throttles back, no room for turns and selected a small landing area directly below. Diving steeply, they made an off airport strip landing.

The ship, now fast as lightening on the ground, bounced up and down due to the rugged hand-hewn short run-way. Too short!

The C-47 crashed into a grove of thick bushes at the end as the nose broke off and the damaged plane tilted sideways.

All strapped tightly, felt the thud of instant stop. Dirt and debris flew about as the men took stock of their physical being.

"Ow! Bruised ribs." The Navigator released the tight belt that saved his life.

"Better bruised ribs than a dead body!" Radio Engineer George immediately began working on communicating their demise with Air Waves. Contact was immediate. "Stay with plane. We'll find you!"

Feeling lucky, each took a long deep breath and unstrapped belts and head gear. Than—

"HOLY SHIT!! Look at this," yelled Ears as about 100 Warrior Lo Lo's, mounted on stout Tibetan ponies, surrounded their ship.

HOLT, head of intelligence for this crew, had advised them about Lo Lo's. *"They're very dangerous and only respect authority. If you see them coming at you, act brave. Don't run. Devise a plan of escape, or you will be chopped liver!"* Mitch sat thinking for a short while as they heard shouting and jabbering outside. Pounding on the plane from sharp objects hastened their anxiety. Mitch made a plan. "You three get out and bow down on one knee to greet me as I leave the ship last. This might work." They nervously rehearsed as quickly as possible.

Ears, Navigator, and Flight Engineer climbed out of the damaged plane slowly one by one. Each began to kneel on one knee and bow with head down. Plan was to not look up as Mitch unloaded. Fortunately, the heavy rain had quit and only a fine mist gathered around the herd of snorting mounts.

Mitch, shoulders back, standing tall as possible in the door way, lifted his chin a bit to face the crowd. He looked them over hesitantly from left to right. In his right hand he carried his oxygen mask, a foreign object to the Lo Lo's but another prop to add to his distinguished air of authority. *"Just like in the movies,"* he thought. His heart thumped loudly in his ears as he continued the act.

His crew did not look at him as they continued looking down at the ground while bent on one knee.

It sold.

The Lo Lo's backed away mumbling adamantly to each other. The Chief joyfully accepted the gifts that the crew now handed out, per plan—the oxygen mask, a clip board with pencil attached by string, an extra old jacket with multiple snapped pockets. From the safety pack, the compass, flash light and snacks of raisins and nuts completed the gifts.

The Lo Lo's became like kids with the fun of new items. They were Native Warriors from the mountains and had never seen the marvels of these contraptions.

Four Warriors got off their mounts, handed the braided leather reins to the crew men, and waved for them to follow the group. Mitch led as the other three followed per their act of respect for authority, Ears said, "On the map there is a small landing strip not far away. It's in the same direction we're going."

"I like it," said Mitch. "We'll make radio contact there for pick up."

The killer Warriors became congenial while feeling important at the same time.

"So this is war," Flight Engineer George commented as the sure-footed Tibetan ponies moved at a quickening pace, spurred on by the lead.

After the crew reached the British out post, the Lo Lo's departed.

Mitch noted immediately the missing normal courageous cheer of *esprit de corps.*

Instead, the Brits were morose, and gloomy. They were speechless until a Captain delivered the horrific news quite hesitantly.

"A plane fully loaded with crew, medics, and 30 nurses, crashed while landing." A long pause, then "NO SURVIVORS."

A shocking silence of grief was heard around the world.

CHAPTER THIRTY-SEVEN—June 1944

After hearing the horrific news, WEN WU and HOLT almost went into shock.

NEWS FLASH! PLANE OF 30 NURSES CRASHES UPON LANDING. NO SURVIVORS!

This was the single most tragic happening in the ATC-AIR TRAFFIC COMMAND, so far. Massive grief was worldly. Experts traveled to the site with numerous questions.

"How could this happen?"

"Why so many nurses on one plane?"

"Who's at fault?"

"Where's the blame?"

All questions went unanswered. The desperate attempt to find the blame dwindled among the entire group of experts. This was a bloody War. Nothing would bring the fatalities back to life.

HOLT and WEN WU sat on their bunks in the main barrack next to Headquarters, thinking—not talking. Of their total experiences, nothing surpasses this catastrophe.

"Son-of-a-bitch!" HOLT lit his pipe, took a few puffs, sat it down on the small chest of drawers and opened a bottle of whiskey. He poured a good amount in each glass—his and WEN WU'S.

They, along with the entire thousands of ATC crews, loved the nurses. They were the young recruits from the states. They handled the sick and bloody bodies of everyone. They were tender, young and hardworking. Most were volunteers.

Sadly, and most of all, they were the sisters, aunts, cousins, and moms of crews working this bloody campaign.

HOLT, the go-to man for problems, did not want one like this. He heaved a heaviness with each breath. A pain that would not go away. He thought of the beginning when he was a Flight Officer—an F/O on the first cargo ship of its kind, the C-46. If he could just go back to his original crew, to the innocence of pre-war.

Now a senior with the most experience, he has to ride out this bloody, stinking, ungrateful War. He thought of his past:

HOLT, senior officer with 6 aircraft and crew;

HOLT, liaison officer to executive headquarters; HOLT, base navigator and main officer in operations;

HOLT, commanding officer of squadrons—330 men.

The tragedy brought back memories of every bad experience he wished to forget. Tears welled in his eyes. *He sniffed. Too tough to cry.*

Sitting on the edge of his bunk, head down, both hands gripping the glass of whiskey turning it round and round slowly, he thought of the most haunting parachuting memory. The last of his crew to face the Chinese Officer aboard with forty laborers on the doomed flight of the spiraling plane, he heard again:

"Where you go Captain?"

"To get help." HOLT'S only reply. As he turned to dive out of the hatch to safety he heard—

"You good Captain!"

These words would haunt him forever.

His chute opened to the terrible boom of the ship as it blasted into the mountain and disintegrated.

Now, tears welled again as he remembered the confident look of the poor, innocent Chinese Officer.

"Damn War!"

WEN WU came over with his glass of whiskey and sat next to HOLT. After lighting a Lucky Strike, he looked down at his tired feet somberly.

"Good news. You know BOBBY'S been found." Shifting on the cot, HOLT wiped his eyes and said, "Now that's a bit of a lift."

"And", continued WEN WU, "Mitch and Ears made it off a crashed plane. Saved by the Lo Lo's I hear."

HOLT made a muffled sound, a sad chuckle and said again, "Now that's a lift!"

"Ok, go get the clip board. We need to brainstorm the recent monstrosity."

"Sabotage," said WEN WU.

CHAPTER THIRTY-EIGHT—June 1944

WEN WU and HOLT got the word out about Chinese laborers accepting large sums of money from the Japanese to cause major havoc.

"Sabotage is where you least expect it," said WEN WU now taking charge with the tasks of weeding out the culprits. First order of plan is brainstorming sessions in headquarters, tents and barracks involving all personnel including Chinese police and staff. These sessions will be produced by local and reliable men of the ATC communication systems.

Because of the language barrier, HOLT let WEN WU take charge. He read his notes from impeccable English and translated them to Mandarin, the most common language. All notes will be communicated over the air waves as produced by the ATC. Locally, their audience is now at a large tent set up near the barracks.

"First of importance, planes must be guarded by military at all times and not by miscellaneous personnel. We need to find the bad guys and how much the Japs are paying them."

A hand raised and an airman added "We need to offer material goods instead of money. Soap is their number one love!"

Laughter and comments followed with "very true," and "happened on my run."

WEN WU continued, "Always check your IFF-Identification Friend or Foe before changing any original directives. The enemy is extremely cunning. For example, they paid mixed groups of Natives and Chinese to help set up dummy homing stations in Himalayas to throw off the instruments and cause C-46 crashes." He looked around and felt confident standing next to HOLT as his anchor and asked, "What else?"

An airman stood and stated loudly, "We need to find and destroy mobile transmitters hidden at landing strips for Japanese bombers to home on." WEN WU shaking his head yes, kept translating for all the Chinese leaders, the trusted ones who wanted to help. To them, a local countryman working against his country is considered treason, and all wanted to weed out the culprits.

"Check who is hand pumping your gas so they are not shorting you," said a crewman. "I landed once on fumes from an emptying tank. I landed, but didn't make it to the end of the runway."

Someone added the importance of firmly tied horses and mules. "Once, an untied horse almost brought down our ship."

HOLT intervened, "If you are out on the landing strip in any way, watch the edges where laborers are working with carts and animals. There was an incidence of a worker wheeling a cart in front of a landing plane."

He paused for emphasis. "Was it an accident? Or was it sabotage?"

The brainstorming session went well. Everyone made verbal notes of suspicious activity that happened to them and others.

Tribal leaders needed to be contacted and informed. The Chinese were willing to take on this task.

All knew that the native tribes were ignorant of the War purpose and didn't take sides. Now, they need to be helpful and more similar to the Gurkha Warriors, native to Nepal and immensely helpful to the ground War effort. Troops operated behind enemy lines in areas of dense jungle helping the British.

HOLT finished with, "First of importance, notice who is on or near your plane before your flight. No persons other than crew should be allowed. In the past, oxygen air hoses were found loosened and the F/O and Co-Pilot almost passed out before landing. Double check everything."

He noticed how all the crew now shared their experiences among one another.

"You did a swell job today," said HOLT to his number one interpreter. "The word is out!"

"Now, let's go see BOBBY. I hear he's back."

"DING HAO!"

Among the masses of listeners to the loudly broadcasted message, some poor Chinese peasants looked at each other with both knowledge and contempt.

CHAPTER THIRTY-NINE—June 1944

Milly, surgeon Tom and staff on the field with the trauma patients, were finishing their tasks quickly before the sun went down.

A larger tent had been erected to administer aid, free of the drizzling rain and near the landing strip. Patients were being flown out, including the young Air man who refused to let go of her hand as he moaned in pain.

"You will be ok," she said heartily, proud of the medical staffs' emergency work.

She patted the top of his hand, as another C-47 came thundering in loudly, all lights blazing in the darkening night.

She let go of his hand as he was prepped and carted away to the recent arriving cargo plane that was empty of passengers except one, and ready to board the last few injured. The small team of surgeon Tom, med technicians and five nurses including Milly, were eager to leave the stench of the sweltering field.

Lone BOBBY hobbled off the plane to great his friends and to exercise his now fully wrapped left ankle. He should feel happy. He was almost home, here with the Americans.

Gathering everyone around him, he felt the need to be the bearer of the horrific news. Somehow, they had not heard the bad news. Being too busy saving lives and administering emergency first aid to the injured, they paid no attention to the chatter communicated on the air waves.

It was pitch black.

It was now pouring.

They were tired and ready to go home on this plane that landed to retrieve all of them.

BOBBY hated to be the one to tell them what happened.

It was easy to tell by their excitement to be flying out, that they did not know about their friends and co-workers perishing in the crash.

Waiting until he and the small staff were last to board, he told them everything while out on the tarmac. The injured did not need to know right now. It was the omen Milly feared that came true. They felt the devastation as they all stood hugging each other and weeping. Shoulders slumped. They stomped around in disgust and disbelief.

"Damn War!"

"Jeezus Carrist!"

"No! No! No!"

They thought of the F/O, Co-Pilot, Peasants, and bandaged unknown War heroes swabbed for healing, that were now gone forever. Knowing some of them personally by name, made it worse.

Loss of the 30 nurses was too much for Milly to bear. Swaying and losing her footing, she was caught by a staff member who promptly put her on board.

All wept silently on the two hour flight back to Assam where medical staff personnel were diligently waiting.

Milly felt a devastating loss for her friends and also for herself.

Where will she go now?

What will she do all alone?

In sorrow, everyone huddled closely on the droning plane.

CHAPTER FORTY—June 1944

Mitch, Ears and crew boarded a C-47 for fly back to Assam from the British Outpost. They became the crew of the ship waiting for fly out. It had unloaded earlier with medical supplies and flown in by a crew too tired now to man the plane back to Assam. This worked equally well. Likewise, the Brits knew how to accommodate the Lo Lo's. Having worked the India Tibet areas in years past, all the natives became familiar to them.

Most importantly, plenty of hand soap and chocolate bars are kept for these weird occasions and are handed out plentifully. Thankful no one was hurt or killed, they all shook hands and the Lo Lo's disappeared into the thick jungle. As always, they knew the trails adequately in the darkness.

After takeoff and with the ship on a steady course, Mitch and crew became solemnly quiet.

And then:

"Oh, my Lord!"

"I can't believe it!"

"How did it happen?"

Mitch breathed deeply then slowly said, "It was Milly's field group." It hit him like a bomb. He pictured her soft brown hair and heard her baby voice. *"I just turned nineteen."*

Because they had the Lo Lo's to deal with earlier, their remorse had been delayed.

All went quiet as the plane droned on. They were now an hour out of Myitkyina (Mitchi-NAW) Burma and heading to Ledo with supplies for this stretch of Stillwell's Road which will eventually connect with the Burma Road. Heading north, they could see the Patkai Range ahead and the Chindwin River south of it. Crossing the Chindwin, they thought of BOBBY and his crew.

"I hear they never found Walt," Ears said, being the first to break the silence.

"They'll get him," Mitch stated with a superficial confidence totally aware of the dangers everywhere. "You never know. He could be going from village to village stunned from the crash."

"PALOOKA and Chuck are combing the crash area closely." Then Mitch added, "He could be a coma patient somewhere with lost tags."

"Hopefully the Brits have him."

"Good thought!"

"But we would have heard from them by now."

They were on the Easy Route after crossing Charlie and heading toward Ledo, Assam when the tower at Shingbwiyang started calling for a "three ball" alert, meaning enemy planes are in the immediate vicinity.

Mitch took the plane to a higher altitude and kept all lights off.

Navigator got traffic control on the radio for directions to a new field.

Traffic Control was having troubles as nearly all fields south of Assam had been hit by enemy bombers.

"They're re-routing us over to Fort Hertz which is about one hundred miles to the north-west of Ledo, Assam. Keep flying blacked out!" Since it is after midnight, and no moon in the sky, Mitch and Ears are on instruments only.

Japanese bombers hit in continuous fireworks on a field to the left.

Mitch and Ears kept the plane at a steady 14,500, thankful to have enough fuel for the re-route.

Chatter on the radio emphasized the stress of workers on the ground trying to get some emergency runways open and free of deep craters. The total black night made it more difficult.

"Mayday!"

"Mayday!"

Repeated at regular intervals, stress calls only added to the tension and the men were silent in desperation.

Airplanes were stacked over Ft. Hertz at 500 foot intervals and radio tower was taking them off the bottom of the stack for landing as fast as they could. Plus, the crew heard the tower warn about landing on the south half of the runway as "it is torn up for repair".

Suddenly, the tower started calling the airplanes by number to check their IFF (Identify Friend or Foe) which was time consuming.

Mitch and crew got the bad news.

The runway lights ahead and below of them were turned off and it was obvious they were scrambling two P-61's (Black Widows) stationed there. An enemy fighter was among them trying to get a shot at Mitch and crew in their huge C-47 cargo plane, carrying fifty pound barrels of high octane.

Since coming down from the high altitude in preparation for landing, they were now within shooting range from the blunt nose Zero.

With a pounding heart, Mitch stationed the Radio Operator on one side window and the Crew Chief on the other side for lookouts.

Within two minutes the Radio Operator sighted the Zero coming in at a fast climbing turn. Mitch waited until the last possible second as the Zero was rolling out on his tail, than dumped the gear to a slow speed and split out in a downward turn.

After the loss of about two thousand feet, he spurred the C-46 back to its assigned altitude and held that position for about thirty minutes as the P-61's, airborne now, flew through the stack chasing the Zero off.

Runway lights below came on and the tower started landing planes off the bottom of the stack. The narrow strip, bordered by craters caused from enemy fire and weather, could present a problem. "Wow," complained Ears. "Good luck to us!"

Rolling in to a stop, they were one of many transit planes parked all over the place.

They had just cut the engine and shut down the radio when the field klaxton sounded a screaming warning.

After opening the cargo door, they all jumped to the ground without a ladder and while bending low, ran to the side slits along the pitiful runway.

The Zero came down the runway all guns firing and not striking a thing.

It disappeared in the dim of the early morning light and never returned.

In the blue-gray dawn, the men secured cots in a nearby tent. Too jittery to sleep, they mumbled back and forth.

"Word has it that BOBBY'S party is still on." To this, Mitch made no reply. With his hands under his pillow, he turned his back to the others. His eyes open in a gloomy daze, his thoughts were only of Milly.

CHAPTER FORTY-ONE—June 1944

HOLT, always in touch with his crew buddies, kept contact the best he could. While he, WEN WU and crew are flying to the area of the recent fateful crash for full assessment, they mumbled the whereabouts of buddies.

"Mitch is in Ft. Hertz after a fortunately lucky landing."

"PALOOKA and Chuck are searching for Walt around the Chindwin River."

"BOBBY is resting in Sookerating while writing his adventures for brass and notes on 'HOW TO SURVIVE IN THE JUNGLE.'"

"Good luck with that," said HOLT. "Mud pack saved his ankle."

WEN WU added, "We all need to read it and add a whole lot more."

"Damn," said Bill the navigator. "Why in hell did Stillwell stock our plane with horses, mules and workers? I feel the plane shifting all the time." "The Chinese laborers in the far back should be controlling them," added Rick the radio operator. HOLT, noting the problem, had trouble keeping the plane as steady as possible. "In their defense, these tired laborers have been working non-stop for weeks and need to go to the area we're headed to relax a bit before getting back on the job. They'll be working the other end of the Ledo Road. When we get the Japs out of Burma, the Burma Road will be one-long-highway for transporting supplies to China."

Earl the co-pilot, now noticed cold seeping into his electric flying suit. "I put this on for warmth. I need to check it out when we land. Wires could be crossed."

"Or snipped!" WEN WU whined. "Ok."

Notebook in hand he told the crew, "List problems you've seen that could be possible sabotage. I meet with Captain Chang tomorrow to discuss our dilemma."

HOLT added, "The meeting we had yesterday was quite successful. All problems and ideas were transferred via the air waves. Our powerful radio beacons that dot the Hump air lines are well regulated by the ATC."

"And the co-axial cables around the Assam Valley and Calcutta are manned by wire sweepers," WEN WU added.

"How does that work?" Bill the Navigator was fairly new to this area of the HUMP Theater and found 'wire sweepers' a fascinating concept.

The young Chinese interpretor continued. "The wire communication system is handled especially by the Signal Corps along the Ledo Road. Workers with long sweeping handles do their best to clear the spiders off the wires before the webs get wet with dew and short out the wires."

"Can you believe it was all put together last year, 1943, to establish a radio network!" HOLT continued, "Now all air bases in India and China are interconnected."

Bill interspersed with "Next, they need to complete Burma and be aware of the Japs intercepting our call letters from their pill boxes in the canyons." Now at 8000 feet, HOLT turned the controls over to Earl as he stepped out of his seat to crawl into his electric flying suit for warmth. He fit the oxygen mask to his flight cap easily but had trouble getting into his heavy flight boots due to the movement of the plane caused by the mules and horses. He fell back near WEN WU, who could barely move, and squeezed into a make-shift seat behind the cockpit. "Check on the animals' tie-downs in a few minutes. We don't want a loose animal bringing down the plane," HOLT barked.

He got back in his seat and attached the electric suit to the plug-in. After connecting his built in microphone to his oxygen mask, and testing the indicator, he was all set and took over for the co-pilot who had to go through some of the same procedures. WEN WU always wore his extra thickly padded suit when he accompanied HOLT on his many expeditions. He too attached his oxygen mask for their short adventure over the south tip of the Himalayas. HOLT planned a quick trip because of the animals and workers. Without enough oxygen, the men would become light headed and pass out or vomit a great deal.

Coming down from the high elevation allowed WEN WU to unplug his oxygen mask and check on the horses.

"What's that smell? Is it smoke?" HOLT was yelling by now. "Son-of-a bitch!" He pinched the bridge of his nose.

WEN WU yelled back over the loudness of the engines. "The workers have started a fire in the back of the plane to stay warm. I'll take care of it!"

Still yelling, he instructed the Chinese workers to put out the fire and reminded them of a possible explosion. "We always carry high-octane petro on planes. Pooff", he made huge hand gestures, "we could have an explosion!"

Instantly, and with great fear, the workers stomped rapidly on the flames. They chatted wildly and swayed with dizziness. The entire operation so foreign to them, they again needed reminding of whose side to support.

"We are the good guys," shouted WEN WU making sure they all heard over the frightening snorts of the animals and stomping of hooves.

"Double check tie downs," he shouted to the men as he tried to get through the shifting horses. Getting wilder, the animals kept moving in a white eyed panic due to the smoke, so he had trouble getting through them.

"Everyone help now!" His order loud and clear emphasized desperateness.

Everyone pitched in to help, except two. Everyone grabbed a halter and tried vainly to calm the animals, except two.

The crew empowered the instruments on the huge cargo plane keeping it on task.

Putting out a fire anywhere is a major job due to smoke thickness that seems to hang around. WU and others stomped fiercely on the last remnants of hay and flaming tarp, except two.

The shifting and whinnying ceased in frequency due to the workers soothing voices and head pats. And WEN WU, thankful for the coldness, realized the barrels would be less likely to blow from the low heat of the fire which was dissipating now slowly.

"This could have been a disaster," he wailed while waving his arms in great circles. "POOF!" They cowered.

Except two.

CHAPTER FORTY-TWO—June 1944

It is a messy, sloppy, dirty, stinking day in Shingbwiyang, south of the Patkai Range, a couple hundred miles from Ledo and Assam. An earthly, fetid odor of rot permeates the air.

The rain is coming down in torrents pounding on the tin roofs of shanties and shacks lining on both sides of a muddy track of a roadway, packed with rickshaw drivers, small scooters, fat pigs, skinny dogs, scrawny rats zooming about and boxes used as hovels for those dry seekers.

It is an ordinary day for the people of this land who never mind the months of torrential rains, especially now during June.

Numerous natives hobble about trading beads, feathers, wood trinkets and leather goods while ducking under make-shift shelter and sloshing in the mud.

It is a colorful market! Indoors are rolls of silk, tobacco, pipes, cigars, liquor, hush-hush opium, garden vegetables, and tea pots. Lots of colorful tea pots line shelves above the numerous teas harvested here and previously planted in abundance by the British, eons ago.

These natives from the surrounding hills and mountains of Northern India and Burma are the Kachins, Abors, Mishmi, Lo Lo's and Nagas. It is a mixed group, all here to trade, or sell their wares. They are the hawkers of the region.

Accepting the rain, all are dresssed quite bare. Distinct colorful beads, short belted tunics, weird leggings and chopped black hair, differ per group. Most are friendly except for the Nagas who are split in two groups, the friendly helpful ones and the bad. The bad are the head hunters of the mountains and compared to the Lo Lo's, most feared by everyone. They all teetered and waddled when they walked. Short legs, adapted for speeding up and down mountain trails, now find it difficult to walk flat footed on straight streets.

BOBBY and small group of friends, jeeped in from Ledo, crossing over the Chindwin River on the only bridge possible. LUCKY LARRY drove the

Willys accompanied by lovely Loretta in the front seat. "I'm so lucky that you can come along," he had said earlier.

"What a break!" She heartedly exclaimed. "I am now bandaging soldiers in my sleep."

Larry looked over at her longingly and decided that before the day was finished, he would play with her long dark shoulder length hair fingering it back into her G.I. cap. To him, she was a piece of art work much like those he painted on planes. He smiled at her. She smiled back.

BOBBY, Bonnie and WEN WU squeezed tightly together in the back. Each had an agenda, a purpose, and a ride-along-get-away permit endorsed by HOLT, their leader, their pal, their mountain of support.

BOBBY, still on crutches, refused R and R in Darjeeling, wanting instead to help LUCKY LARRY plan the big birthday party to take place in Sookerating, date extended for next week. Though masked as a twenty-first birthday party for BOBBY, it is to be for everyone. Thus, the importance. "We need a mood-climber," was LUCKY LARRY'S chant pushing the importance of a gathering. "After all, I piece the planes together that you guys wreck. And who paints the best babes in the entire ATC?"

Upper Brass was always accommodating with G.I. desires. "Good incentives," the Majors and General agreed. "Makes this hellacious war barely bearable!"

"Swell! We need a party. Party, party, party," was the premier chant as the five first drove out of Ledo heading for Shingbwiyang.

Now they are quiet. The poor, poverty stricken area, amass with buyers, sellers, and raggedy beggars half-naked and bold, frightened the young women. Bonnie, never away from the airports with her job of jeeping crews around, had never seen the real squalor like a market place in upper Burma. Her chatty, smiley demeanor gone now, she scooted closer to BOBBY. "How's your left foot? You need help walking, let me know." She was now shouting to be heard over the pounding rain on the Willys' canvas top.

He shook his head Ok. Looking over at her small face, he wondered how her hair curled more when wet. "Not a perm," she had told him last month. "Just a family investment." Then, they had laughed. Now, both are quiet.

"LUCKY LARRY, are we headed in the right direction?" Loretta shouted. "What's the name of the shop?"

"Parts and Pieces. But, I'm turned around in this rain. We need a side road or track as they call it." Just as he turned the corner, a beggar wearing shreds and carrying a medium size basket, stepped in front to stop him.

The jeep spun a bit, throwing mud and slop everywhere. Grinning, the toothless beggar started opening the lid.

WEN WU shouted at him too late as a swaying snake head appeared over the edge.

Simultaneously, the ladies screamed, LUCKY LARRY stepped on the gas, and the beggar flung the basket while stepping out of the way.

The snake hissed on the wet ground deciding which way to slither.

Loretta coiled next to LUCKY LARRY, grabbing his right arm and curling her feet around his ankle.

He smiled broadly.

"This is not the break I needed," she simply babbled.

"It gets better," added WEN WU. "I know a British run tea house a few blocks or mud holes away."

The beggar scooped up his snake in two slippery slides, enveloping it in the basket and lidding it all in one quick motion. He glared at them as LUCKY LARRY stepped on the gas and the Willys spun away down a side track of narrow road, twin to the one they just left.

"Good decision," WEN WU said. "The British Tea House is near this area. I recognize this place." Soon they reached a shop set aside from the street hovels, with a large rectangular painted sign hanging above wooden steps, "Darjeeling-Tea." An overhang provided shelter to those sitting on a long wooden porch, watching the rain and mud filled stream out front. British uniforms were the masses, smoking, drinking whiskey or tea.

Parking close, the five ran to the shelter. Because of the heavy downpour, more soldiers than normal sat outside at small wooden tables under the overhang, absorbing all action.

The five nodded as they walked inside, deciding to find a table in the spacious interior. Nods of tired smiles and grins half-heartedly worn on every soldier's face greeted them. No one cared where they were from. No one asked.

WEN WU ordered a large pot of Darjeeling.

"You know, this is called the 'Cadillac of Teas'," he announced while setting the service for them in the center of the round table. Raised as an infant by British parents, he had learned good tea etiquette and now was the time to show off his skills. Teasingly he bragged, "You hold your cup like this, and you pour from the pot like this. And you put cream in your tea like this!" He shuffled his fingers in mockery.

The entertainment was sorely needed as they laughed and mocked each other over proper tea etiquette.

"Now, for our agendas." WEN WU pulled out the small note pad from his Marine green service bag and began to write. "BOBBY needs to find the two young Burma boys who helped him survive. LUCKY LARRY needs ice cream machine parts, and I need to meet with Chang, the Chinese Chief of Command to discuss sabotage problems."

"We cannot separate," Bonnie murmured softly while rolling her young blue eyes around the room and touching BOBBY'S shoulder. "In here, peace. Outside, not."

Loretta shivered while nudging more closely to LUCKY LARRY.

He beamed. "All agree!"

BOBBY began. "I know that the two boys were separated from me here, near this town, when the British scouting team found us. Let's go to the British Consulate that's here."

"It's next to Chang's office," WEN WU added.

"First comes ice cream!" They all agreed. Suddenly, a loud raucous occurred at the open door followed by yelling.

A British group previously sitting near the opening, forcibly prevented a short, squat, swaying native man from angrily entering.

The group of five looked over at the entrance. There stood *NAGA MAN* snarling at them and pointing. Around his neck, tied with a cord, was the harmonica. In his hand he held a freshly severed head.

CHAPTER FORTY-THREE—June 1944
Shingbwyang

"Holy Mackerel!" LUCKY LARRY blurted while grabbing Loretta by the shoulders and pushing her away from the scene.

"What the Bloody Hell," screamed a British Airman. Sitting back hard in his chair tipping it over, he fell with a thump and rolled over on his back all in one motion.

"Get out of here!" Someone yelled.

"Out! Out!" They all yelled waving their arms trying to force NAGA MAN back.

Next, they took their Ghurka Knives out of their shafts pointing at him forcibly.

He didn't move but stood there unfazed, swaying. Staring straight ahead with a fiendish grin for BOBBY, he held the severed head high for all to see.

Bonnie ducked behind BOBBY.

Loretta clung to LUCKY LARRY.

The Brits kept yelling. Now pulling out their guns, they were ready to use them if necessary.

Like a stone, NAGA MAN did not move from the doorway, and no one wanted to touch him to push him away. He had no fear.

WEN WU jumped into action. With an explosive dialect, he grabbed a Ghurka knife from a Brit, and began attacking the intruder with short jabs to his chest. In its casing, the sharp dangerous knife could do no real harm, only bruises.

Although the tactic worked, the entire group was soon rescued by the good Nagas, those sympathetic to the War effort. They had been following NAGA MAN earlier and now pushed him, shoving him away, all bellowing and cursing.

Then, the unthinkable happened. NAGA MAN, heavy in a kind of stupor, heaved the bloody severed head at BOBBY while babbling incoherently. In a wide arc overhead, the wrinkled face spewed blood everywhere before landing on the table where the five had been sitting.

"Bloody Hell" yelled several Brits as they all stood now in a helpful force supporting the good Nagas, yet standing at a distance from the gross scene. A few young Brits went outside to vomit. These natives were the good guys, helpful in every way with the ATC's War effort. Efficiently, they cleaned the entire mess while everyone stood back. Removing the head was their first goal. Seizing the crazy native and whisking him away was their second.

Harshly they pushed NAGA MAN out. By this time, the native could barely stand because of the heavy dose of opium or some other drug he had consumed earlier. He was part of a group of renegades who lived deep in the mountains robbing for food and trinkets as a means of survival. They severed heads for control of their enemies.

BOBBY and other service men had seen these trophies grossly mounted on a heavy board and displayed in the market for all to see.

Warned by upper brass about this group, they were every pilots fear when parachuting out of a crashing plane.

The five paid their tea tab and moved out on the porch where a few others were sitting, happy to leave the disgusting scene inside but still interested in talking to others about the two boys, and getting on with their agenda.

WEN WU chatted loudly with the Nagas, interpreting the conversation for the Brits and his own group.

"This is the man who chased our military pilot after he parachuted out of a crash high in the Himalayas."

The good natives shook their heads in understanding and were excited to have an interpreter who spoke their language. They commented that this unpopular Naga, a renegade from his village, should be locked behind bars. "He is a danger to himself and everyone else. He thought the soldier's blond hair was some kind of gold."

As things calmed down a bit, WEN WU explained why they were here in this area, to both the Nagas and the Brits. "The two boys who saved our friend's life, we would like to find them."

The soldiers were standing now, milling around trying to de-stress from the despicable scene they witnessed earlier. They refilled empty whiskey glasses, smashed half smoked cigarettes and lit new ones.

A pacing Brit loudly blurted, "What the FFF-Friday night was that? Here we are 1944, the Twentieth Century, and we see stuff from the Eighteenth Century." He walked in circles a bit before sitting. "Ghastly, I say!"

A Brit who had been jiggling coins in his pockets came forward. He looked at BOBBY and said, "I remember you and the boys. They cherished the retractable cup and few gifts you gave them. At that time there was a road crew heading to Ledo to help with Stilwell's road. It's a mixed group from Burma and they joined them. You'll find them around the Ledo area." He was quick and brisk with his answer and continued pacing the wood floor. "Cards anyone?" He shouted.

The Nagas left with a short salute. Needing to handle the situation with the bad guy, they hurried out.

BOBBY came forward. "I too remember you and your group who saved my life. Can't thank you enough! PALOOKA and Chuck were on the other side of that swiftly flowing river and it would have been treacherous to raft over."

"Knowing where and how to cross these rivers to save Airmen is what we do proudly!" The Brit kept pacing.

"Cheers!" All raised glasses for whiskey refills. The five raised refilled tea cups. "We have an agenda to finish before leaving and the daylight is disappearing."

The Brits started their card game and the group of five found a quiet table in a corner to continue their thoughts. But, before leaving the Brits, they invited them to the party at Sook. Party date and time noted by all. "Last Saturday in June at the Swing Canteen. We'll be there!" They all shook hands.

"What did we do? They're babe stealers." LUCKY LARRY sighed. "Ah hell! This is a good day now." Re-convening, they sat close, very close, as WU, with notebook in hand said, "Good news! Agenda number one crossed off. Now we find the 'Piece-and-Parts' shop for ice cream machine." LUCKY LARRY lifted his glass, "Homemade ice cream coming up." Loretta hugged him delightfully. Bonnie added the important news of knowing where to confiscate canned milk and fresh eggs. "No more powdered 'eggus' and powdered milk." They all looked at her skeptically.

"I jeep around." She raised her eyebrows and glass simultaneously. BOBBY'S laugh, a head back fist thumping on the table, was an invite for Bonnie to quickly move to his lap.

"What a lucky day," he said putting his arms around her waist.

Suddenly, the two British Airmen who previously went outside for fresh air during the fiasco, came hurrying in.

"Hey," looking at the five. "We chased two Chinese away from your jeep. They had knives in hand ready to slash the tires."

"Thanks!" The group hurried out.

"On with our agenda. Chang's office is around the corner from the parts we need for machine," said LUCKY LARRY.

"DING HAO!"

CHAPTER FORTY-FOUR—June 1944

Ft. Hertz

MEANWHILE, Mitch and Ears followed orders to re-route octane from Fort Hertz Valley in Burma back to Ledo. Stillwell, while losing his patience over the weather delays, became a Frankenstein force to deal with.

It was early morning when they awoke to the crew giving orders for flight preparation. In the streak of dawn they prepared in silence due to lack of sleep from the trauma of last night and few days before with the Lo Lo's attacking. Noting that the Zeroes had been chased away by the P61 Black Widows during the night, they felt reassured for a safe upcoming flight.

Now, jeeped to their newly fueled plane warming out on the runway, they thought of their orders to fly one hundred-sixteen miles to Sadiya, 16,000 feet on the Able Route due to temporary good weather. Trucks at Sadiya are to carry octane down to Digboi and then on to Ledo near the Patkai Range.

In the warm cockpit, the four crew members plugged in their oxygen masks and re-checked lines for leaks. Once, a line had a small break and the F/O almost passed out from lack of oxygen. This important double check, was a major drill.

Last, Mitch and Ears checked all flight controls for free movement. After take-off of 115 miles per hour, they were climbing.

"I can't do this anymore. I want out. I hope the damn Burma Road gets finished before the war is over!" If he were in his tent instead of the cockpit, Mitch would be banging his fist on the short chest of drawers near his bunk.

"Who you sore at?" Ears realized his mistake when Mitch had no answer, only a sorrowful grimace. "What a tragedy." He half whispered.

Seeing the last ridge ahead, they started a gradual descent by reducing the power settings. Finally crossing the last ridge and the flat valley of the Brahmaputra River below, they were in the Province of Assam.

With heavy oxygen helmets off, they felt like talking.

"I'm for turning on the radio. We need some music!" Ears needed to control the mood from somber to cheery.

Ralph the radio operator was ready to give it a try. "Sometimes I can get a clear station from San Francisco." He worked the dials.

"You made me love you, I didn't want to do it," came through loud and clear, and static free. "Morton Downey Orchestra," said Ears.

"Geezus! Turn that off," moaned Mitch.

"Holdit! We need ideas for the Swing Canteen," one of the crew members complained. "How about Glenn Miller's *Stardust*"?

"Yeah, that's a body crusher." Ears smiled broadly. "And, I can play the tune. I'm part of the band."

Mitch rebounded with, "I'm more in the mood for '*Casey Jones*' by Spike Jones and his City Slickers." "Turn on ole' Tokyo Rose. She's a ghost but the station plays great American music," said Ears.

Soon Benny Goodman's clarinet resounded clearly in the small cockpit to everyone's peace of mind.

Idle chatter began to burn time.

"Say, I hear that BOBBY'S looking for those two young boys who saved his life."

"They're around somewhere. He'll find them." "Sad part of the War is that the Japs are paying groups to cause problems for us. We need to turn that around!"

"How do we do that? These poor people need money and they don't care how they get it."

"Constant communication. Handing out food and trinkets of all kinds helps."

"They love chocolate and cigarettes….jeep rides."

"Don't forget. WEN WU is working with Chang the Chinese Commander. And, because he speaks different native languages, he'll get to the bottom of the problem." Silence.

Then, "My beautiful, innocent, little Millie. Such a young thing!"

"Oh hell, Mitch! You only met her briefly. And you're only twenty-three yourself!"

"Twenty-two. I'll be twenty-three next month." "This plane is sure having troubles," complained the navigator as the rain and hail pounded on the wings.

"What happened to our good weather?" "Ole' Dumbo can make it," said Mitch the F/O. "No way do I want to hit the silk today. We're almost there."

Ears added, "All our tent mates are back except for Walt. He may never be found."

"Hope he didn't have a run in with the Lo Lo's," said Ralph. "He should hide out in a soggy little village and escape the HUMP duties."

"Back to BOBBY." Navigator Tom looked at the other three quizzically. "He had an entire month of R & R coming to him in Darjeeling. Why didn't he take it?"

"Maybe he lost some marbles in the jungle," commented Tom.

"Making it down the mountains and through the jungle is no picnic I hear." Ears now stomped his feet for re-circulation after leaving the higher elevation and the extreme cold.

"I hear BOBBY'S running around with Bonnie, the jeep loader."

They all whistle.

"What a knock-out!"

"She's a Babe!"

"LUCKY LARRY has a free model for nose art." "Today, WEN WU, LUCKY LARRY, BOBBY and two girls are jeeping to a village not far from where we're flying, to question Chang. And one of the girls is Bonnie," said Ralph.

"How do you know all that?" Ears wanted to know.

"It's part of the communication system. Remember the lecture we had about sabotage? It's all part of radio operations' attempt to keep us aware of hazards."

"So you gossip?"

"You damn right! That's the fun part of this job, flying over the roof top of the earth."

Soon a saucy voice interrupted. *"Hello boys in c-46. This is Tokyo Rose playing 'Lilly Marlene' for Mitch and Millie saying—get out or get dead!"* Mitch came unglued. "Holy Shit! How does she do it?"

"Hold on," Ears yelled.

"She doesn't know you," Ralph remarked. "It's coming from an insider somewhere. Remember, there are some workers who understand English and get paid for any information they hear."

"WU better weed them out quick!" Mitch shook from anger.

"We need to keep our socks on. Her wise cracks are only talk to agitate us," added Tom.

Ralph said, "Let's change the subject to the party. It's the last Saturday of this month. This gives LUCKY LARRY time to finish that ice cream machine."

Tom added, "Remind everyone to wear their shirt with the CBI patch in case of fights." "I'm not going," mumbled Mitch.

Ears said, "If we have enough dames, there won't be any fights."

"Spread the word."

"Also, Chaplain Ray plays a mean boogiewoogie piano."

Near Sadiya, the heavy downpour, together with the wind, shook the plane as it prepared to come in for a landing. Wings swayed side by side, sometimes dipping down from left to right and vice versa.

"Hold it steady. We can do this!"

"There's Ledo below and Sookerating in the distance."

They taxied to a loading revetment where crews were ready to unload the barrels of high octane and load supplies for the next HUMP trip. The tired crew were jeeped to their tent.

"Home. We have a stock of new tales to trade at the party."

CHAPTER FORTY-FIVE—June 1944
Shingbwiyang

HOLT and crew delivered their cargo of horses and mules to Shingbwiyang, Burma. The Ledo Road out of Assam, India, painstakingly traverses south over the Patkai Range, through the dangerous Pangsau Pass and is now treacherously close to Jap held, Myitkyina, (Mit-chee-NAH) Burma.

Supplies for this section of the Burma Road are sorely needed if Chief Engineer General Lewis Pick and General Joe Stilwell want to soon taste success. Known as "Vinegar Joe", Stilwell relentlessly pursues his task.

Mud slides and removal of heavy boulders are daily threats for the thousands of workers and heavy equipment needed to shape a resemblance of a road. Too many face death due to Malaria and injuries caused from working in the sweltering heat.

Now, as the CATF-China Air Task Force, a volunteer group unloads the cargo, HOLT, Co-pilot, Navigator and Radio Operator decide to Jeep into the market place of Shingbwiyang. The June rain slowed to a drizzle as HOLT sloshed the Willys through deep mud puddles here and there.

"Believe it or not," offered Blair the co-pilot, "I find this refreshingly fun considering where we just came from." He held tightly on the front bar as the jeep skidded over bumps in the road.

"We have a surprise waiting for us!" HOLT forced a smile while roughly steering and shifting with his left hand. Both hard to do while balancing his pipe in the right, like a cup of coffee.

"I know what's going on. Your friends are here in town. Radio Operator knows all," laughed Cecil as he lit a cigarette. "I'm king of the AACS—Army Airways Communication Service." He waved his hand like a wand.

"Holy Moses," laughed Orville the navigator in the back seat both arms like wings grabbing bars. "HOLT! Where'd ja get your driver's license?"

"Ahhh youth," he said while slowing down. "In this marketplace around the corner, watch out for hawkers seeking your attention in every way but legit. They line the road with cripples to steal your attention and your wallet. All to deflate your ego." "What ego," smirked Cecil. "I left it on the HUMP! And, could you give me a quick two minute briefing about the Ledo Road? I need to know why we're killing ourselves."

"The road out of Ledo to the west, is supposed to meet the Burma Road coming out of the east from Kunming, China. They intersect at Lashio in Burma where all supplies come in by rail from Rangoon to support China." He held his pipe between his teeth to join his hands for explanation. "The danger zone is Pangsau Pass where it's very high and difficult. Hell-of-a-task!"

"And," added Blair, "Rangoon is controlled by the Japs."

HOLT stopped the jeep in front of an empty shack to quietly explain important news and to re-light his pipe. "A secret attack is planned within the next six months to chase Japs out of Myitkyina which is on the route to Rangoon. Combat cargo task force is planning an air armada of about seven hundred thousand men, a mix of American, British, Chinese, Indian, African and Kachin. This six nation force, called Operation Grubworm, follows the assault from three months ago called Broadway." He stopped, puffed on his pipe and continued. "It's hush hush because some of these beggars and natives are traitors in disguise. That's why our friends are here with the task of weeding them out." HOLT stopped talking, looked at his tired crew and with a heavy sigh said, "I need some tea."

"How about British Tea," remarked Orville nodding towards the road sign <u>Darjeeling Tea</u> pointing toward a side muddy rut of a road. A quick right turn and they were there.

"What a lucky day," blurted HOLT as his crew met LUCKY LARRY and WEN WU rushing in a hurry toward them, jumping off the porch of the British compound.

"Whoa, what's going on?" HOLT bolted out of the way too late as his two pals jumped off the steps knocking him over.

"Oops!"

"Sorry!"

Though slipping and sliding, they sprinted fast toward the back of the Brit's barracks soon to disappear around the corner.

CHAPTER FORTY-SIX—June 1944
Shingbwiyang

Next, HOLT and crew met BOBBY and the two ladies coming out the door looking anxious. Bonnie and Loretta quickly secured a table on the porch and pulled together chairs vacated earlier by a few Brits. "Son-of-a-bitch! That looked serious!" HOLT brushed mud off his khakis while searching for his pipe in the mud.

"Hey, good to see you!" BOBBY hobbled over to HOLT, both all smiles.

"You look debonair," said HOLT. "Maybe you should jump out of a plane more often."

After greetings all around and shaking hands, the men's eyes were on Bonnie and Loretta. The young Airmen drooled as they rearranged their caps off and on several times. HOLT simply cleaned his pipe on his shirt and started relighting.

"What just happened?" After his first puff and pulling up a chair, which he quickly straddled, explanations began.

They all started talking at once.

"Two Brits caught natives trying to slash our tires," said BOBBY.

"They were the Brits who went outside to vomit after the severed head!" Wide eyed Loretta had a quick answer while flipping her head back to adjust the navy blue hair ribbon holding back her long, dark brown hair.

"What!"

"A native came in holding the bloody mess!" Bonnie's huge eyes and waving arms illustrated the excitement.

"What!"

"This was the NAGA MAN that had chased me all over the mountain side." BOBBY said quietly while trying to calm the situation.

"Well, this makes no sense," stated Orville. He, Cecil and Blair standing there quietly listening, hands on hips, waiting for an explanation, are new to the group of old friends.

"Ok, this is what happened." BOBBY began a full account of what had taken place as everyone standing now decided to grab a chair and form a crooked circle.

"NAGA MAN...stood at the door like a wooden Indian from Arizona...then...swinging...bloody mess... Good Naga group came in and saved the day."

HOLT took the pipe out of his mouth and roared with laughter. His heavy, heaving shoulders shook with convulsion as the chair began to teeter. Grabbing his chair, Loretta said, "Hey, I'm off my duty. Not nursing a broken arm today."

"I haven't seen this side of you," BOBBY said inching his wrapped left ankle away from his old friend.

"Now, I've heard it all. I'm ready to go home. There's no excitement left to compete!" HOLT, still chuckling, stretched out his legs, took off his cap and dusted it on his knee.

Staff Bonnie and Nurse Loretta quickly volunteered to bring more pots of tea to the outside table to now accommodate the happy mood. "We're all going inside," said BOBBY. "Too many flies and bugs out here."

Always per British style, a small tray with metal pitcher of cream and mason jar of sugar were brought over by a waiter from the kitchen. "Our compliments," he said while anxiously explaining the use of the Mason jar. "Keeps bugs out."

"So, where's the cake?" HOLT quipped to no one while securing his chair on the end of a long rectangular table.

"Ahhh, this is too good," remarked Radio Operator Cecil, sipping and savoring the aroma of hot Darjeeling.

And for a brief five minutes, silence echoed quietly from the barrack walls as the hum of an evaporative cooler from somewhere, softly vibrated the wooden floor.

Cecil continued, "Wait till I tell my favorite radio operator at the ground station in Jorhat. We have a story contest titled, Unbelievable Tales." "You'll win," said co-pilot Blair.

"They'll make a Hollywood movie about this day," Blair suggested while looking at HOLT.

"NO, NO, NO!" HOLT firmly commented. "Their movies are so fake! I saw one where an army soldier sat down during a march and took of his boots to fan his feet."

"Not good."

"Not good."

"Not good."

"Not good." Each repeated the negative. "So," HOLT continued. "I only go to the movies for the cartoons. Bugs and Popeye are my favorites." As they began the good spirit of sharing cartoon stories, and laughing, LUCKY LARRY and WEN WU came panting in with a distinguished looking Chinese man.

LUCKY LARRY began. "We didn't catch them, but we brought in the best person to help us with this dilemma."

More chairs were scooted over, and the ladies went to get more cups.

"This is Chief Commander Chang in charge of this entire area. He recognized the two men as they ran around the corner of his office."

Per each introduction, Chang added a small humble bow. Though hesitant, he spoke good English with a strong British accent. Dressed like a Brit in dark grey gabardine short sleeve shirt with matching shorts, he exemplified a man of duty.

"We need a list of what's 'beeeen' happening as this may lead us to the front group." He looked around, making eye contact with each person. "Location is important," added WEN WU. "This could pinpoint the main saboteurs."

HOLT'S idea was best. "We need thousands of pamphlets announcing our purpose and denouncing the presence of the Japs." With the stem of his pipe between his teeth, his words were slurry but meaningful. He leaned back in his chair and put both hands behind his head cradling it tiredly. He tried not to be cynical to the very young group, but words spilled out fast. "I've been in this war zone too long." His remark created silence and a great deal of sentiment.

Looking down at his half drained cup, "Death here, death there, death everywhere." Then looking over at Chang for sentiment, "And now, saboteurs, the invisible ghosts, the invisible enemy"

"Where's PALOOKA our personal surgeon. You need a pill."

Miraculously, everyone in the barracks became enthusiastic with ideas, a camaraderie enterprise indicative of War time downs and ups.

Cecil began. "Let's get a note pad and spill out ideas to put over the Army Communication system since it interconnects all bases in India and China." "I've started a list," said WEN WU. "With the groups notes, Chang and I will put together a pamphlet to be air dropped by the thousands." Chang shook his head benevolently.

Brits pulled chairs nearby to help with the communication. One noted problems on the runways. "Last month as a loud C-47 was trying to land, a worker pushed a heavy cart with a fire hydrant into the lane. The plane did a nose dive, but luckily no one was injured."

"Note: Better security on runways."

They were a small group, bundled together in a foreign land of strange people, strange sounds, and strange fetid smells.

HOLT and his crew need to fly out in the morning with new orders.

LUCKY LARRY and group of five need to put a spin on the Willys for a long drive back to Ledo. They still need to go to Pieces and Parts for ice cream machine fixing.

But, here they were writing all the complaints they could think about and listing past happenings that served as warnings.

"This will save a lot of lives," someone said.

It was a laborious twenty minutes before everyone began to disperse. "I need some whiskey."

"I need more tea."

The clink, clank of dishes and shuffling of chairs broke the monotony.

Looking at Bonnie and Loretta who had been silent during the entire discussion, HOLT changed the mood with, "I have a cake recipe from home for the party."

"We'll bake it," they said simultaneously.

BOBBY lifted his half-healed left foot, put it on a vacant chair and added loudly, "We all need a little piece of fun!"

Through the open doorway loud and clear, came a tall handle-bar whiskered Brit holding two small raggedy Chinese workers by the back of their necks. "Here's your piece of fun." He roughly threw them down on the wood floor.

"Spitz," blurted HOLT.

CHAPTER FORTY-SEVEN—June 1944
Shingbwiyang

Chang hurried out of his chair and furiously began scolding the two laborers who are now kneeling and ducking their heads in extreme fear.

Chang and WEN WU spoke in Mandarin.

WEN WU added, "You are working against your own people." He got close face to face in a forceful movement. "I would like to shoot you right now." His voice so loud and clear, echoing out the doorway, down the muddy track of a road, created a bit of chaos among the hawkers and gawkers.

All the men circled near, curious to hear what the two laborers knew. HOLT, the one usually in charge, decided to quietly sit there and let others take over, especially WEN WU.

Bonnie and Loretta, arm and arm, backed away from the scene, but not too far.

"These are the two tire slashers I saw," said a Brit.

"I saw the chase," said Spitz. "Next, I found them hiding behind whiskey barrels in the alley." Chang and WEN WU, both in a rage, pulled their large Gherka knives from holders and shouted, "Talk!"

The two raggedy workers shook with fear and while ducking their heads, began to tell all they knew.

"The Japanese are everywhere in the villages and towns offering good sums of money for any damage we can do. They hand out a list of what we can do and how much each obstruction pays". "Where are they located," demanded Chang. *"No special place. They loosely walk among us like ants. They are out there now."* They both tossed their heads toward the rutty roadway.

"How does the system work?" WEN WU was writing notes.

"If we take money for an obstruction, and we don't finish it, we get shot!"

"You put your own lives in danger for a little money?" Chang purposely stood dangerously close to the shaking two.

They meekly whispered, *"We have very little food and medicine. They pay well."*

Chang raised his Gherka knife, hit it hard on the back of a chair and shouted, "You are helping the wrong people!"

WEN WU added, "You need to help us now and you will be well rewarded. Sit!"

A chair was provided near the large mixed group. "Tell us what you know. We need a long list." WEN WU had worked with Commander Chang for the last ten years and greatly respected his efficiency for getting results. But, never has he seen him so angry.

WU was ready to write.

Chang was not finished. He spoke loudly and harshly for a full five minutes waving his arms in disgust.

Everyone, Brits included, froze where they were, standing or sitting.

This time in perfect English, Chang slowly added, "Tell us all that know or you will be shot."

Ahah!

All listeners noted with amazement that the raggedy pair understood the English language. They now began to babble in English and WU began to write.

Everyone participated for a while. Soon, some Brits and other air men began to taper off in their own groups. The final decision about pamphlet airdrops put them at ease.

Some departed with "thanks," and "we are all now more aware of the dangers from these vagabonds." No one left without shaking Commander Chang's hand and acknowledging the importance of what they just learned.

WEN WU carefully shoved the small tablet into his gear bag, buckling a rain tarp over all.

HOLT said, "The most important item on the list is fuel pumped by hand from the fifty gallon drums. It is an easy way to bring down a C-46 Commando or C-47 Sky Train if fuel is short changed on the long haul of five hundred miles over the HUMP from Assam, India to Kunming, China. Fuel gauge should show a capacity of 1,796. WU, put this as number one of importance on your list."

Chang decided to take the two workers back to his office for further questioning and some jail time. But first, Bonnie and Loretta had an urge of sympathy for the two workers and offered them pieces of chocolate from LUCKY LARRY'S and BOBBY'S gear bags.

They humbly bowed, took the chocolate and hurried out with Chang.

The men smirked disapprovals and gruffly cleared their throats as they now reconvened back to the original table to finish out the day.

"Let's complete our list," said BOBBY. "We need to head back to the base barracks before dark."

"And, LUCKY LARRY added, "we will have a tenting good time." His smile was as wide as his gait when he shifted chairs back to the table. "Come on. Let's go get those ice cream machine parts!" He grabbed Loretta's hand to hurry out.

"You need chaperones too," said HOLT'S crew. "I want to check the markets for any Chinthes, the mythical Burmese Monster, half dog and half lion," said Blair.

"Holy mackeral! You'll get a lot of girls with that gift!" LUCKY LARRY laughed.

"No. Gift is for my dad," Blair shouted. "He's Canadian. This is the emblem that the RCAF (Royal Canadian Air Force) chose. My dad says they are the best paratroopers in para drop operations." They shuffled out fast to hit the markets for their lists.

"Hell! Is there a War going on or not?"

HOLT'S comment was just that. His half-hearty tone, accompanied with a corner-of-the mouth smile, invited Bonnie to change the subject.

"Cake! You said we need cake for our party." She looked at HOLT and jokingly elbowed BOBBY as she sat very close to him and his elevated left foot.

"Remember, I have ways of getting top ingredients. What do you want? Devil's food, chocolate, marble, lemonnnn." Her sing song voice trailed higher and higher.

HOLT'S tired look became dreamy. "I have an Applesauce cake recipe memorized because I made it almost every Sunday."

"Ok, let's have it. I'll write it on the back of this tea menu." She took a small pencil from her bag. "One cup butter, one cup brown sugar, one cup sugar, two tablespoons cocoa, one tablespoon cinnamon, four teaspoons soda, two and one half cups flour, one quart applesauce, and nuts and raisins. One cup each if possible. The recipe calls for black walnuts if you can find them."

With sparkling eyes she teasingly said, "Remember, I jeep around." She reread her notes back to HOLT.

Suddenly, the loud sputtering of a low plane in trouble broke the peace.

"Low fuel?" BOBBY yelled.

The boom of the crash so close shook the tea barrack and a waiter raced frantically about uprighting dishes.

HOLT violently pushed away from the table. "Back to the War!"

CHAPTER FORTY-EIGHT—June 1944
Shingbwiyang

In an increasing down pour and with hearts thumping, the two groups made a mad dash to their jeeps. Fortunately, LUCKY LARRY'S shoppers were still in the jeep, so they sped away quickly to the crash.

Billowing smoke, much too close to the old busy village and Brit barrack, swept through the shops, curling around in all the corners like a snow storm. Smoke glued to now vacant webs as spiders disappeared to the unknown.

"This is not good," yelled Orville hanging on tightly while HOLT manipulated the little Jeep through the not-so-busy crowd while honking continuously.

Some of the young scrawny natives hanging on to the sides, ran along with the jeep eager to see what happened. As the road cleared, HOLT felt the need to speed for emergency reasons and the clingers let go.

LUCKY LARRY, two inches ahead, honked and waved hawkers out of the way, while WEN WU shouted orders in different tongues.

Hope, hope, hope, was the theme as both jeeps sped closer.

Hope for survivors.

Hope the crew parachuted out.

Hope it was not MAETS—Medical Air Evacuation Transport Squadron.

Most of all, hope it was not close friends.

Flights over the HUMP usually started near Shingbwiyang, a busy hub of numerous types of missions.

Pamphlet air drops and food drops by the PT-19 are a regular daily routine in the area.

The P-40 fighter planes flew consistently in the dangerous environment taking out small bridges. Used as dive bombers supporting ground troops, their hazardous flights are the miraculous safety nets when called upon to perform. They are the best!

The wreck is that of a two passenger PT-19. Its nose, buried in thorny bushes, is flaming a red hot upward tower. Thrown clear is the pilot lying in a twisted heap close by. Everyone learned later that the deceased passenger in front was a friendly Naga Chieftain. It was a pitiful state of affairs for the military. Condolences were high from all the different groups taking part in this ugly War. Yet, deaths were so numerous, an understanding among the natives developed. It was an acceptance of the small negative circumstances that could alternately lead to victory.

Now suddenly, help came from everywhere. The stunned pilot was lifted away from the smoldering wreck, his legs dangling strangely, his body still numb from the trauma.

An entire village of people is at the scene offering help and also suggesting how handy they can cart away airplane parts for their use.

LUCKY LARRY however, is on the job, master minding parts for repairing planes.

HOLT quickly roped off the area making a huge ring around the wreck like a circus tent.

The crews are on their phones transmitting to military offices and to Air Evac about the pilot's situation. Although the hospital is in Shingbwiyang, all outlets need to be notified.

Nurse Loretta with Bonnie's help, tended to the injured pilot. From the medical kit in the Willys Jeep, pain killers are administered as the pilot begins to gain consciousness moaning loudly. *"Buzzard flew in props,"* he gasped.

"You're in good hands now," said BOBBY remembering his own crash and bail out.

A medical team from the base gingerly loaded the injured pilot and took him to the hospital where it was discovered that he had two broken legs along with other bruises.

"What the hell are we doing hauling around a Naga Chieftain?" Blair's question was not meant for others to hear as he quietly asked navigator Orville standing next to him.

"It's part of the War effort," Orville answered as he stared at the smoking plane. "They're on our side. They want chocolate, our cigarettes, and plane rides."

WEN WU, overhearing the two men's discussion, sighed and said in punctuated phrases, "These hillside tribes of North Eastern Assam are friendly. They're semi-Burmese, semi civilized, and most of all harmless. We want them on our side. We'll compensate the Nagas for loss of Chieftain."

"What a day," HOLT complained warily. "It's getting dark. We can't extend our leave too much longer. Tomorrow we fly to next assignment and gather the injured from Kunming." Back in the Willys Jeep he yawned, rubbed his forehead and repositioned his pipe behind his ear while waiting for everyone to gather their wits.

The unanimous decision is for the two groups to stay at the barracks near the Shingbwiyang base. In the morning, HOLT and crew to fly to Kunming, and LUCKY LARRY'S group of five to drive back to Ledo.

"I'll figure out a make-shift hand crank for the ice cream machine when we get back to Ledo," he said tiredly.

At the barrack, they secured cots, pulled them in a close group of nine, and passed around shots of whiskey. Shoes and boots were taken off and set on top of dressers away from crawling intruders. Belts were loosened.

HOLT hid a smile when noting how the seven cots automatically circled the two girls' cots and thinking how they must love the attention and all the security.

In the dark just as lights were turned off, HOLT asked, "Where in the hell is PALOOKA?"

CHAPTER FORTY-NINE—June 1944
Patkai Range near Assam

PALOOKA Penny, AKA 'big red', flew in and out of canyons, low to the river's edges from the dark green jungle to crevasses of snowy mountains searching for Walt and other "Mayday" crash victims.

Chuck with binoculars kept an eagle eye busy looking for white parachutes and shroud lines tangled in the vicinity of where he, BOBBY JOHNSON, Walt and Harry went down.

Walt, the short, stocky, handsome lad of Welsh descent, so proud of his curly, dark brown hair, always grinned from cheek to cheek when the nurses teased him about his curls.

"Sleep in curlers again Walt?"

"Who gave you your perm?"

Had Walt met Harry's fate? A broken neck and tangled body far away from all activity, only to be buried days ago near the Chindwin River. Chuck had no other choice after the crash. It seemed the right thing to do. Not wanting him to fall victim to the elements, he found a pointed rock and feverishly dug a large hole. After covering the body, he looked around for some kind of marker, some kind of scenic value to the grave later for family retrieval. In his hands were identification tags, and the Airman's jacket. The family would want these. He had said prayers, and cried over the site when finished. At the same time, he wept for BOBBY and Walt, not knowing where they were.

It has been days since the crash. Hope is always alive. Crews have been found days later while skirting the fearsome native mountain tribes, floating across swollen rivers in make-shift rafts, and finally found by British Outfitters searching on foot familiar with the terrain.

Word was out about Walt's disappearance. An interconnection of Army Air Communication System frequented word about missing crew members repeatedly.

WEN WU made sure that volunteers like him spread the news in their different native tongues. Though regions are vast with treacherous terrains all over India, Burma, and China, peoples of all types cover the territories.

Hope is always present.

"Today, we'll find him," said PALOOKA. "Let's start again with the mountain crash."

He pointed the little L-5 up away from the river canyons and headed towards the snow covered Patkai Range.

"Good luck," said Chuck. "Today we have bright sunshine and the whole area sparkles with aluminum pieces—like an aluminum highway."

"It's a mangled mess of green with an outcropping of rocks here and there." Chuck mumbled while keeping the binoculars focused and active. "I wonder where I buried Harry. I left a pile of rocks like a cairn as a marker."

"A what," laughed PALOOKA.

"A cairn is a pile of rocks that usually mark a trail head for hikers."

"Forget a hike," PALOOKA said wiping the sweat off his brow. "I need a swim in a back home water hole."

PALOOKA flew the L-5 low to the ground for better visability and not to compete with the larger planes in the higher altitudes. Also, number one reason is to avoid Zeroes.

"Nothing looks familiar," whined Chuck. "What's the matter with me? I should be able to locate that mountain area where we crashed."

"I found you close to the Chindwin River after you probably walked for twenty-four hours. So, let's head back down to where I think we found you and trace upward."

Now flying low, the two didn't see the danger coming toward them as the Jap Zero flew in head on. The bend in the river obscured the blunt nose monster roaring toward them full speed of 350 mph all guns blazing.

PALOOKA temporarily left the safety of the tree top level to assist Chuck's spotting for parachute shrouds and any other airplane debris. Only a few seconds above the tree tops put them immediately in the Zero's path.

Neither had time for anything but a quick intake of air and grip of plane side.

PALOOKA instantly banked the plane vertically hoping not to flip but stayed low taking off a few top branches. The versatility of the L-5 allowed for this maneuver, but both men gasped loudly.

As a few bullets penetrated the cockpit, he felt a biting sting on the right shoulder tip where a bullet hit.

Straightening the plane, he decided to stay in the middle of the river where he could find an obscured bank for landing. Tea fields flashed through his mind as Chuck yelled, "Zero turning around and heading in again from the left."

The monster coming toward them carried two 7.7 MM machine guns with 600 rounds above the engine plus two 20-MM-type cannons with 100 rounds each, in the wings. This info flashed through their minds as quickly as the bullets they were about to receive.

They were close enough to see the machine guns of bullets coming from each wing but saw only smoke as the Zero pulled up frantically and headed upward.

"Out of ammo," PALOOKA heard himself whisper in a gasp while flying the little rescue plane keeping the tires from skimming the water. "Holy shit!" Chuck wailed. "There went my bowels."

"You shit your pants!" PALOOKA laughed tearfully.

"Now I get a crud ribbon from the club," said Chuck so happy to be alive.

"Not any more. Upper brass learned about the secret club and outlawed it immediately. It had many members."

"I saw death right there at my window," Chuck sighed.

"This happened to a buddy of mine flying a C-46 a little lower than usual, when a Jap Zero flew next to him a few feet away. Then, the pilot grinning menacingly, his white teeth flashing in the sun, flew off."

"Apparently out of ammo," said Chuck. "Luck does happen," remarked PALOOKA. "I hear all kinds of wild tales of near misses."

"Hey, you're bleeding all over the place. We need to land quickly and get you to a medic—Doc!" "I have a medical kit in the back and a good sopping rag. It's just a nick, but let's head into Shingbwiyang."

"Now that we're safe, we can talk about that crazy Zero." PALOOKA was so riled from the narrow escape, he needed to talk. "Their quick agility is due to their light weight. However, the designers sacrificed pilot protection for this light weight." "Such as?" Chuck was curious.

"Lack of armor plate. The heavy stuff. But the latest good news is that we now have the Grumman F6F-5 Hellcat which is faster than the Zero and can out gun it. Plus, our pilots are under a tough sheet of armor and can make it back home after a fight." "How do you know all of this," Chuck asked.

"HOLT....Where the hell is he anyway?"

CHAPTER FIFTY—June 1944

Shingbwiyang

"It's getting dark. Let's tent in Shingbwiyang and leave for Sook in the morning." PALOOKA'S sleeve now a bloody mess, concerned them. "Sookerating is seventy three miles from there. We also need to learn how the Ledo Road is coming along and what kind of doctoring needs to be done." Chuck realizes the difficulty they both now face, flying through the canyons of Jap pill boxes. Also getting through Hell's Gate Pass near the Patkai Mountain Range, then over the Naga Hills, is a triumph of its own.

"Diseases and accidents among the workers are daily events. We might have to transport a few critical cases." PALOOKA groaned now from the shoulder pain as he called base for a landing. This was a negative.

"Field lights out. Can't land. Swarm of Zeroes attacking."

"Where are P-40's?" Chuck asked.

"Ground radio party needs contact with P-40's," PALOOKA blurted. "Hope Jap canyon pill boxes didn't get them!"

PALOOKA continued. "The Japs are like mad ants because of our major attack and take-over of Mogaung, south of Myitkyina (Mit-chee-NAH). By the end of August, we'll have Myitkyina. A major campaign of all Allies are participating in the attack." "Good. Then we can go home," Chuck added sarcastically. "Hey, we need to land somewhere quickly and treat your shoulder before you bleed to death. Put this bird down."

"And before we run out of fuel," PALOOKA shouted due to the stress newly encountered. He contacted base with "Mayday, Mayday." Bleeding to death here and now was not his intent, and crash landing for lack of fuel would be suicide. *"Setting down L-5 between barracks and tents away from field....need medical assistance."* He relayed to field base.

Familiar with the area from many landings, he knew that the few lights from grass bashas and barracks outlined a flat spot for landing. A short quick runway was to the right and he could squeeze the small plane there, landing lights out. He depended on it.

"Base to PALOOKA...p-40'S and Black Widows now active. Fly low and note campfires."

Landing as planned became a nightmare due to truck loads of tea pickers scattered about and away from the runway escaping the horrors of the Zeroes. The tea pickers worked nightly and the Zeroes focused on every nook and cranny of the entire area including the landing spot the two airmen had planned.

PALOOKA twisted the Stinson away from a truck and did a slow shuttle toward tent city, stopping at the entrance after a nose slide into the opening of the large tent.

"Whoa Sally," yelled HOLT jumping off his cot where he had been playing gin rummy with the group in the dim lamp light.

"Grand Entrance," LUCKY LARRY chuckled, the first one to recognize the crew in the plane as he rambled over.

"Hallelujah we made it" PALOOKA shouted as he opened the cockpit door and sat there not moving. Than looking at BOBBY who had just hobbled over, "Sorry we were on the wrong side of the river. Glad you made it out!"

Chuck had already jumped out and hurried around to help PALOOKA as did everyone else after seeing heavy amounts of blood on their good friend.

"New landing strip?" HOLT smirked.

"Planning on a quick bed down?" LUCKY LARRY snickered while helping his increasingly weak friend out of the plane.

"Hell-of-a-note!" PALOOKA babbled. "I had no other choice."

While everyone was busy tending to the bloody shoulder, rounds of introductions were made to the new crew.

"What happened?" Loretta, the field nurse, was all hands with Sulfur, bandages, and other meds on the bloody wound. Not until she was totally finished did they mention his status as a field surgeon.

"Well doc," she said, "how did I do?"

"You're hired. We have a long, long War going on."

Adding two more cots, they bedded down again, all shoes and boots on top of a desk. With cots in a close circle, they relived the day's events.

Blair's Chinthe, the mythical Burmese Monster, lay next to him on his pillow as he re-explained its purchase and significance to PALOOKA and Chuck.

BOBBY and Bonnie held hands, cot to cot.

Likewise for Loretta and LUCKY LARRY, smooching and whispering.

HOLT'S crew discussed tomorrow's plans to fly out to Kunming after ditching the Willys Jeep at headquarters.

PALOOKA and Chuck are to head to Ledo in the morning to meet with Stillwell about problems. BOBBY'S group of five plan to Jeep back to the Ledo area for new flight orders and to find the two native boys who helped with the big jungle escape. WEN WU fell asleep with hands under his head reciting the contents of the air dropped pamphlets warning about sabotage and thinking, *This is a good plan.*

DING HAO!

CHAPTER FIFTY-ONE—June 1944
Shingbwiyang

With punctuality, a barrage of village roosters crowed tent life awake. It is their moral obligation as they twist their heads here and fro looking for a compliment, a dare, yellow eyes seeking trouble. "Just like home," someone whispered.

Aromas of breakfast coming from the twenty-four-hour-all-night kitchen in the barrack next door, replaced the dank odor of moldy dampness inside the tent.

HOLT looked at his watch. "Time to move out; it's 4:A.M." he announced to the sleepy group.

"Wash room facilities in barrack next door. Meet you all there for coffee and 'eggus' in thirty minutes."

He and WEN WU were quick to grab packs and leave.

"Put some tables together," moaned LUCKY LARRY stretching and searching the floor before throwing his feet down.

"Too early," someone complained.

"What a swell night," Bonnie said with a smile. "I never felt so secure in my life," she laughed while counting all the guys getting out of their cots.

"Surrounded by handsome hunks," Loretta added. "We'll tent with you Airmen any time."

"Hubba hubba," said LUCKY LARRY being quick to hand Loretta her boots.

"We loved our all American campout," winked BOBBY. "And we're not sharing with anyone else!" He handed Bonnie her gear pack.

"Nope" PALOOKA shrugged. "It'll always be just this special group."

Everyone was pulling out dry socks from their gear bags and replacing them with rolled wet ones. The loudness of planes warming for flights a short distance away hastily awakened the crews with a sharpness of where they were, quickly replacing the merriment with the drama of War.

They met at the long, long rectangular tables after securing trays of food from the hot buffet of powdered scrambled eggs, corned beef hash, and handmade biscuits.

HOLT and WEN WU, with the help of the service staff, were placing large mugs of coffee on the middle of the tables within everyone's reach. Someone else walked about setting cans of evaporated-milk here and there, usually by a large sugar bowl per table. "Sit!" Everyone told the two girls. "You perform your duties out on the fields. It is our turn to help you."

The place was louder than usual this morning as khaki uniformed personnel rushed about preparing orders for the day. Flight plans, cargo plans, fuel plans, all needed to be addressed, important orders previously prepared by various teams of the ATCAir Transport Command.

"Luckily I was here by 4:30 to put these two rectangulars together for the group of us," HOLT mentioned to his crew as each grabbed a chair with left hand, food tray in right. Olive colored oil cloths on tables had previously been wiped clean of crumbs.

Chatter began crosswise and every which way with each person addressing the day's events. "WU, when does the *pamphlets air-drop* begin?" HOLT asked loud and clear.

"Today. It's all at the print shop as we speak." He broke his biscuit in smaller pieces and began to butter each.

Next, HOLT addressed BOBBY and LUCKY LARRY. "Is your jeep secured outside? You practically parked it in the tent last night with worry." "I paid a local Burmese native with two bars of Lux soap and a package of chocolate to be on the lookout for trouble. But, I think the Lucky Strikes did the trick. He was able and more than willing," said LUCKY LARRY as he noticed Loretta had finished eating and was drinking her coffee. "May I?" He asked as he coupled her tray with his, loading the used dishes on top.

Feeling the need to finish, all followed his lead. "We have a War to win," said HOLT clearing his area and getting ready to leave.

All headed out the mess hall with reminders of Sookerating Party—"last Saturday of this month." "Somebody contact Mitch and Ears to remind them," said BOBBY as he and his group headed out to the Willys Jeep.

"You able to fly?" Chuck asked PALOOKA who was moving his arm and shoulder up and down as if in pain.

"Hell yeah! Takes more than a shoulder nick to ground me! Just doing a little warm up here."

Walking out, HOLT met Byron, an old friend from Navigator-Radar Weather Bureau and inquired about today's weather.

The news was a negative.

"We were able to fly the B-25 through the worst monsoon weather we've seen so far. I don't recommend it for your cargo plane. Too risky today," he said in a serious tone.

"The rain poured all night," mumbled HOLT shaking his head. "But, we could take the Charlie Route to the field hospital in Yunanyi, and then fly over to Kunming, China. I'm loaded with a big shipment of supplies for the allies and have word about evacuees needing transport back."

"Watch your safe elevation," suggested Byron. "Japs are out and about like fleas, and if they don't get you, the weather will."

"Geezus! Thanks old fried friend."

They both puffed a quick smile, a hint of laughter as Byron walked away with a half salute.

"We fly prepared with chutes on," replied HOLT more loudly than usual, wanting his crew to hear while lighting his pipe with fresh tobacco.

His young crew now standing next to him and listening to Byron speak about the weather, became distraught. Awareness of crashes caused by weather invaded every Airman's mind.

"Have you ever had to bail out?" Cecil, the youngest, became tense.

"No, but almost. For that experience, you need to quiz LUCKY LARRY. How do you think he got his name?" HOLT showed little concern as he indicated with his pipe in hand, for Cecil to talk to his close friend about the experience of bailing out.

Helpful LUCKY LARRY always good at down playing drama to young crew members, spoke calmly. "When the F/O orders to get ready to bail, be prepared. Figure out before hand the few steps necessary to the cargo door. EASY! Keep in mind that storms are plentiful this entire month of June and about four hundred planes per day are up there flying in the soup, crews all prepared for a crash." Loretta and Bonnie standing close, quietly showed remorse of having experienced trauma of some sort. Both remembered dear friends of the thirty nurses who perished in the plane crash. It is forever on everyone's mind.

What happened?

Can it happen again?

HOLT, noting the loss of positive spirit, spoke abruptly to the small group who are still mingling. "Fear, getting in the way of hope, can not prevail." Then again to the group, "PALOOKA, get your job done in Ledo and we'll see you in two weeks in Sook. LUCKY LARRY, drive that Willys fast through the deep puddles on your way back to Assam." Adding with a crack of a smile, "Everybody have on your work boots for pushing a stuck-in-the-mud Jeep." "Not going to happen," said BOBBY.

"I'm doing the look-out for problems," WEN WU stated as he jumped over and into the back of the Jeep.

As the eleven dispersed for work with all belongings in place, HOLT pointed to Bonnie and said loudly, "Cake!"

CHAPTER FIFTY-TWO—June 1944
Shingbwiyang to Ledo

LUCKY LARRY headed the Willys and crew towards the long drive to Assam Valley, India, taking a northern back route of narrow trails for jeeps only. Coming down the Patkai Range had been easy, but driving up would be challenging. He would not attempt such a dangerous journey without prior knowledge of the trail's condition.

"Easy for a jeep." Said one.

"I've done it many times." Said another.

"This is the cut of land that Stilwell is widening for his Ledo Road to connect in Wading with the Burma Road," said WEN WU unfazed by the rawness of the land after leaving Shingbwiyang. "I wondered where it was," shouted Loretta to be heard above the pounding rain on the canvas top. Hanging on to the side bar tightly while keeping an eye on the narrow trail kept her occupied. Sitting in front, LUCKY LARRY designated her "the automatic boulder sighter".

"Just in case I miss one," he said with a sigh thinking about how lovely she is sitting next to him. BOBBY added, "This little jeep can surge through any small river crossing." Looking at Bonnie's whiter than usual face and bobbing wet curls, he added, "Not that we expect one, but have no fear." He noticed how her hand had tightened in his.

The fearless five are a youthful group of skills and talents, getting accustomed to the challenge of War and death all around them. A seriousness prevails as they now face Wartime realities and the work ahead in this dreadful, deadly War.

LUCKY LARRY talked about the flotilla of planes he and his crew are to fix. "They need to be up in the air and not sitting around getting rusty." The road, now a narrowing lane with thorny bushes brushing the sides, prompted him to warn everyone. "Keep your arms in."

Actually, with the rain pounding the sides, they were hovering towards the middle of the back seat like a can of sardines. Bonnie in the middle of the two men, never felt so safe.

"Don't forget that big boulder that we had to swerve around getting down here," warned Loretta.

"Yes commander," smiled LUCKY LARRY sitting tall in the driver's seat, knees from his long legs almost against his chest, feeling good, feeling confident behind the wheel of a vehicle that he knowingly can take apart and rebuild.

Loretta smiled.

He smiled back.

BOBBY suggested, "When we come to the boulder in the middle of the road, let's get out so the jeep won't tip over as it edges around it."

"Good idea," they all agreed after eying the drop of the land along the narrow road.

They wanted no dilemma on their half day's journey back to Assam Valley and insisted they wouldn't have one. The jeep was full of gas; the tires were in good shape and LUCKY LARRY'S tool kit for all emergencies was under the back seat. And per requirement, they had notified check points along the air waves of their travel. Basic check points would call them if Jap Zeroes were about. *"They're as mad as a busted nest of hornets since Mogaung was taken from them. Be prepared to hit the bushes,"* warned radio.

"Remember," said BOBBY, "we need to call in every forty-five minutes because the check points purposely are weak to avoid Jap usage."

"Whoa tiger," ordered WEN WU sighting a running rivelet. "We need to get out and push through this next stream crossing so we don't get stuck. You ladies stay put!"

"Nothing doing," they spoke simultaneously as they each jumped out.

"We'll push next to BOBBY to help with his bad left foot."

The rain was coming down in sheets but the narrow stream was shallow due to the steady upward elevation. Flat land would have been a problem.

"All in?" LUCKY LARRY asked before gunning the jeep upward on the sloping hill preparing for the switch backs.

"Onward" he shouted happily. "Home before dark!"

"Hold it!" BOBBY yelled. "I hear something!" "Shhhhhhh!"

Meanwhile, PALOOKA and Chuck are heading towards Ledo in the heavy June rain, flying low and watching for a wayward Jap Zero. Chuck called Bed Post to hear if the enemy is in the area.

"Not yet. We have fighters out and about keeping them contained."

This favorable answer was welcomed. "I'm hearing from Stillwell that I have to play medic when we get there. Lots of injuries."

They flew upward from Shingbwiyang following along tributaries that led down to the Chindwin River. Below was an occasional hut on stilts. Natives out cleaning fish along the streams waved to them as small boys ran along playfully trying to find the fast shadow of the L-5 as it flew above.

"After Ledo, we'll head towards Sook and our tent," PALOOKA said with tiredness. "We'll tend to the injured on the Ledo Road for about four hours, my usual time."

"Christ! I'm so ready to get out of this business," whined Chuck with binoculars at his face, wincing sporadically due to the heavy cast on left foot.

The heavy rain pelted the small plane as PALOOKA struggled to keep it upright. Wings wavered a few degrees when the L-5 hit air pockets easily bouncing the two men around like ping pong balls.

"Never ending rain! Japs everywhere! Crashes daily! Walt! Where is he?" Chuck continued his rampage for a few more minutes. "Such a good buddy!"

To this, PALOOKA added a shadow of truth. "I know a great number of crew members who are constantly sick. Afraid to fly, so they fake it."

"Swell," added Chuck. "If I wasn't here with you, I'd join them. One crash is enough for me." "You are designated my permanent medical assistant. No more rock pile for you!" PALOOKA insisted. "HOLT will clear it with brass."

Chuck sighed. "I shouldn't complain. These natives who live such simple lives have been gracious. The Mishmi and Abors who live above Ledo in the Brahmaputra River Range want to be helpful. These natives taught us how to catch fish in the many river streams."

"This is what keeps crews alive after crashes and walk outs," added PALOOKA. "Especially when the food supply in our packs runs low."

"The Kachins down by Myitkyna (Mit-cheeNAH) and the good Nagas have been known to carry wounded Airmen for many miles." Chuck added. "I think those two young native boys that BOBBY wants to find in Ledo, actually carried him over fast running streams."

The two Airmen mumbled a progression of positive thoughts as the small plane struggled in the malevolence of wind and rain.

After the last current of wind sent their bodies bumping the sides of the plane, PALOOKA stated, "Within thirty minutes we should meet Stillwell and his road crew. We'll land on the road and pull over to the field hospital nearby where a landing strip is available for treating injuries."

PALOOKA flew low expecting to be brought down by the stormy conditions or a Jap Zero. "By the heavens above, we will not crash," he insisted.

Meanwhile, HOLT, and crew of Blair, Cecil and Orville, filled out the flight check list and each bundled their gear of chute, emergency pack, and oxygen mask, ready for the jeep to ferry them out to their waiting C-47 Sky Train. They stood a few minutes on the tarmac, wearing their large clear plastic parkas always helpful against the rain.

After boarding they ditched their parkas and began chatting.

"We head west on the Charlie route to Yunnany, then west again to Mike which will head us south into Kunming, China." HOLT mumbled while reviewing the chart he held in his hand.

"Over three hundred miles," said Cecil, the Radio Operator, as he adjusted his equipment.

"Correct," added Orville the Flight Engineer also known as Navigator. "Phew! Long route ahead. Get the chocolate ready."

"Kunming is large. Get ready for a late steak dinner," remarked Co-Pilot Blair.

All four checked oxygen plug-ins for masks. Pilot and Co-Pilot discussed do's and don'ts of flying the big Sky Train as per management written by HOLT. *F/O must always co-manage with co-pilot before takeoff.* They assumed the inconsistencies in the past, crashed planes.

Field crew had previously started the big R-183092 Engine per pilot's check list, and now the crew of four made preparations before takeoff.

HOLT began with Blair's assistance. "Landing gear control handle from neutral to down then back to neutral."

"Check!"

"Mixture to auto rich for take-off and climb positions."

"Check!"

"Carburator heat COLD."

"Check!"

"Propeller pitch control-FULL LOW PITCH"

"Check!"

"Tail wheel LOCKED."

"Check!"

"Tighten Throttle Lock."

"Check!"

"Check all Flight controls for FREE MOVEMENT."

"Check!"

"And away we go!" Cecil and Orville announced. Again as always, silence dominated during the big drama of takeoff with Engine RPM at 2700. And it was not until they gained the desired cruising speed of 120 MPH with Engine RPM at 2150, before they relaxed and began a conversation.

"You young Airmen really keep me in good spirits," HOLT began.

"That was a good time we had in the tent and at breakfast," Orville replied. "Those two ladies are really pretty."

"Good Joes you might say," added Cecil.

"Cooperation in this ugly War goes far. I hope they make it to Sook for the party."

Blair added coldly, "I hope we all make it back to Sookerating!"

The reality of daily disasters aggravated positive situations like a needle poking at a filled balloon. Time was the main essence everyone faced flying in the 'soup'.

There was a stiff silence as each attended to his task at hand.

The wind blew harder and the rain pounded louder.

CHAPTER FIFTY-THREE—June 1944
To Kunming

HOLT started the conversation about the party at Sookerating to lessen the stress they were feeling as the storm pounded from every direction. The C-47 wobbled and seemed to put up a fight.

"Don't forget to wear shirts with CBI patch on the sleeve so you won't be confused for a Brit if a fight should break out; since everyone is wearing khaki we are one big blend."

"Huh?" Cecil was confused.

"When American military start waving batons to break up fights, you won't get hit!"

Severe turbulence threw them to the right. They fought the controls.

"True. It's red, white and blue with the star of India and Sun of China in the design."

The C-47 shot up and down fast in the fierce storm.

The men paled with sweat which would freeze if they were any higher. Each tended to his particular duty.

"What are we hauling?" Orville asked timidly as the plane surged.

"Heavy pipe. Explosives. Fuel. Most importantly, medical supplies."

Taking his pipe from his pocket, HOLT slapped it on his knee before shoving it in his mouth empty. "Main purpose is to bring injured back with us to Assam."

Cecil looking stressed asked, "Did you ever have to bail out?" While looking straight at HOLT, lightning flashed through the cockpit as thunder rolled on top and around the plane.

"Once I lost both engines….left a cargo of Chinese workers behind as I chuted out!" His voice was low, almost a whisper due to a lump in his throat and the sad event he will live with forever.

"Have you flown the Hump the required 650 flight hours?" Cecil wondered.

"Yes, and many more." His jaw line tightened as the plane bobbed up and down in a frenzy.

The four crew members felt both desperate and small in the huge cargo plane pitching up and down, now taking over independent of them.

"May Day! May Day!"

Fire flames circled the propellers and did their evil dance.

No answer from base as the desperate crew manned the instruments.

Soon they passed over a town that looked like Kunming.

"Wait! This can't be! We have another thirty minutes to Kunming," yelled Cecil.

HOLT turned the ADF (Automatic Direction Finder) to R.Q. (Roger Queen) Kunming, and watched in amazement as the needle swung to a strange direction, to the town they had just passed over.

"The wind is pushing us a good 120 MPH faster than we figured and in a few minutes we'll be in the danger zone of the Japanese and beyond contact with our homing station."

"Don't doubt the accuracy of the magnetic compass," said Blair as he and HOLT began to correct their position turning the ship around.

"Instrument flying is a life saver," added Orville when the gyro instruments tumbled as they hit a terrific gust.

HOLT and Blair manned the flight controls with all their strengths as the turbulence worsened and the controls fought their grips.

"Let's bring the ship down lower where the wind gust is less," HOLT shouted.

They all agreed knowing full well the Japs flew the lower elevation.

One or the other could be their destiny.

Meanwhile, LUCKY LARRY'S group of five quietly strained to hear the sound coming toward them, a sound so different from the loud roar of the huge cargo planes high above. Although the rain relentlessly pounded the jeep, the unmistakable sound of a Jap Betty, shrilled loud and clear in their direction.

They leaped out on both sides scrambling into stinging shrubbery, prickly and thick.

BOBBY had been sitting in the back seat, goodright-foot near the jeep door making it easy for him to scramble out while pulling Bonnie with him. They all scooted and wormed quickly under the side brush hoping to be safe while leaving the Jeep behind. From the Willys Jeep they heard contact from a nearby base loud and clear, *"Enemy in the air. Fighters scrambling."*

Meanwhile, PALOOKA and Chuck kept the L-5 heading to Stilwell's camp near the Ledo Road where they are to land, tend to the injured, and continue on to nearby Ledo, then Sook when work was finished. "Our fighter planes should be out and about in this area keeping the Japs from bombing the road construction," PALOOKA mumbled while stealthily searching the skies for a wayward enemy plane.

Too soon he saw one.

They both shouted, "Out in the distance to the left!"

PALOOKA radioed for help. He knew that P-40's of the fighter aircraft group were in contact with ground radio parties and were out and about blasting enemy machine guns' positions. Also, P-51's and P-38's served as flying artillery in coordination with Stilwell's infantry keeping Japs' lines of supplies from heading north near the Ledo Road.

The enemy's goals are many. Keeping the Ledo Road from developing is a top priority. They hated the thought of a serviceable route for supplies to China.

Since the Chinese-American-Kachin forces protecting the Road are many, PALOOKA had faith that the P-40 Warhawks are fighter ready and in the air nearby.

Now diving near vertically from a high altitude, one came out of the blue and attacked the Jap Zero coming toward them about one mile away from their L-5.

An explosion, with debris exhilarating near, prompted PALOOKA to pull up immediately.

"Remarkable," exclaimed Chuck.

"Twenty minutes remaining," shouted PALOOKA. "Get ready for home base number one!"

CHAPTER FIFTY-FOUR—June 1944

"Chute up" yelled HOLT as the air currents shook the plane uncontrollably.

"These down drafts are tossing us up and down," whined Blair fighting the controls with HOLT as they worked to lower the plane.

"Kunming is closed because of the violent storm," Orville yelled back listening to reports. "Yunanyi is open and we're directed to fly there."

HOLT turned on the auto-pilot control and let the "arm and legs" do the impossible as the electrical gyros held the plane a little longer from a disastrous plunge. "We're about 110 miles out."

"Cecil," HOLT yelled. "Make sure every crew member is buckled tightly in chute. Double check!" In a frenzied rush, the four member crew doubledouble checked bindings and knew how to bail when HOLT gave the order.

Previous disasters flashed through HOLT'S mind. Some he experienced, and some he heard from others during discussions in tents while whiskeyed down.

A pilot plummeted to the ground for failure to buckle in. Well known fact.

Another crew member's chute got caught in the jump line and he fell with a broken neck. Well known fact.

"Be careful jumping out if I give the signal," shouted HOLT. "Pay attention."

Again he contacted bedpost for help desperately giving his bearing as the plane wavered in uncontrollable dips.

Then, *"This is Baker Jake 520. I have your bearing. I'll call you in. Sit tight. Other planes stacked above. Stay low. You'll make it."*

"Lights ahead," someone yelled just as the plane nosed down violently causing Cecil the radio operator to plunge to the side hitting his head, knocking him out.

MEANWHILE, LUCKY LARRY'S group lay low in the brush not worried about being scratched to bits. Each scooted as far away as possible from the jeep knowing it would be an easy target. They snaked through stickers, mud and grime rapidly.

LUCKY LARRY lay on the far left worried about Loretta who had scrambled out on the right. Now they were split.

"Fighters scrambling" were the last words from the jeep radio.

BOBBY lay on top of Bonnie shielding her face with his chest, his hands under her head and feeling confident they would be ok as the roar and rat-a-tattat of shells dispersed above too close. Their dark marine green and dirty brown clothing protected them in a masquerade of color that blended with the surroundings.

Now, burning brush and sulfurous smoke, along with the odor of wet rain filled the air in a suffocating stench.

WEN WU did not move as he lay about 30 feet from the jeep while listening to a battle above, close, too close. Hearing broken glass as a bullet busted the Willys' wind-shield, he held his breath fearing the worst, that they were next, torn to shreds by the many bullets radiating from the Jap Zero coming in at 350 MPH.

Two machine guns with 600 rounds were located above the engine, while two cannons of 100 rounds each, shot from the wings. These terrors flashed through his mind in a mini-second as he heard the unmistakable sound of a blast approximately a quarter mile away. Crashing sounds meant flying debris in their direction.

"No, No, No, No," he groaned in panic.

CHAPTER FIFTY-FIVE—June 1944
Shingbwiyang to Sookerating

WEN WU dare not lift his head to see what was coming towards friends and him. Overcome by dizziness, he held his breath awaiting doom from the flying debris of rocks and shrapnel.

Did he pass out? All was quiet except for the faint buzzing in his ears. Breathing deeply three times, slowly, he shook all the while. He was alive!!

"Hey," he yelled.

In unison there were four more "Heys." Two female. Two males.

They sat up, looking around, then scooted together joining hands. Hugging each other tearfully with pats on backs they had escaped death only two seconds away.

"That's as close to death I ever want to be," wailed LUCKY LARRY wiping away dusty, dirty tears getting too close to his mouth.

"Dirt from bullets flew around us," added BOBBY while hugging a shaking Bonnie. "You're full of mud," he added as they muffled a very nervous laugh. He gingerly wiped mud from her face with a pocket handkerchief. "Always a handy spare," he said while looking at her longingly. "You're as good as new and ready for a dance."

From nervous laugh to sobbing, she whimpered "Sorry".

Loretta hugging LUCKY LARRY said, "I'm so relieved no one was hit." She began wiping debris from her face with the heel of her hands.

"Whoa-whoa….the jeep! Let's have a look." The air began clearing. Billowing smoke and dust, pushed away by the soft wind, left a bent-outof-shape piece of transportation within sight.

"I can put this Willys back together piece by piece if I have to." Circling it, LUCKY LARRY happily announced that the spare gas can didn't get hit. "What a miracle!"

"The thrust of the bullets hitting the mud around turned it sideways," said BOBBY. "It may not be damaged other than windshield glass breakage." The five stood there staring at the sideways jeep, taking deep breaths and feeling stronger. Losing the numbness brought on by their close call they echoed, "We can do this."

"Let's get it back on the road and try to start it," someone said. They pushed and shoved getting it half way on the rutty road.

"Stand back while I try to start it," said LUCKY LARRY.

The Willys Jeep sputtered, spewed and hissed.

NOTHING.

"Ok. Let's get it fully on the road and push it backwards down the hill," suggested someone.

All agreed while positioning it on the road to LUCKY LARRY'S command. They knew the day was darkening and they had at least two more hours to make it to Ledo and then on to their barracks in Sookerating.

After ten minutes of pushing and shoving, the engine turned over and the mighty-little-military miracle was ready to roll.

"Hubba-hubba, our War hero," yelled LUCKY LARRY slapping the driver's door.

"Jump in," voiced the men urgently. BOBBY assisted Bonnie with his hands around her waist. Loretta jumped in the front right seat as LUCKY LARRY grabbed her hand with a steadying motion. They were like five shaking lizards, so happy to be alive. He geared a fast forward. "Hold on everybody. We have some lost time to beat."

"What's today?" BOBBY the F/O of the group asked bouncing in the rear right side.

"Thursday." Someone yelled.

"Saturday's my twenty-first birthday party. We're going to be there!" He gave Bonnie a fast kiss on the cheek as she clung by his side happily squeezed in the middle of the two men. "Seventy-three miles from Shingbwiyang to Sook. We've done about forty. We can make it before dark"

"DING HAO!" Yelled WHEN WU.

"DING HAO!" Echoed the youthful group.

CHAPTER FIFTY-SIX—June 1944
Shingbwiyang to Yunnanyi

HOLT and Blair fought controls feverishly as the C-47 Sky Train plummeted nose downward, a forceful speed of engine and gravity towards doom led by the fierce storm.

"NO-NO-NO" in unison they yelled fighting controls.

Gear DOWN

Control NEUTRAL

Latched GREEN LIGHT

Extend FLAPS

Ahead the dimly lit field of Yunnanyi dulled in the dark night. Jeep lights lit the ends while flairs lit the edges of the rugged field.

Like a cork bobbing in high seas, the ship leveled out as quickly as it had plunged downward. Waving to and fro, up and down, skidding sideways doing a little dance, the Sky Train landed nose first at last stop.

"Son of a bitch," HOLT belted out after killing the speed.

The three men sat stunned, bowels gurgling, adrenalin taking over, the usual.

"Cecil," they shouted.

No answer. Then "A groan," said HOLT. "That's good."

"Let's do this," said Orville the navigator. "We've landed."

So grateful to be down, HOLT and Blair voiced aloud what needed to be done before jumping out to meet the emergency water truck led by the First Aid Jeep both speeding towards them.

Propeller-LOW PITCH

Flaps-UP

Tail wheel-UNLOCKED FOR TAXIING

Cowl flaps-OPEN
Mixture control IDLE CUT OFF engine at 1000rpm
Ignition-OFF
Landing gear lever-DOWN

A crew outside swiftly tied down the wavering plane as gusty winds worsened. Like always, a first aid group met the wayward plane, anticipating problems the crew endured due to the uncontrollable weather.

"Cecil," called Orville closest to the stunned airman.

"Huh?" Cecil sat weaving back and forth.

"Up and at-em!" Orville and first aid group lifted him helping to secure him with arms all over the place as blood trickled down his face due to a small cut above the brow.

All jumped in the jeep and headed towards main barracks.

HOLT changed plans with other officers. "This C-47 needs to head back to Kunming when weather clears. It's loaded with much needed War supplies—fuel, ammunition, medicine."

The officers listened intently to HOLT'S version of their treacherous flight from Kunming area to here in Yunnanyi. "Impossible to land."

After learning of crew's plans to make it back to Ledo and then on to Sookerating, it was decided that a plane switch would work. "A flight coming in from Ledo within the hour would be a good switch for each. We'll unload here and that crew can fly to Kunming when weather permits," said an executive officer of the base unit and a good friend of HOLT'S. Director of Operations filled in the paper work after deciding HOLT'S crew needed to wait till the A.M. for a safe flight to Ledo. He nodded at the newly patched Cecil.

Wearily the four exhausted crew headed for the Officer's Club for chow before bunking down for the night.

The stressful flight had left them exhausted and with a new tale for the men when whiskeyed-down. "Where in the hell is PALOOKA?" HOLT'S last words after placing his empty pipe on the short table next to him and flopping down on the cot.

CHAPTER FIFTY-SEVEN—June 1944
Shingbwiyang to Ledo Road

PALOOKA and Chuck wearily rode the L-5 the last 20 minutes to touchdown at the small landing strip carved out of the jungle for Stillwell's main camp of supplies. Evading the Jap Zeroes became less treacherous the closer they got to the camp. P-40's and P-51D Mustangs did the heavy tasks of chasing away Zeroes.

Warhawks, used numerously by the fighter squadrons covering India and Burma, became a large part of the CBI Theater whose number one objective of keeping Zeroes away from Stillwell's Road met with success. Along with the P-51D Mustang equipped with six 50 caliber guns and the 1540 H.P. Rolls Royce Merlin Engine, the two fighter planes controlled the area. In the 400 mph class, the P-51 outran most other planes.

Knowing these aircraft circled above gave PALOOKA and Chuck the confidence they desperately needed.

"The Japs come in like fierce fighter bees knowing that we're closing in trying to chase them out of Burma," said PALOOKA.

"How's that going?" Chuck asked, forever keeping the binoculars at his face following construction efforts below. Occasionally, he shifted his left foot relieving the dead weight of the heavy cast.

"End of August," HOLT said, "we'll take RANGOON."

PALOOKA kept the plane low following the newly carved dirt road. Below, hordes of men on foot, some driving small Jeeps and large trucks, worked together as a military team carving out a road engineered to meet the Burma Road, the latter completed in 1938. "When Stillwell's Ledo Road meets the Burma Road sometime next year in '45, the two roads will have taken seven years to connect," stated Chuck.

"How do you know this?"

"I looked it up."

As usual the Stinson L-5 let down easily in the small area of Stillwell's camp. PALOOKA edged the plane to the far side away from the hustle and bustle of nurses and medics tending to bandaged patients, some on cots, others on tarpeted ground. Moving heavy boulders took its toll on the small bodies of the Chinese workers even though they worked in unison, pulling long lines of ropes or pushing rocks, large boulders and heavy bushes out of the way. Though big bladed machines carved the road, much had to be done by hand and no man worked alone. Hence, many injuries.

After landing, the two airmen shuffled about, good to feel their legs on the ground surveying the action here and there while side stepping over debris. PALOOKA slapped his shirt pocket containing the cigar butt wrapped in wax paper and decided to wait.

Good enough that it's there.

From a table nearby, there are coffee and biscuits. "Help yourselves," said a young nurse, a petite brunette with brown waves ringing her neck. She pointed to the table while rolling a long bandage into a ball.

Surgeon O'Neil and two medical assistants tended to a blood splattered young Burmese.

"Hey PALOOKA. You need to take him to the hospital in Ledo for stitching. We'll load him in about fifteen," he said wiping his hands meticulously on a cloth of rubbing alcohol. A tub of used soapy water swished close by, a bar of Lux soap on its rim. PALOOKA and Chuck poured coffee in paper cups and each took a warm buttered biscuit never taking their eyes off the scene before them.

The young nurse looked at them and added, "There's canned milk over at the Red Cross station." She pointed at a large wheeled cart about 100 feet away.

"Say, don't I know you?" PALOOKA looked closely at the young nurse who now stopped rolling the box of gauze in a ball and changed task to arranging supplies in a cart. She stopped and stared.

"What's your name?" Always up front and straight forward, shyness was not part of his makeup.

"Millie."

"Yes. Mitch's tent. You're his girl!" He pointed at her with the hand holding half a biscuit as he spoke.

Her face cornered a bit of a smile. "I don't know about that," she shyly said. Then looking at Chuck, "What happened to your foot?"

"Plane crash. C-46."

Now everyone close by looked at him listening. Likewise, he looked at everyone as he spoke.

"BOBBY JOHNSON the F/O made it out. We're still looking for Walt."

All was quiet for half a minute, a customary pause so in tune with the tragedy of plane crashes. "We're loading now." O'Neil and two medics gingerly lifted the injured young Burmese to the flat bed behind the pilot's seat, an area especially designed for patient pickup.

PALOOKA shouted to Millie while he and Chuck rushed to the plane. "Sookerating….Swing Canteen…birthday party Saturday for BOBBY'S 21st…Be there!"

"And bring more nurses," Chuck yelled while smiling. They both threw her a kiss.

"Don't tell Mitch." Her voice trailed away heard by no one.

Millie stared a long while at the small plane flying away. Yes, she remembered the husky, loud voiced red head, mustache and all, entering Mitch's tent where she had spent some free time. Sentimentally she remembered the empty bed Mitch had pointed to. "BOBBY JOHNSON," he had said. "Not heard from him in days." Now, she was so happy to hear that he was alive, a brightness in this dark War, a glimmer of hope for all.

Mitch. She thought about him daily and especially at night when she hugged her pillow. Back then, at his tent in Sookerating, he tended to her every move, every moment while he described all the war planes to keep her attention. Or, was he just a lonely young Airman so far from home. Maybe she reminded him of some old girlfriend. But, she remembered his kiss, so special. Instinctively now, she covered her mouth with her hand. Could she see him again? Would she?

Her mood darkened as she remembered BOBBY as the bearer of the bad plane crash. She had almost joined the 30 nurses on that flight. They were her closest friends. Frequently when alone, she sobbed uncontrollably.

Surgeon O'Neil came over to her noting her lonely mood. With both hands on her shoulders, he turned her toward him.

"You have worked so hard tending to these injured." He nodded toward the suffering group. "The War will not miss you for a day. Go to the birthday party." With a heavy sigh, he turned toward the bandaged group and shuffled off.

Millie looked out at the road a close distance away. A pair of huge convoy trucks met while traveling in opposite directions, gathering riders for one reason or another.

One was headed north, to Ledo and then on to Sookerating. The other was headed south, on down the road of heavy construction.

She paused.

CHAPTER FIFTY-EIGHT—June 1944
Ledo to Sookerating

PALOOKA and Chuck flew from Stilwell's Camp sight to the hospital in Ledo with their patient, a blood splattered young Burmese boy. A long cut across his chest needed stitching. Surgeon O'Neil had taped it together for the fifteen minute flight.

"You good?" Chuck asked looking back at the pale young boy who was somewhere between twelve and sixteen. His eyes closed obviously in pain, he tried to look brave and blinked heavily before answering.

"I'm good. Had some aspirin for pain."

"It's a short flight," PALOOKA remarked while keeping a steady eye on the sky for trouble.

Chuck put down his binoculars, turned to the boy and asked, "Have you heard about the Japs paying money to locals to cause trouble for us airmen?"

"Yes sir. That's how I got slashed."

"Tell us about it. We're trying to figure out the best way to deal with the trouble makers. We call it sabotage."

Not shy, the boy somberly began. "Two peasants, not part of the road crew, slashed tires on a big convoy truck. I yelled, 'Hey, get away from there' and got attacked. The doctor said, cut is quite deep." The boy sucked in air, a big sigh of pain.

Chuck gingerly patted the boy's face with a provided wet cloth given to them by the medic, and continued.

"What happened to the two peasants?" "Military took after them. I don't think they caught them. They really know the jungle trails." "Thanks for your help." Noticing the young boy breathing deeply with eyes now closed Chuck added, "You'll be fine. We're almost there." He patted the youngster on the shoulder.

PALOOKA knew where to park after landing and pulled into the hangar labeled *EMERGENCY ENTRANCE.* Field radioed ahead, a first-aid team met them with a stretcher. Heavy greetings were had by all, so accustomed to PALOOKA'S Search and Rescue.

"We need all info for WEN WU," said PALOOKA while getting out his clip board outlined: name, date, problems, comments. "Let's hobble in and get info down before heading to Sook. I think the boy can tell us more while being stitched."

Looking down at Chuck's cast, "You think you can make it?"

"Hell yeah! They might have doughnuts here." "And new cigars," added PALOOKA throwing away an empty ball of wax paper he took out of his pocket. Walking in and heavily greeted again by staff rushing around taking care of injured patients, he looked over at a nurse he knew well who always greeted him warmly.

"Hey big red! What's going on?" Nurse Polly had just looked up from helping a heavily bandaged soldier who needed a great deal of assistance. "Why the shoulder wrap? Played tennis with a Zero?" "Five of them," he said. "I got the better of them."

Spirits are high around sobering patients. The staff talked briskly with an occasional laugh. So thankful for lives saved by Search and Rescue, the staff members are forever accommodating their wants and needs.

"Cigar, PALOOKA?" Polly handed him two, then tore off a piece of wax paper, folded it, and slowly put it in his shirt pocket all the while making eye contact.

"Hey, you flirting with me?" All smiles, he stared closely at her dark brown eyes that soon pooled like chocolate. As was his usual ritual, he placed one side of her long brown hair behind an ear. "Pure silk," he said.

"One hundred strokes a night. Brushing keeps me out of trouble." Coyly she turned her head sideways and more hair fell over her eyes.

"You're a regular Veronica Lake," he said as they briefly stared at each other chest to chest before getting back to work.

A heavy sigh from a chair nearby, sat Chuck. His big foot with cast extended out brought sympathy from working staff. Three or four came over with questions.

He again told the tale of crashing and also mentioned Walt. "He could be anywhere, unconscious, or heavily bandaged."

"We forcibly seek I.D.s in every way possible," said someone. "We refer to the growing list of MIAs daily," said another staff, overhearing a short distance away as he scrubbed his hands at a tub. "Hope is necessary and always present." "Damn War," Chuck murmered.

Two nurses sensing his depression came over and smilingly asked, "Can we sign our autographs?" "Only" he sparked, "if you come to our birthday party celebration at the Swing Canteen, in Sookerating tomorrow night." "Who's birthday?" They asked.

"It's for BOBBY JOHNSON, and anyone else who has a birthday this year." Wow! He felt sharp as he extended his foot.

Surgeon Kelly attending the young Burmese boy was so astounded by the depth and force of the blow to the young man's chest said, "had to have been a Gurkha knife."

An aide helping him said, "The Gurkha Warriors from Nepal, are fierce, loyal supporters of our campaign and team with the British Army. However, their knives are used widely by all sides."

"Make note to Brit's headquarters to keep a closed door on this vicious weapon if possible," added Kelly.

"It's time," said PALOOKA extinguishing his cigar and wrapping it away in wax paper. "Lift off in ten minutes."

Goodbyes began.

"See you later."

"Not if I see you sooner." "Save a dance for me."

"Sookerating, here we come."

CHAPTER FIFTY-NINE—June 1944
Yunanyi to Sookerating

The restful night for HOLT and crew reinvigorated their desire to fly to Sookerating, their home base for much needed R & R for however long their schedule could permit.

"Rest up as much as possible while in Sook," HOLT mumbled. "Big attacks planned against the Japs the end of this month."

"What's happening?" Orville asked. "I heard you mention code name Broadway." He, Blair and Cecil hurried getting ready for the last leg of their flight. Gear, boots, packs, are shuffled into a waiting Willys secured by HOLT.

Showered and shaved, they all left their tent and drove to the mess hall for breakfast.

"As you notice," HOLT began, "the Chinese forces are everywhere here in Yunanyi. They are headed to Yunnan to meet with other allies and then on to help the Chindits take Mogaung from the Japs. Stillwell's forces are coming down from the northwest to help with the attack. Time line is the end of this month."

Cecil feeling the bandage on his forehead mentioned, "This War has got to be coming to a peak. Chindits are the Burma soldiers?" HOLT shook his head affirmative.

With coffee cups in hands, they were trucked to their prepped and waiting C-47.

As always, they repeated the entire process:

BEFORE STARTING ENGINES: They completed the list of 20 items; wheels chocked, landing gear pins installed, check fuel quantity gages, prime 2 to 3 seconds with outside temperature 40 to 60 Fahrenheit, ENGAGE STARTERS—ETC.

DURING WARM UP: Warm-up at 800-1000 RPM

Master battery "ON", ETC.

BEFORE TAKE OFF: They completed the list of 13 items: Mixture in "AUTO RICH", propeller pitch control "FULL LOW PITCH",—ETC.

Check all flight controls for "FREE MOVEMENT".

HOLT mumbled, "After 650 flights over the HUMP, this is such a blur in my head."

Airborne, he continued with one last statement, "Once Mogaung is secured, Allies head south to Mandalay and then the final goal, take back. Rangoon."

Blair added, "You know the Japs took it over before Pearl Harbor in '41."

HOLT sighed. "Everything's in the hands of Commander Bill Slim."

"Afterwards, this is when we HUMP pilots can go home," said Orville.

"Getting close," added HOLT wearily. Looking at his watch, "It's now 5 A.M. We should get to Sook by 8."

"This area is a real hot spot," said Blair, copiloting while looking out the slanted windows. "Planes above, planes below, jeeps in sight everywhere. In the far distance, I can get a glimpse of Stillwell's winding road. It's zig-zagging down a mountain." Orville added, "It's going to get hotter. At least we don't have boots on the ground. That's got to be a real jungle torcher."

"This entire upper Burma is a hornet's nest. Japs want it. It's their gateway to a China takeover," HOLT summarized.

As the plane burped and seemed to jump over a bubble, HOLT added, "And all during the great monsoon! Let's bring her down out of the heavy clouds ahead."

"Too much radio static," whined Cecil. "Probably jammed by the Japs. We are in a Hornet's nest."

"At least our plane was double checked for sabotage problems inside and out—lines cut—fuel shortages—oxygen hose cut. Did anyone grab the list of sabotage problems for awareness?" Blair stressed, raised his voice a notch.

HOLT, always with pipe in hand, pointed at a clipboard nearby. "I grabbed a few for us." "Woopie," yelled Cecil the kid of the group.

"Dim lights ahead."

"Sure want to see the old gang again," HOLT mumbled. "Home-made ice cream. Cake."

Then from Bed Post: *Fighters out. P-51's, p-40's, p61's, British spits—*

"P-61 is the Black Widow Night Fighter. We must really be in the mustard," said Orville.

"Son of a Bitch!" HOLT chewed on the stem of his pipe. "Japs too close to our destination."

Cecil radioed Bedpost, "Coming—heading to Sookerating with supplies."

Static: "Have you in sight. Upper altitude necessary. Stay put until cleared."

"Christ! Black clouds ahead," blurted HOLT.

"Hang on," he shouted.

Heavy sighs all around.

CHAPTER SIXTY—June 1944

Ledo to Sookerating

The packed large Army truck heading to Sookerating barely had room for one more. So Millie sat on a soldier's lap in the front seat. She felt nervous but had no other choice. Her quick decision barely allowed time for her to join the group.

"Come on! Jump in," said Tom.

"How long a ride?" She asked wide-eyed and hesitant.

"About an hour," said Tom near the window as they squeezed together. "You're ok here in the front. How much you weigh anyway, ninety pounds?"

"I have to meet friends in Sook." She lied but worked extra hard not to show it. All her friends had died in the recent plane crash, and now she is heading to the main office for questionable duties, all new to her. She looked out the windows at the scenery ahead while holding on to the loop that hung from the top of the side door near where she sat. The bumpy ride allowed for much body jolting now and then.

"You ok?" She asked in her embarrassment trying to look back at her comfortable provider.

"Life couldn't be better," uttered the young soldier. "We're moving away from the tedious road work on to Sook for some R & R." We switch crews now and then. "Say, what are you doing later?"

"I hear there's a big dance this Saturday at the Swing Canten. A birthday 21st for BOBBY JOHNSON. I might go to that," she softly said.

Her low trailing voice lacking excitement, and duly noted by the soldiers in the truck, prompted the driver to ask, "You a nurse?"

"Nurses' assistant," she answered.

The soldiers said no more for about ten minutes. The heavy silence breathed the loss of the 30 nurses and medical crews, news heard around the world just a week ago.

Heavy noise overhead of fighter planes keeping the area cleared from Jap Zeroes, reminded them to be alert for shells. The four were on edge as they rambled along.

"Soon," said Frank the driver, "we'll be in safer territory. The enemy is viciously trying to eliminate Stilwell's road to Burma."

"Ouch!" Yelled Hank as they hit a bump. "That jarred my foot. Do you people mind if I take off my boot? My ingrown toenail is probably infected." Frank slowed the big Army truck as Hank proceeded to free his foot of boot and sock, a gigantic task while squeezed in the middle.

"Let's put Sulfa powder on it for now. When we get there, soak your foot in Epsom salts," Milly said opening her gear bag at her feet.

"You have to clip your big toenail into a "V" to eliminate this problem from happening. That's why we have clippers in our gear bags," said Frank.

"I forgot to do that. Blame it on this busy War. Now, I have to get well so I can dance."

"Who's playing," someone asked.

"I don't know," said Frank, "but the Hep Cats have been playing there pretty steady."

"Yeah. Chaplain Mike plays a mean Boogie Woogie piano; with LUCKY LARRY on Sax and Ears always on drums, what could go wrong?" "Wait. Ears a friend of Mitch?" Millie became excited.

"Oh yeah! Great talent."

The empty Army truck sped along more quickly than usual as the need to be free of imminent danger controlled everyone's thoughts.

Soon, "We're pretty clear. Sook is around the bend," said Frank.

"Say! My toe looks like Rudolph's nose." Somehow, the youthful Hank was able to hold it high within view.

Their laughter was more of a relief from the danger above, than his quip.

CHAPTER SIXTY-ONE—June 1944
Shingbwiyang to Ledo to Sookerating

Nurse Loretta constantly aware of jungle problems, hammered the Willys' crew to be on the alert for mosquito bites, ticks, and leeches crawling on them.

"Malaria is so prevalent among the British Armies marching through these thick jungles; I hear that more than half the men of Britain's 14th Army led by Mountbatten are in field hospitals."

"We not only made it through a Japanese air raid, but now we have attacks from the ground," remarked BOBBY.

Each was holding on to something in the Willys while LUCKY LARRY drove like hell through the rambling road. "I'll get us there before dark," he promised.

"Five minute break," yelled WEN WU to be heard above the overhead noise of fighter planes attacking Zeroes. "Let's inspect each other's hair, and boots. The leeches crawl into the shoelace sockets." Adamantly they began with no shyness.

"Holy mackerel! Pass the salt. What a War! We're being attacked above ground and from it," LUCKY LARRY added with alarm. "I have problems on my ankles."

Salt was shared from kits and rubbed vigorously around ankles and waists.

"Alcohol anyone?" Bonnie held a bottle of rubbing alcohol from which she poured a pool in her open palm to rub through her locks.

"Pass it around," said Loretta. "We need to all rub some on our scalps. Won't hurt."

"Five minutes gone," said LUCKY LARRY.

"Hang on!" They all prepared as he surged forward. "You're playing in the band HEP CATS?" Loretta asked.

"You betchum! Put in your request." He was top of his game now and kept busy thinking how he would paint a picture of Loretta on the nose of a C-46.

"I hear that 'Lili Marlene' is playing all over Europe," said Bonnie.

"Such a tune! It's everywhere," offered BOBBY, his arm around Bonnie's shoulders bracing her as they bumped along.

"Crazy Tokyo Rose plays American music on all the air waves when she likes to taunt us for attention," added WEN WU. "HOLT'S good with finding reception on long flights above the HUMP. We heard Guy Lombardo one time coming all the way from San Francisco."

BOBBY'S suggestion was the best. "Play all the slow tunes you can think of. How about, 'You Made Me Love You' by Morton Downey Orchestra." "Good choice," said the girls.

"Star Dust' by Glenn Miller is new too," said LUCKY LARRY.

Jovially they bumped along, thankful for being alive, totally aware of dangers today, tonight and tomorrow. Soon they saw the sign: *Ledo 2 km. Sookerating 15 km.*

They were a popular sight as the Willys of five came roaring in to Stilwell's camp in Ledo, Assam. The late day heat circling about them in the humid jungle did nothing to dampen their spirits.

"We made it." LUCKY LARRY was the first to yell as workers at the base camp clapped them in. All are aware of the Zeroes dangerous noise above and a little too close. Fighter jets in abundance added to the drama.

Crews shuffled over to greet BOBBY heartily, all aware of his life or death adventures after the crash. He had been a popular Airman as followers learned from the airwaves the dilemmas he faced while trying to make it back. They each had been through 'Maydays' of some sort and empathy was always there.

Back pats, hand shakes, and "Long time no see."

"How's the foot?"

"Sorry to hear about Harry."

"And, Walt. I can't believe he's disappeared."

"They'll find him for sure."

"Hey, I hear Chucks helping PALOOKA."

Then aware of Bonnie holding BOBBY'S hand, smiles began. Surgeon Kelly came forward. "Now, about the big birthday party dance tomorrow night, I'll have to dance with your partner to help you out." He stood tall, proud, both hands on hips, being the great Surgeon Kelly, happy this small group of friends are alive. He and others knew Bonnie as the 'cute jeep girl' who hauled crews to their flight zone.

"We're heading on to Sook," BOBBY said before adding, "I'm looking for two small native boys about 10 or 14 who helped me survive. I was told they came this way to help."

He looked around at crews of men who were everywhere. Some moving rocks off the road. Some near the water station set up by the Salvation Army. Some standing around just catching their breath.

"They could be anywhere," said a crew leader. "Check at the water station." He nodded, turned and pointed a thumb over his shoulder to that area.

The popular station manned by a crew of young service women, all volunteers, is a busy sight of workers needing a break from the heavy toil of creating Stilwell's Road out of heavy jungle bushes and rocks. Rocks and small boulders are pushed aside by machine and mostly man power. Therefore, the Salvation Army cart on wheels is a popular sight that follows the work units, station to station. Stress from ground work, plus stress from Zeroes overhead strafing the road, are never ending.

BOBBY and group had an immediate all important mission. To find the two boys who helped keep the young pilot alive over difficult and foreign terrain, is now a chore they each took seriously.

WEN WU kept busy talking to the road crew in their particular language, whether native or Chinese, asking questions.

The group followed WEN WU along and quickly pantomimed the sizes of the two boys as he spoke. After walking down hill for ten minutes, they turned around and went back up hill to retrieve the Willys and continue on with their goal in mind.

There was a commotion at the jeep. Several workers were jabbering angrily and pointing to a lone worker who kept something hidden, cupped between his two hands.

Frightened by the forceful nature of others, he opened his hands to present an aluminum cup to BOBBY. It was the cup that folded down flat to a one inch size. Looking like an accordion, it could be pulled up again to an eight inch drink cup, able to bear a leak proof beverage.

"Ahah! I gave this to the boys to share while we were staying in a hut on stilts by the Chindwin River." He turned it over and over. Flipped it up and back down again checking its flatness.

"What a clever item," Bonnie mentioned taking the rustic metal piece, cradling it in her hands like a toy. "It even has a flat surface for setting it down on something."

"Fits perfectly in a gear bag," said Loretta.

"How did you get this?" WEN WU asked ready to translate.

"They asked for a free ride here to help out and said they wanted me to have this."

"Where are the boys now? Any ideas?"

"They said they were heading north since Stilwell didn't have much work for them. They left this morning, walking."

"Load up! Onward!" LUCKY LARRY threw the Willys in gear and they surged ahead to their goal. BOBBY left the accordion cup behind with the native who bowed with gratitude.

DING HAO!

CHAPTER SIXTY-TWO—June 1944
Sookerating

PALOOKA taxied the Stinson to its usual parking spot, close to home—a tent, cot, and personal chest of drawers allotted for him and a couple others. Especially for PALOOKA, the professional, tough, Jungle Walla, this was home base. Known as the king of Search and Rescue, no job is neither too difficult, nor treacherous, and it is a popular known fact that all crews flying the HUMP feel a bit more at ease knowing that many Search and Rescue crews will never quit looking until everyone is found, where ever the dilemma.

"Have your shoulder checked again," said Chuck noticing PALOOKA'S grimace for the first time as he tried to raise his left arm.

"We're a party pair. With my shoulder and your foot a mess, forget the dancing!"

"However, expect a pitiful amount of attention. These are wounds of battle," Chuck remarked. "You can slow dance with one arm and I can do the same only holding a crutch. Where's the problem?" He bent down reading the signatures of the two nurses on his cast. "Have to remember them at the party." They threw their gear bags on their cots, did a quick clean up and decided they would wander around after entering necessary paper work at the front office.

In the waning dusk, busyness was everywhere. A large hangar sat between two barracks, one for dining and one for all military operations. Small groups of uniformed men and women sat typing orders, notices, and airplane jingle. Clacking Royal manual typewriters filled the atmosphere with Wartime seriousness. Next door, maintenance crews worked tirelessly on airplanes in the hangar and outside. Labeled parts were shuffled about on tall carts, all stolen parts rescued from wrecked planes, the necessary items to keep the planes in the air.

Soon, "Hey PALOOKA, where's LUCKY LARRY? We need him for this problem we're working on." A tired mechanic came walking toward them while wiping his greasy hands on a rag. "You know how fussy Mr. Fix It is! All tools have to be placed in a specific order and facing a certain direction," big smile.

"You mean that guy?"

"Yes, that guy."

"It's got to be his artist side." Chuckles all around. Known for the nose art he paints on planes with perfection, he is quite popular.

"He should have been here by now. He's driving a jeep from Shingbwiyang."

"Zeroes been extra heavy today. They must suspect something going down the end of this month," the mechanic added, hands on hips, rag thrown over his shoulder, looking up at the darkening sky. "It's been a long day. Been trying to fix this fuel filter forever." He sneezed.

"All fuel problems can be a result of sabotage," PALOOKA suggested. "Look carefully. Read problems they cause from the list put out by WEN WU."

"We all have copies," the mechanic said. "Who to trust and who not, is the problem!" He and the maintenance group called it a day as they shut down work area, covering parts with large tarps and pushing wheeled carts under shelter at the hangar entrance.

"Let's head back for a game of poker. I'm tired," said Chuck.

"Tomorrow we'll grab a rickshaw and get around a bit." PALOOKA yawned, then added, "or use the Willys. Hmmm, where is that gang?"

In the dark tent, and before lights were turned on, a shuffling noise startled the two.

"Hey, what's going on?" Chuck instinctively turned around elbowing someone hard in the face.

A quick cry and then, "OK Joe!"

The younger of the two held a dirty hand over a bloody nose. The elder stood stunned by the sight of the blow, fear in his eyes.

"Sorry, sorry," said Chuck trying now to be helpful.

Surgeon PALOOKA to the rescue, immediately wiping blood away from the young boy's face, said "So good to find you two."

"OK Joe," they each said with frozen faces.

"Say, these are the two boys who helped us find BOBBY." PALOOKA, elated to have found these two gems he knows his friend is looking for, decided to keep them close. "They saw us fly in, recognizing our plane."

The men decided their first task is to get the boys out of their torn and dirty clothes, showered and redressed.

"Onward to the medic station." With hands on each skinny boy's shoulder, they led them to the building of nurses and volunteers, a station open 24 hours ready to assist where needed, both eager and accommodating in all situations.

"Please feed them too and bring them to our tent. They are the two who helped save BOBBY JOHNSON. We'll have space ready for them." Nods and smiles all around almost completed the evening for the tired Search and Rescue pair. After one last trip to the dispensary for the free 2 ounces of whiskey allotted each crew member flying in, the two crashed on their cots in contentment, with smiles in their hearts.

Overhead *'Maydays'* will wait until tomorrow.

CHAPTER SIXTY-THREE—June 1944
Shingbwiyang to Sookerating

In the darkening, rainy night, HOLT and crew entered the black clouds at an attitude of 12,000 to avoid Jap Zeroes buzzing everywhere. Plus, they needed their C-47 Skytrain out of the path of the fighters honing in on the chase at lower levels.

"Look for the silver lining," said Orville.

"Here we go again," said Cecil rubbing his bruised forehead.

"We can do this. We're just 45 minutes away." HOLT sighed. His duties were basically in the Offices of Operations and Intelligence. Why did he insist on flying in this dangerous War. He looked over at Blair the co-pilot. So young! So eager! So earnest! Was this him ten years ago? He talked aloud, "I'm done."

Still connecting to his long career, he continued. "When I started flying at age 15, the only problem I faced was getting over the telephone wires. They were everywhere."

"What you say?" Orville could barely hear due to the loud roar in the cockpit of the plane. "I'm finished flying. I've accumulated an excess of hours over the requirement trying to make up for the grounded pilots too scared to fly," he said sarcastically.

"It's true," added Orville. "The Himalayas are littered with pieces of aluminum from crashed planes. This is no pony ride! I have pilot friends who begged to do land jobs."

"We're not too far from Sook," said Blair while tuning in T.K. (Sook).

Although the weather consisted of a torrential rain, they received the station from bed post loud and clear.

"Hey, what's going on here?" Cecil loudly complained that the needle on the ADF (Automatic Direction Finder) swung far off to the right, away from the destination they were headed. "This indicates we are off our route. We need to follow the needle."

"No, we don't!" HOLT demanded. "The instrument is wrong. Some dummy station is trying to pull us off course. We stay on our route."

Within minutes, the needle on the ADF swung back around to the plane's nose.

They yelled with the excitement of relief that only imminent danger can explain.

"I heard about these Japanese dummy homing stations set up high in the Himalayas to pull planes off course to crash in the Rock Pile. Wow! It almost happened to us." Blair shook his head in disbelief. "Something to talk about at the Swing Canteen. Everyone needs to be on the alert. It will only get worse." HOLT sighed heavily. "You know that they infiltrated our regular homing frequencies, using our call letters. In the beginning, we lost a lot of planes."

"How do we avoid this problem?" Blair was nervous as he adjusted his oxygen mask again and double checked instruments. "I have many flights ahead to accumulate flight hours before I go home to Uncle Sugar!"

HOLT simply said, "The routes are studded with Bed Post frequencies. Always call in if you feel there's a problem."

Orville added, "First, check your plane carefully for sabotage before you even board. We need to memorize all the items from WEN WU'S list and make sure all the new guys are aware."

"Like at the Swing Canteen this Saturday," Cecil offered.

"Hell yeah! Lights ahead. Sook, here we come!" Next, HOLT radioed in loud and clear to his group of friends at tower control. "Ship's arriving!"

CHAPTER SIXTY-FOUR—June 1944
Sookerating

It was midnight when the group of four came roaring in to the camp of tents, all the while zigzagging through busy crews, some walking to the mess hall for a taste of coffee and late night biscuits, and some working on plane maintenance.

Avoiding the office headquarters and row of half boarded latrines, LUCKY LARRY buzzed the Willys quickly to the final destination of home among the tents, all sandwiched in between barracks where day crews were snoring and night crews were stirring. Roofs of palm thatched huts edged in rows surrounded the compound. Rickshaws are parked outside in a waiting perimeter ready to help and eager for a few coins; the nearby drivers sit on stools of rocks always alert. Hawkers handy with baskets of exotic wares, sleep close by with one eye open.

"The War never sleeps," said BOBBY.

Among the midnight buzz of activities were fully lighted maintenance crews, late shifts working to keep the planes in the air.

"Hey, LUCKY LARRY. Grasshopper legs," someone shouted. "Our Aircraft Maintenance Officer. Get over here and look at this problem." "Holy mackerel! Give me five. I've been working all day!"

"Yeah, we see that." The crew, led by Jolly Tom, all mouthed a tired smile while looking at Bonnie and Loretta.

"Hey BOBBY, welcome back!" A lot of hand shaking and back slapping began.

"Your left foot keeping you from a mean game of poker?" Jolly looked down at the cast.

"Not unless my jar of nickels disappeared." "It's been growing interest since you've been out hiking in the jungle. A nickel a day," said Jolly now wiping his hands again on a rag flung over his shoulder. "Since you're lame, I'll have to dance with your beautiful friend here," looking at Bonnie. "I heard about the birthday bash at the Swing Canteen." "I'll save you one soldier," smiled Bonnie. "I'm always accommodating."

Jolly feigned a salute and walked back to his crew.

Loretta and Bonnie grabbed their gear and with quick "See you in the morning," left for the women's tent, not far from the main barracks. Here they met Millie, the new helper among the crew of medics. They agreed after quick introductions, to exchange War talk in the morning. They bedded close by to avoid the emptiness of the huge tent due to the missing nurses.

Before entering their tent, the two men discussed concern over WEN WU.

"He knows what he's doing," said LUCKY LARRY. "We were being followed, no doubt."

BOBBY and LUCKY LARRY quietly found their home spaces. In the dimness of the night, due to large lights not too far away as a protective measure for foreign creatures--both animal and human, the men settled down. They recognized PALOOKA, Chuck, Mitch and Ears in their sleeping quarters among the cots, tired and loudly snoring.

Not too far away, nestled among pillows were the two young native boys whom they would surprisingly meet in the morning.

WEN WU, the youngest of the entire group, jumped out of the jeep about a quarter mile before the compound in Sookerating. "We are being followed," he had said. "Every time we stop, I hear them and see their lights among the thick bushes. They are not the friendly ones. We stop. They stop. Something's wrong. Go ahead. I'll meet up later. HOLT's flying in anyway with his crew."

Although ten years younger than HOLT, he had been by his side as the number one helper and interpreter since the War effort began here in the Himalayas.

Among his many styles of uniforms, it was decided that he would dress as a Chinese peasant when he rode earlier with the Willys' group to Shingbwiyang.

"Just in case!" And now this decision would come in handy. He walked along the narrow strip of a road and decided to hide in the bushes before accosting the followers. Fortunately, he was armed and ready.

Although it was close to midnight, planes roared above, flying low ready to land at Sook. Buzzing of midnight insects, thickly harbored among the bushes where he hid. From a can of repellent, he swiped some liquid around his neck under his collar. Soon in the short distance, he heard the distinct sound of a motor bike.

He waited.

CHAPTER SIXTY-FIVE—June 1944
Sookerating

The midnight darkness turned a murky gray from an accumulation of the many flights over head, search lights near the landing strip, and circulating flood lights near the occupied tents and barracks not too far away.

This dim visibility allowed WEN WU to see the pair approaching on a motor bike.

Loudly they came, fearlessly shouting due to the noisy cargo planes coming in for landings one by one. Their hurriedness and stealth reeked with evil intent.

From their loud language, WEN WU knew them to be Chindets, Burmese Soldiers highly respected for their War efforts collaborating with the British and Allies fighting forcibly against the Japs.

Yet, the actions of incognito and stealth from this pair were not normal. Obviously, they did not want to be seen nor heard as they stayed a good quarter mile back from the occupied Willys. What kind of renegades would he be facing?

He knew they were following the five since leaving Shingbwiyang. Often, LUCKY LARRY would stop the Willys thinking the approaching cycle would come around the bend and he would let them pass.

Nothing.

Only their head lights, shooting like a star through the bushes and trees every now and then, reminded the group that they were being followed and the pursuers were in a hiding mode.

"Not good!" They all agreed.

So, WEN WU jumped out of the Jeep and told his crew of friends to proceed without him.

"You sure?"

“Be careful,” the girls whined.

“See you soon,” were his last words as they sped away.

“We’ll be back to check on you,” they shouted, knowing full well HOLT’S friend was physically capable of anything dangerous. He learned to be a Jungle Walla with PALOOKA. “We practiced together,” he would often brag.

WEN WU hid in heavy brush near a mud puddle knowing this terrain would keep the mystery pair occupied and unprepared for an ambush. Also, the winding road made a swift turn near this same area encouraging the driver to slow and pay attention to the road or off the edge he would go.

Now parallel with the bike, he jumped from the brush as planned, thrusting a long heavy stick into the spokes of one whirling tire, both in a spontaneous motion.

The bike flipped, landing hard on the Chindet driver, thrusting his face into the mud. His feet stuck weirdly through the spokes of the back tire as the momentum of the cycle continued to drag him along.

The passenger thrown free and half dazed was no match for quick WU, who was now pulling out two weapons, a gun in his left hand and Gurkha knife in his strong and steady right.

“Don’t move,” he shouted to the half dazed Burmese now sitting on the ground. “Throw me your gun!” He stood close by waving both weapons; the dangerous Gurkha knife glinted in the hazy moonlit night as he held it high. “Who are you and why are you following us?” No answer.

“Throw you gun far into the bushes and put your hands behind your head.” A quick glance to the right showed no movement from the driver meaning he was unconscious or dead as he lay face down in the oozing mud.

WEN WU stepping back, posed a defensive fighting stance, his gun cocked and ready while waiting for the mystery soldier to throw away his weapon.

The soldier slowly threw his gun with his left hand far into the branches than swiftly turned fiercely swinging a knife at arm’s length near WEN WU’s head.

He expected this action after watching the soldier use his left hand to throw away a weapon and not his right. He knew that soldiers needed to be right handed for all combat.

Simultaneously, he ducked very low, threw out both feet hitting the wayward Chindit below the knees knocking him down. Before he could scramble upward, WEN WU twirled, and using the heel of his left boot kicked him hard under the chin knocking him out.

Next, he tied the two men together back to back with heavy duty fishing twine taken from his pack. Twine, a necessity in every soldier's emergency pack, was known to have many uses.

Both men now unconscious, one possibly dead, added to a heavy weight as he dragged them into the bushes for hiding. He moved the muddy twisted cycle from the road and shoved it next to the bushes near the men. Although it would be a short walk to the barracks, he was tired and his feet felt heavy as he started walking.

Fortunately, he heard the Willys coming fast toward him. Too fast!

Lights from the Willys shot in all directions with each twist and turn of the road. The starless sky with clouds shooting passed the full moon lent a hand in the surreal scene. All factors racing toward WEN WU as he stood next to the edge of the road, prompted him to set the twisted bike close as to be noticed, and he decided to hide out of sight. "Caution" was his training, the heaviness of this bloody War never to be forgotten.

Although word was out that the fierce-fighting Japs had retreated far south out of the Assam area of India to the middle of Burma, he decided to be wary. This is War and he knew to be prepared for the unpredictable.

HOLT needed to slow the Willys for fear of driving passed his friend and best helper whom he worked with closely from the beginning of his Pacific assignments.

Earlier, after landing the C-47, he checked on the whereabouts of his family of friends, and learned from LUCKY LARRY that his friend had decided to stay behind and catch their pursuers.

"That sounds like what he would do. I'll see what's going on," he said as he jumped in the Willys parked nearby.

"Me to," said Cecil.

Headlights first found the upturned, twisted bike, its silver stripes glaring back as the Willys honed in.

HOLT stopped and shouted.

WEN WU stepped out of the thick jungle edge where he had been hiding.

"Hey!"

"Hey"

Half smiles all around. "Climb aboard!"

"I have two bundled guests. They'll need questioning."

"I'll say. Let's load them in back."

The three jabbered all the way to the barracks. After depositing their bundle of hate with the Military Police for safe keeping and questioning first thing in the morning, the three headed to their barrack and crashed on cots.

"Home!"

CHAPTER SIXTY-SIX—June 1944
Sookerating

A noisy early Saturday morning in Sookerating awoke everyone within the half-mile complex of hustle and bustle. Activities among crews were hurried and tense due to War worn and weary personnel and flight crews. Heavy plans in the air involved chasing the entire Jap regiment out of Burma with the starting emphasis of freeing Myitkyina (Mit-chee-NAH). Invaded and occupied by Japs in 1942, this was their starting point of taking over Burma.

All Allies, under the leadership of General William Slim in command, are preparing elaborate plans to free Rangoon by the end of next month. Victory means a recaptured and free Burma.

Today, specialized groups and support teams cling together fiercely with hopes of seeing an end to the bloody Pacific War caused by the Japs. Secrets are no longer kept and all squadrons know what is going down, hopefully within the next six months. All will have to do their part.

Gurkha Warriors, native to Nepal and now part of the Gurkha Brigade, are fierce fighters for the British.

They too walk in proud groups among throngs of mighty military men out and about planning future duties while here in Sookerating. Tensions high everywhere introduce a heaviness of ending the War.

Word is out that the enemy on the ground is exhausted. They, like all the Allies fighting them, suffered from thrashing through thick jungle brush and beating off leeches, ticks, mosquitoes and diseases they caused. Malaria, dysentery, and jaundice are never ending. The Jungle won over mankind and only masses of men could turn this around.

At breakfast in the huge barrack, eating arrangements were put together for the group now gathered around HOLT. Spirits are high and emotions are raw in a good way. They are home. They are family.

HOLT and WEN WU arranged tables for the group by 4:30 AM. Much needed to be discussed. Previously, HOLT made sure with Office Brass that his "Company" had the day off. "We'll help interrogate the two renegades who secretly followed LUCKY LARRY'S group. And don't forget big Saturday night social event the guys have been talking about for weeks," he demanded.

"As long as we're invited," winked Officer Nick. "Brag to your boys, 44,000 tons monthly, were air lifted earlier this year."

Because of the dangerous and heavy work loads the young flight crews endure, it is a known fact that Office Headquarters supported much needed R & R for them.

Now, HOLT counted chairs as WEN WU stood for roll call. "BOBBY JOHNSON and Kid Commanders Chu and Lue."

"Ok Joe," they each responded. The two Burmese boys smiled so broadly, their caps tilted. They sat stiffly forward in new clothes provided by the nurses' station. BOBBY and Bonnie sat on their left.

"Loretta, Bonnie, Blair, Orville, Cecil, PALOOKA, Chuck, Ears, Mitch."

"Mitch is doing laundry and said he does not plan to go to the dance," said Ears. "He's depressed over the loss of Millie when the plane went down with thirty nurses. She was on it."

Although Bonnie and Loretta met Millie last night in the women's barrack, they did not hear the above conversation. The noisy breakfast crowd seemed to echo loudly this morning.

LUCKY LARRY hurried in wearing work coveralls, long legs forcing a usual body bounce. "About time soldier boy! I was ready to give away your chair," said Loretta.

He held her head in his hands and briskly kissed the top of her head before heading to the food line. "Let's eat," demanded HOLT. "Coffee alone will kill ya!"

Each had a tray with mounds of scrambled eggs, buttered toast and coffee. Each table contained jars of sugar, cans of evaporated milk, biscuits and squares of butter. Lidded jars of jams were available at the front service table.

Tired and tense, no one talked much while eating.

Glances were made in HOLT'S direction often for further info.

"Today we play. Tomorrow we fight!" He pulled out his small note pad and stub pencil to make notes as he talked.

"Number ONE. Get an available crew to help set up this big mess hall for the dance tonight."

"Words been out for weeks about tonight," interrupted PALOOKA.

Chuck added, "I'll make sure all communications wire announcements again, BIG BIRTHDAY BASH FOR BOBBY JOHNSON."

"No" said BOBBY. "Party is for everyone who has a birthday this year." He put his arm around Bonnie knowing she is very supportive of his cleverness.

All smiled.

"The bands been ready. The usual group will play the latest tunes," said LUCKY LARRY while picking up finished empty plates and carting them away to a bin.

"That's us," said Ears as he followed LUCKY LARRY while doing the same. "Me on drums and you on Sax!"

"Yeah, but I want to dance most of the time." He looked over at Loretta. "Hubba Hubba!"

"Easily done. We have replacements all eager to participate."

PALOOKA looking around, realized Millie had not come to breakfast. His intentions are to tell Mitch that she is here. She is alive. But Mitch left early this morning, "for laundry chores," said Ears earlier, "and he refuses to come tonight." "We will get them both here," said Bonnie.

"And, we'll keep it a surprise," added Loretta. HOLT and WEN WU leaned back in their chairs while the younger crowd bounced around discussing chair set up, band placement, and bar facility.

"Number TWO," said HOLT.

"Oh hell, no ones listening. Let's go to the office and help interrogate the two Chindits."

CHAPTER SIXTY-SEVEN—June 1944
Sookerating

HOLT and WEN WU left the hustle and bustle of the huge dining hall to check with the officers holding the two renegade Chindits. Who were they? Why were they sneaking an attempt to attack the Willys Jeep as they weirdly followed? What was their plan? Clearly, they did not wish to be seen as they kept a short distance away from the Jeep.

The two Chindits were held in a secured jail compound next to the Officers' Quarters. The Officers on duty and in charge of the interrogation, welcomed both HOLT and WEN WU with frowns. "They speak no English," Officer Snyder complained.

HOLT nodded at WEN WU to get started.

It was learned they were part of Bill Slims crew of 9000 Chindits flown in to Burma for <u>OPERATION</u> <u>BROADWAY</u> and other code named tactics to eliminate the Japs from the jungle area around Assam. HOLT knew this is to be the second large expedition utilizing the talented natives.

It also was learned that the two traitors wanted no part of the War and said they snuck away during an opportune time. The death toll was heavy and they didn't want to be casualties. "Bill Slim's group is determined to eliminate the Japanese from the territory by chasing them out of Burma entirely before the monsoon hits heavy."

"Fighting will go on for weeks," one said.

"The Japs will never be defeated," said the other. WEN WU translated their words clearly for HOLT and the two officers.

"Their body language shows they are lying," said HOLT as he watched their eyes dart around fearfully.

"Ask why they carried Japanese guns?" *"We are tired of fighting in searing temperatures and many of us are sick and exhausted,"* said one. *"We helped capture Mogaung and my brother and I stole –or borrowed—the bike and guns from dead Japs,"* said the other with a battered face and one eye shut. *"We had to fight under Stillwell's command and feared he would put us to work on the Burma Road out of Ledo. With the monsoon coming, we wanted out."*

"But why follow us?" HOLT had not cracked a smile during the questioning. "And why try to fight WEN WU?"

To this they had no answer.

"We were trying to get back to Sookerating hoping there would be a flight back to India. We feared the Japanese were still in this area."

Officer Jones, listening to the translations, interrupted at this point. "Noise has it that Chindits are being sent back to India by August. Is this what they heard?"

WEN WU kept the interrogation going onward to the point of exhaustion.

"They look sick and War-weary," HOLT noted. "Aren't we all," offered Officer Jones, second in command. "Ask if they were part of the group that cut the Mandalay, Myitkyina (Mit-chi-NAH) railway back in March?"

They shook their heads "yes" to the questioning. "They have been fighting fitfully for the last four months," HOLT stated, "with both Bill Slim and Stillwell. Now they are exhausted and confused."

"We'll see that they get back with their group." Officer Jones taking off his glasses and cap, began wiping sweat from his forehead with a large brown military handkerchief. "In the meantime they can help the mechanics with cleanup and other issues over there."

"They need to go to the medics first," said WEN WU while listening to the two men apologize. Then directing attention to them he said, "You know that we have a problem with sabotage right now. What do you know?"

The two Chindits looked at each other in thought. *"Keep hawkers away from the landing fields and airplanes. If paid by Japs, they will try to cause accidents on runway by pushing carts in planes' paths."*

"Don't trust helpers with mechanics." WEN WU asked, "Can we trust you?"

"Yes, yes! We just want to go home." They shook their heads up and down adamantly.

"Tell them we'll see they make it home with their crew in August. In the meantime, they need to be honest and useful," he said sternly.

HOLT and WEN WU escorted them to the medics with instructions per Officer Jones.

Hilda, head nurse, noticing HOLT come her way, had many questions about the Chindits as she waved for help from others.

"What's going down? I feel something's about to break in this dirty War." She quit writing vigorously on her hand held tablet and heaved a heavy sigh as she stared at HOLT closely for the first time. "You come and go around here like a locomotive!"

"Someone has to," he said briskly to her pertinence.

"Are you the caregiver?" Not smiling, she continued staring at him, her hands on her petite waist.

"One of my many titles." A spark of sun peaked between shifting clouds allowing a bright view of Hilda's face.

"Emerald green," he whispered noticing huge eyes admiring him from under the brim of an officer's cap.

"What?"

"Nothing!" He waved a half salute, turned around and walked away leaving her standing there staring at his back.

She stood outside the medic tent avoiding the sweltering heat left over from the fans inside. The pounding rain that comes and goes brings no relief. Soon, the heavy June monsoon will arrive in full force and they need to be ready with shelter. The wooden porch, free of the rain, amply provides space for needed cots of the wounded waiting for medical assistance.

For now, she sat down on a wooden bench with a fan in hand taking a break, wondering about the loud music coming from the barrack next door.

She lit a Lucky Strike, inhaled, then looked down at her slacks. "What a mess!" She re-creased both cuffs and shifted her belt. Next, she crushed out the cigarette and said, "I need to quit" knowing it would please her mom back home.

Finding the newly arrived nurse named Milly, is her immediate task. After showing her around, she will ask her to go next door to the Dining Hall and learn what is happening there. She just might find the answer. Hilda felt suddenly inspired to know.

CHAPTER SIXTY-EIGHT—June 1944
Sookerating

Pounding rain did nothing to dampen the spirits of party goers planning for tonight's festival and feast at the newly named Swing Canteen, formerly the Dining Hall.

HOLT, Officers Jones and Snyder, stood back and watched from the open doorway, elated to see a vigorous mood rise above hate and disappointment. Tiredness mysteriously disappeared from the youthful fighters.

"This one day." HOLT shook his head and filled his pipe.

"This one night." Officer Jones followed the short thought, cigarette in hand.

"So necessary," quipped Officer Snyder. The three stood there watching, listening and feeling good.

"Band in that corner," said LUCKY LARRY to his group of helpers as he pointed to an area next to food service, "on a platform to be seen and heard." "Let's get building," said BOBBY JOHNSON.

"Should take only a few minutes," said Chuck. "We have builders in my family." He hobbled over to take measurements dragging his heavy cast. "There's a pile of suitable wood out back," said PALOOKA waving for help. Blair, Cecil and Orville followed.

"Nothing like boots on the ground," someone said as they each tested the sturdiness of the finished platform.

"Yeah," someone followed as they all stood and stared at their accomplishment.

Loud noises never cease from planes overhead, taking off or landing not too far away.

With experience comes War awareness of the different sounds from each different plane. In the not too far distance, the shrill piercing sound of Chennault's P-40 Flying Tigers filled the air above and the scene below.

"What's going on?" HOLT now held his pipe in his hand and looked at the two Officers. "Aren't they supposed to be in China?"

"For a short while they are helping Stillwell's Army fight off invaders spoiling the Burma Road coming out of Ledo," said Officer Snyder.

"It's supposed to be finished next year. According to Churchill, the War will be over before the Road meets up with the tail-end coming out of Burma." They nodded a short laugh, more of a negative snicker.

In the close distance they could see a C-46 Commando used as an air ambulance, unloading stretchers of patients for medics in the next building In the scene before them, all friends working hard in the huge mess hall sucked in a breath of tension at the sounds in the air. With the beat of the War, they moved around rapidly preparing for tonight.

LUCKY LARRY glided by with sax in hand.

"Girls, fun, music, dance!"

Band set up was the loudest.

Ears on drums beat out a short piece.

"Loud enough? Hey you groups in the back, report."

Other band members came in to get ready for tonight. Calvin on Clarinet and Tex on Trombone settled in on the platform.

"We need to see the list of what you're playing." Bonnie and Loretta joyfully headed over to talk with the band.

"Here's our temporary list for your approval." LUCKY LARRY playfully elbowed Loretta. She began to read the list aloud, followed by Bonnie's comments.

Of course, those working in the Hall suddenly became a quiet group of listeners.

"The Man on the Flying Trapez"

"A happy tune for starting. Gets everyone motivated."

"You'll Never Know How Much I Love You."

"A cheeker!"

"California, Here I Come."

"A fast one!"

"Two Sleepy People" and "Stardust!"

"Cheekers! We need a Jitterbug. That's the new dance."

The group was loud as activities increased.

Someone grabbed a chair and began to dance with it. "What about that new comedy band, Spike Jones and his City Slickers? We need some comedy and fast pick-up." Cecil snapped his fingers and did a little foot shuffle.

Lue and Chu eating biscuits in the corner, ducked their heads with laughter.

"Casey Jones came out last year," said Ears.

Band members shook heads affirmative. "We can do it," said Tex polishing his trombone.

"Lily Marlene," The ladies shouted simultaneously.

"It's new this year."

"They're playing it all over Europe," added Bonnie.

"Yeah, and the Germans consider it their song," moaned LUCKY LARRY.

"Doesn't matter!"

"Doesn't matter!"

Loretta was loud and clear. "It's about a young girl waiting at the garden gate for her lover to come back from the War."

Silence!

"It's from a poem that was written around the time of WWI," Bonnie added.

"Play some of the favorites twice. And we need lots of swing." Someone from the audience of workers added.

"Swing to this!" LUCKY LARRY stepped into the middle of the floor and began to play Stardust with a lively beat.

Everyone stopped what they were doing to briefly watch.

Before the other players joined in, he stopped playing to brag. "I learned this tune when I practiced with Glenn Miller and The Army Air Force Training Command Orchestra—briefly!" He bowed.

"How'd you do that?" HOLT laughed.

"With high-frequency radio, I played along!"

"Oh sure," someone said. "In the C-46 Commando."

"I love it," Loretta said as she and Bonnie did a few dance turns.

"Hubba-hubba!" LUCKY LARRY returned back to the band.

PALOOKA at the bar stacking boxes of whiskey, waved for help. "We have permission to bring crates of whiskey from the Office dispensary," he said to BOBBY.

Led by Officers Jones and Snyder, they waved for the two young teens, Lue and Chue, to come and help.

"Ok Joe." They were all smiles in their new clean clothes.

"I have to teach them English," WEN WU insisted.

"And we need to find their family," Bonnie added.

"I think they are War orphans. They told me they have no clue where they're from. They traveled from village to village," said WEN WU. Briefly, his thoughts of the unhappiness he experienced as a youngster because of his predicament will always stay with him. Thankfully, a childless couple from England found him running loose on the streets and adopted him. He looked over at HOLT still standing there with his pipe in hand, watching. He nodded and briefly lifted his pipe, a perfunctory wave before walking over to the band.

"The platform is high. Don't fall off tonight," he said while walking around three areas of the square platform. "Good plan to have the back against the wall." He moved out of the way as Blair, Cecil and Orville came in carrying heavy boards.

"For the steps in front," said Chuck hobbling along seeing HOLT standing there. "Wide and broad so no one falls off."

"Don't bring the steps too far out in front. We need every inch we can get for dancing." HOLT now lit his pipe.

Mechanics from next door came in carrying chairs that they rustled from all over the base in sneaky ways. "If we get in trouble, we'll tell them the brass want all the chairs repaired."

"Line them along those walls," pointed Loretta.

"But, keep them away from the bar," offered Bonnie. "We don't want someone falling into another person's lap."

They walked over to HOLT. "What's the plan for food?"

"Since LUCKY LARRY'S ice cream machine is not finished, free home-made biscuits with lots of butter and jelly will have to do. Otherwise, it gets complicated. This is a free for all dance."

"You can say that again," said Bonnie. "I hear that a huge crowd is coming. It's been planned for a long time."

"What's the timeline?" Loretta asked.

"Dusk to midnight. We'll put a huge poster at the entrance."

"Hope the Brits won't start the usual fights." Bonnie folded her arms in a worried stance. "After all, this is an American base."

"Let's hope our guys wear their C.B.I. Theater patch so when the military police start wielding their batons, we China-Burma-India American flyers won't get hit."

"That's a mouthful."

The racket continued both inside and out. Inside, chairs scraped the floor while being shuffled from one place to another. Whiskey bottles and glasses clicked noisily as the bar crew managed the set up. Loudly, the band screeched a few new tunes while practicing on sax, clarinet and trombone. Ears sitting in back, banged away on drums.

Outside in the pounding rain, there was no break on the tarmac as Commandos and C-47 Skytrains flew in and out.

Not too many miles away, Jap Zeroes as always, are in preparation.

CHAPTER SIXTY-NINE—June 1944

Sookerating

Bright lights outside blinked off and on lighting the large 6x9 poster near the door, anointing the dining hall to a glorified Swing Canteen. Groups meandering through the entrance two, three, four at a time, are met with an intoxicating scent of baked biscuits all planned in advance by WEN WU and his crew of two, Lue and Chue.

Friends not in a rush, gathered outside talking about where they had been, and where they are going next. It is a mixture of old friends from early flight schools and new friends caught in the mix of War turmoil. Few loners light Lucky Strikes or Camels outside while contemplating when to enter.

All men in a sea of khaki visit the bar area first for that boost of jovial confidence. Basically, it is a wave of beige incorporating both badged CBI Americans and British. A few officials from India, Burma, and China mingled among the groups in a welcoming posture. This special night had been on all the air waves for quite a while and joining for a night of fun and pleasure is a break from the fierce fighting. All knew this to be a birthday bash!

Each man had a title.

Each man had a story.

Loudly they were ready to tell old stories to new ears.

"Match this story!"

It became a contest, a huddle of listeners in small groups, some jogging from one group to another. HOLT'S group planned their tables early with designated chairs before everyone arrived. For sure, they kept two empty hoping Mitch will arrive. Loretta and Bonnie were given the job of coxing Millie to join the party. Voila! A romance in the making. Smiles all around.

It took two tables for the large group. The two combined tables sat in a corner nearest the bar so LUCKY LARRY could see them as they demanded tunes and made other comments. Loretta sat nearby. Previously, WEN WU taped names to the metal foldup chairs to keep them at the table and not get lifted by wayward drinkers. Lue and Chue sat on opposite ends as table guards. Their homework learning a new language included pronouncing all the names as pointed out by their teacher.

"HOLT, BOBBY JOHNSON, Bonnie, Loretta, PALOOKA, Chuck, Cecil, Blair, Orville, Mitch, Millie, WEN WU." They laughed when they saw his name printed. Ding Hao!

"You know we won't be sitting long when the ladies arrive and the band begins," said Cecil feeling the bump on his forehead from a few days ago when he fell in the C-47 cargo plane with HOLT at the helm.

"Can you still see it?" He asked Blair.

"Not really. Pull your cap down."

PALOOKA walked over with his sore shoulder in an arm sling. "No! Bare your wounds. Tonight we tell stories." Then after a long sigh and a whisper, "Tomorrow we fight."

They looked over at small groups gathered around a story teller. The big three words of the long night ending too soon would be, "Match this one!" But, one hour into the early night someone loudly said, "Where are the ladies?"

"They're coming in a few minutes." BOBBY JOHNSON looked at his watch. "Bonnie cooked up a surprise for everyone!"

HOLT broadly smiled as Bonnie, Loretta and Millie came walking in, each toting a cake.

"Unbelievable," he said while pulling out their chairs and clearing the table pushing glasses aside from the center to make room for cakes.

"As ordered! Spice cake with black walnuts." Bonnie saluted.

"Wow!"

"Hubba-hubba." LUCKY LARRY sat down his sax to join the group. The rest of the band did the same.

"Break time," yelled Ears.

"But, h-h-how," HOLT merely stuttered as Bonnie interrupted, "I jeep around!" She winked. Others loudly gathered close by while Loretta and Bonnie began cutting small pieces from all three cakes. Millie handed out napkins.

"Wow! Just like home."

Someone said, "BOBBY JOHNSON, welcome back and happy birthday."

"Oo-Rah!"

"For he's a jolly good fellow,"—as the crowd now began to sing, twenty-one year old BOBBY JOHNSON looked over at Lue and Chue who are clapping loudly.

HOLT stood while holding a piece of cake in a napkin and loudly spoke. "This is also one big birthday party. All those with a birthday anytime this year, stand up." Glasses held high, clunked loudly with those nearby. Wine, whiskey, soda seemed to splash everywhere as the band happily played, "Happy Birthday."

Swaying and singing, HOLT suddenly felt two slim arms circle his waist from behind.

"Hey soldier, how about a dance?" It was a demure whisper.

Turning, he quickly put an arm around Hilda and held her close. Hearts beat as one with a short kiss. "Hey yourself! We meet again. Good to see you." They moved onto the floor. "Slow one," he shouted to his friends on the bandstand.

Two hours into the night, with the dance floor packed and walls vibrating in merriment, Mitch walked in.

He stood for about fifteen minutes in the doorway, downcast, wondering why he came.

It was at this time that PALOOKA announced, "This next dance is dedicated to the thirty nurses who lost their lives in one plane crash."

Chuck added with a shout, "And dedicated to Walt and others missing in action."

Silence!

As the band slowly played <u>Stardust</u>, Mitch routed his way through the crowd towards the bandstand to wave at his buddy Ears, busily playing the drums. PALOOKA on the floor with his old friend Polly, saw him and pointed to their table near the band.

Now empty of people, name tags taped to the backs of chairs clearly showed the occupants who were out on the floor.

"What!" He saw his name next to Milly's. "Is this some kind of morbid joke?" He lowered his loud voice and turned towards the band, his close buddies.

After feeling a brisk tap on the shoulder, and a quick turn around, he practically fell into his chair facing Milly who had slipped in.

"Hi," she said after quickly sitting down facing him.

Wordlessly he mustered, "How?"

"I decided not to board," she quietly answered.

Her hands were dainty; her voice was sweet. They sat starring at each other with damp faces until LUCKY LARRY announced, "This next one is for all you lucky ladies."

As <u>Lily Marlene</u> began, every table emptied. Mitch and Millie melted together on the dance floor, "Like butter in a hot oven," someone said.

"Are you my Lily Marlene," he asked.

No answer. Just a long sigh.

Meanwhile, Polly and PALOOKA continued an earlier conversation. "Ok, big guy. You keep it clean and I'll stay here with you. Or better yet, you keep the fist quiet and I'll stay with you forever." She blinked a strong right eye and tilted her head.

"What are you talking about?" He put his arms around her waist and pulled her close in a soft body slam.

"The fighting last time against a Brit?" They rubbed noses.

"Oh, him!" He loosened his hold. "You'll just have to hold me close all night to keep me busy and out of trouble."

"Let's dance! <u>Lily Marlene</u> is my favorite tune." She pulled him out on the crowded dance floor with no resistance.

"Break time," the band announced with a loud beat of drums.

When the group met back at the table, Millie sat on Mitch's lap allowing an empty chair for Hilda. During the middle of the night, four British officers sauntered in. The dance floor split down the middle quietly to let them walk through. Their shirts were medaled and their berets were tilted.

PALOOKA knew them to be troublemakers from the past, and instinctively rubbed his chin remembering their last meeting about six months ago and someone's hard fist.

Two went to the bar and two walked over to PALOOKA who was sitting at the table, whiskey sour in hand.

"Time heals, matey," said one looking him square in the eye. "And we brought our own ladies this time. They're powdering their noses!" He thrust a thick thumb over his shoulder pointing back.

Polly saw him as a big husky guy who slowly shifted his weight from heel to toe and back and forth rhythmically.

She tightly wound her arm through PALOOKA'S. "Where's your buddy?" PALOOKA was skeptical remembering the fiery little Brit with fists of iron.

"You mean the one you pulverized?" He paused and spoke slowly. "Plane crash. Didn't make it!" PALOOKA swallowed hard. Most at the table listening, took a sip from their glasses at the very moment.

Ears to the rescue banged on the drums, 1-2-3-4! LUCKY LARRY went to the mic. "Who's got six Pence?"

The jovial crowd almost yelled out their song as all sang along swaying together, arm and arm.

"I've got six pence, Jolly Jolly six pence,
I've got six pence to last me all my life!
I've got six pence to lend, and six pence to spend
And six pence to send home to my wife, poor wife.
No cares have I to grieve me,
No pretty little girl to deceive me
Happy as a King, believe you me,
As I go rolling, rolling home—

End of song, LUCKY LARRY yelled "Break time" as he noticed too many getting a little 'pie-eyed'. Before coming down from the band stand to join his friends he announced "Don't forget the biscuit table" as he pointed to it.

Chuck went to the mic next. "Ok, I'm looking for Sally H. and Linda T." He read their names from his foot cast. "You owe me a dance."

The two nurses walked out of the heavy crowd to chat with Chuck. "Good to see you again." "Pull up a chair," he said.

Chue and Lue were sent to bed a long time ago so there was ample room. But, since Sally and Linda were accompanied by four soldiers all sweaty from dancing, they said, "One promise full filled." And the three went out on the dance floor taking turns and carefully avoiding his cast. The four soldiers went to the bar for drinks and water.

It was this kind of night. More guys than girls but a robust feel for sharing. The music was loud, the drinks were plentiful and the War stories were non stop leaving a significant impact on comradeship. It was a "been there, done that" kind of atmosphere in a horrific War that's been going on too long.

WEN WU kept busy helping clear the table of extra glasses, keeping chairs near table, and helping with miscellaneous band chores. He was forever mindful of the heavy duties each of his friends endured. They were his family.

Respect rampant, he remembered Surgeon PALOOKA picking up bodies out of Ledo on the Burma Road and packing them into his L-5, then rushing them to the nearby hospital, hopeful a few would make it. Now, it's so satisfying seeing him dance with Nurse Polly.

And he thought how important he felt when putting together a warning list of traitors, a list that was printed by thousands and air-dropped all over India, Burma, and China.

He was happy for the young couple BOBBY JOHNSON and Bonnie dancing together. What a miracle that he survived the crash and has harrowing experiences to tell. From tragedy there is a little good as he thought of the two young boys who would now be his helpers, as always under HOLT'S command. As the ladies left to go powder their noses, he looked over at HOLT and did not like what he saw. HOLT had the depressed downward look that WEN WU knew too well. His face expressionless, he started tapping the butt of his pipe quietly on the table while staring in space. Soon, he got up and left.

The band members watched him regress emotionally, and they were concerned.

Cecil and Blair dancing out on the floor watched him walk out alone. They were concerned.

Everyone who worked closely with HOLT now worried about him. With double the War experience, he was the "go to" man for problems and other leadership.

Now, why was he down?

Hilda felt his mood change when she left with the girls and decided to watch him carefully. Her nursing experience took control. Prompted to hurry back, she saw him slip away with no goodbyes to anyone.

CHAPTER SEVENTY—June 1944

Sookerating

He lay there on his bunk, arms behind his head staring up at the high ceiling. Dripping wet from the short walk in the rain, he didn't care as he pulled the olive-brown blanket over him. On the short end table by his head, his empty pipe lay in a tray. His dancing boots dripped mud on the floor by his side. He whispered to no one. *"I can't do this anymore. I'm done. I want out!"* Thoughts of harrowing past experiences and losses of buddies filled his head. Thoughts of Walt and other lost pilots and crew members who crashed while caught in the soup and their existence never found, were too devastating. What about their families at home?

And the thirty nurses who bravely boarded that ill-fated flight. What about their families?

Most of all it was his own crash that brought him down. The question from a Chinese Captain would haunt him forever.

"Where you go captain," as HOLT had on his parachute gear and was about to jump out of the dying plane.

"To go get help," he answered.

"You good captain," the Chinese said.

Two minutes later while hanging from shroud lines clear from danger, the plane exploded as it hit a mountain peak.

As he crunched his swollen eyes together hard, he felt someone lift his blanket.

"Scoot over," she ordered.

Hilda crawled in next to him, snuggled her head in the crevice of his upturned arm, and threw her other arm across his chest in a tight hug. She sighed, closed her eyes and waited one full minute. "We miss you." Silence.

"Christ, I need out of here," he softly murmured while rubbing her arm. "This War keeps going on and on with no ending."

"You are not alone." She tucked the blanket over them motherly. "And, you are not responsible." She felt the warmth of his chest and heard the beating of his heart against her ear.

He whispered again. *"Within the next two months, thousands will attack the Japs in a major siege to take back Burma. And thousands will die. We are all involved."*

Hilda's experience refused to let depression take hold. "I have been at this game for a long, long time," she spoke slowly. "I feel an ending coming soon!"

"I want to go home and 'root' for the Brooklyn Dodgers," he said. "And start a family. Hell! I'm thirty years old."

"Hey," she cupped his chin in her hand. "Those are my words, except I'm twenty-seven." Silence.

"Hey Soldier Boy," she whispered. *"Let's go dance."*

He spoke quietly. "I'm reduced to Soldier Boy. Of my many jobs: Commanding Officer of squadrons, Air Craft Commander, Group Operations Officer, Senior Officer with six aircraft and crews, Liaison Officer to Executive Headquarters, and most importantly F/O who has flown THE HUMP over seven hundred hours; I am now reduced to Soldier Boy."

He kissed her forehead as a waft of Channel No.5 scented his way. He slowly smiled, and said aloud, "I'll take it."

A swirl of activities greeted them as they walked into the Swing Canteen, and they had to push their way through the crowd dodging flying arms keeping pace to a fast number.

"Slow one," someone yelled.

"Slow one," someone echoed.

LUCKY LARRY left the band stand to join Loretta on the dance floor as the clarinet player began the tune, <u>Forever and Ever, Our Hearts Will Be True.</u>

WEN WU sat at the end of the table with a biscuit in one hand and Whiskey Sour in the other while watching his friends, his family, holding each other tightly to music. BOBBY JOHNSON and Bonnie, PALOOKA and Polly, LUCKY LARRY and Loretta, and best of all his Captain HOLT and Hilda were all together.

"Ding Hao" he said aloud while looking towards Mitch and Millie.

Hilda whispered to HOLT, "You're my hero." "During War, everyone's a hero," he answered. At the end of the number, Ears on drums started pacing a chant. Everyone joined in loudly as the Swing Canteen's walls vibrated.

"HOME ALIVE IN '45!"

"HOME ALIVE IN '45!"

Also by Dot Jay Gomez

<u>Blakely High PHOTO PLAY</u>

A young teacher, Gina McHenry, becomes entangled with danger as she searches for answers to a kidnapping, a terrorizing car chase, and a mountain trail ride shooting. The quest for answers to hidden secrets take you from the CAVE CREEK desert to the high country of the RIM and into the BLUE RIDGE forest.

<u>Blakely High and the VOODOO PHANTOM</u>

The principal, Dr. Shieter, wishes he could rescind the order of "African Studies Across the Curriculum" when a VOODOO PHANTOM causes havoc all over the town of Cave Creek, Arizona. As body parts start showing up everywhere, some of the miscreants start taking bets as to where the next one will appear... Where is the body? Who are the saboteurs? Gina's family and friends, Pop, Dixie, Nancy Lopez, and Richard/Raquel spin around in circles solving the mystery of... THE VOODOO PHANTOM!

<u>Ghosts of the Superstitions</u>

GINA McHENRY and her group of teacher friends innocently decide to extend a trail ride through MASSACRE GROUNDS, haunted by an array of GHOSTS since 1848. Hundreds of skulls and skeletons found by Army Cavalry and foot soldiers in the 1860s indicated an abundance of death and terror.

Ghost weary WRANGLERS, hired to lead, abandon the group of thirty riders when spooked horses stampede, leaving RICK DEL RIO to guide his group out of the Superstitions, *late* at night, *during* a storm, and *stalked* by an unknown entity.

A myriad of colorful characters enhance the finale!

Research Acknowledgements

China Airlift - The HUMP

Copyright 1980 - China Burma India HUMP Pilots Assoc.
Inc.
Poplar Bluff, Missouri 63901
Produced & Designed: David Turner & Assoc.
P.O. Box 3101, Paducah, KY 42001
Printed: Taylor Publishing Co. - Dallas, TX

Aircraft of the World - The Complete Guide

International Masters Publishers AB Aircraft of the World
444 Liberty Avenue, Pittsburgh, PA 15222-1207